Silver Screen Cowboy

Starring Latigo Brown

Books by Rod Miller

Rawhide Robinson *series*
Rawhide Robinson Rides the Range
Rawhide Robinson Rides the Tabby Trail
Rawhide Robinson Rides a Dromedary
Rawhide Robinson Rides a Wormhole

Novels
Cold as the Clay
Father unto Many Sons
Pinebox Collins
Silver Screen Cowboy

Coming Soon!
A Thousand Dead Horses

Silver Screen Cowboy

Starring Latigo Brown

Rod Miller

SPEAKING VOLUMES, LLC
NAPLES, FLORIDA
2023

Silver Screen Cowboy

ISBN 978-1-64540-662-4

For my friend T.C. Christensen,
who knows how to expose film.

Acknowledgments

People sometimes ask how long it takes to write a book. There is seldom a definitive answer. For instance, *Silver Screen Cowboy* is, in a sense, the work of a lifetime, or at least several decades.

The writing about rodeo results from years of personal experience. Many of those stories were inspired during my time hanging out with the "Rounders" while a member of the Utah State University Intercollegiate Rodeo Team, and other cowboy compadres.

Over the course of my career in advertising, I wrote and produced more television commercials and other film projects than I can remember. Most of my education in how film production works came from the many days spent working with my favorite director and cinematographer, T.C. Christensen, who always brought my ideas to life better than other directors and better than I expected.

Some of the stories about making Western movies and television programs were inspired by reading, primarily *Company of Heroes* by Harry Carey, Jr.; *The Western Legends Live On* by Charlie LeSueur; "DeMille and Danger: Seven Heuristic Taxonomic Categories of His Hollywood (Mis)Adventures" by Anton Karl Kozlovic in *European Journal of American Studies*; and others sources.

And it cannot go without saying that I, like many young boys of my generation and adults of my acquaintance, have spent many an hour watching Westerns on television and at the movies. Notice of the many "silly" aspects of Westerns came from my late father, a cowboy who knew better.

The inspiration from these and other sources helped in the writing of this book, but it is, after all, a work of fiction and a product of my own imagination. None of the people or incidents recounted in its pages represent or reflect anyone or anything real, past or present, and literary license and inventions of the author are in play.

"People are always asking me why
they don't make Westerns like they used to."
—*Roy Rogers*

"Nothing ever changes as far as
Westerns are concerned. They are
the same today as they were years ago."
—*Glenn Ford*

"Westerns are a type of picture which
everybody can see and enjoy. Westerns
always make money. And they always
increase a star's fan following."
—*Randolph Scott*

"In Westerns you were permitted to
kiss your horse but never your girl."
—*Gary Cooper*

Prologue

War cries shredded the air like arrow points. Pounding hooves from the pinto ponies carrying the circling Indians raised dust clouds that blended with smoke from the burning stagecoach. Through the murk, the horseback man on the ridge saw bodies scattered around the flaming coach, the feathers of prickling arrow shafts fluttering in the wind.

Standing within the chaos, lost and turning slow circles, stood a woman. Ruffled petticoats bloused a full skirt, glowing white like the form-fitting bodice—and what a form it fitted—above. Strands of honey-colored hair, untucked from the lustrous coiffure crowning her delicate head, glinted when struck by shafts of sunlight that penetrated the haze.

The horseman tugged the wide brim of his hat, settling the head covering down tight, and, with a simple lift of the reins, signaled his mount into motion. The horse trumpeted shrilly and reared up on its hind legs, forelegs pawing the air, then bugled again as long, sure, strides carried it down the ridge toward the disorderly danger below. The silver-mounted saddle horn glistened in the sun; silver-dollar-size conchos glittered from saddle skirts and jockeys and the headstall, as silvery bit chains chimed as they sparkled.

The palomino horse, flaxen mane and tail streaming, passed through the ring of shrieking, bloodthirsty braves as if they were not there.

"Don't worry, Miss, we'll make it through," the horseman said. He reached down and firmly, yet gently, grasped the upper arm of the maiden and lifted, seating her sidewise behind the saddle. "Grab aholt, Miss, and don't let go."

Arms wrapped around her rescuer's waist, she hung on as if her life depended on it—which it did—burying her cheek into the man's well-muscled back.

With a touch from the rider's silver spurs, the palomino stallion reared, pawing the air as it bugled a warning. The horseman dropped the reins as the horse's front hooves reached the ground and, with gloved and gauntleted hands, drew a pair of gleaming silvered revolvers from the silver-studded holsters on his hips. As the horse wheeled and spun, he snapped off shots, white smoke spitting with fire from his gun barrels. Each of a seemingly endless number of bullets from his pistols found its mark, warriors falling from their horses even as their arrows and bullets missed their target. Their ranks thinned, the surviving Indian braves flowed out of the circle into a retreating line, hoofbeats drumming across the desert, war cries and futile fire trailing behind.

The horseman watched the retreat, guns at the ready, until satisfied the Indians were gone for good. With two puffs of air, he blew away the feathery smoke still wisping from the gun barrels, spun the pistols around on his trigger fingers and, in perfect unison, slid them into their respective holsters. Without a word to his trembling passenger, he reined the prancing palomino around and rode away from the burning stagecoach toward the setting sun, the fiery orb shooting flames of its own into the western skies.

"Cut and print!" came the cry of the director, stirring the film crew into action.

"Get me down off from this damn horse," the woman said, her accent bespeaking Scandinavian origins. The horseman reached behind and hooked an arm around her waist and lowered her easily to the ground.

He smiled at his erstwhile passenger and tipped his hat with the touch of a gloved finger to the contrasting leather stitching edging its broad brim. "Aw, c'mon, Miss Eriksson. You'll hurt Nugget's feelin's."

With a snort at her rescuer and the horse, she lifted her skirts, spun around, and hurried off toward the tents in the distance.

The horseman smiled again as he watched her go. He watched the camera crews dismantling their equipment and the other members of the company going about their business. Then, with a gentle lift of the reins, turned the prancing palomino toward a cluster of workers bustling about as they disassembled lights and platforms, and removed a bulky movie camera from the crane assembly upon which it perched.

The horse stopped a few feet behind the canvas chair with DIRECTOR stenciled on its back, snorted once and pawed twice. The man in the chair, clutching a megaphone, dressed in riding boots and jodhpurs, cravat at his throat and safari helmet on his head, slid out of the chair and turned to the mounted man.

The horseman smiled, showing a mouthful of even, white teeth. "Was that okay, Mister McGill? If not, I'm happy to give it another shot."

"Oh, no. That will not be necessary laddie," the director said with a shake of his head. "It was fine. Brilliant, in fact. First rate."

With a nod and another smile, Latigo Brown turned away on the palomino stallion he had called Nugget from its youth, but which would appear on the screen under the more illustrious moniker, *El Fuego*. He rode toward the corrals where the horse enjoyed a private pen of its own, shaded by a canvas fly and attended by a personal groom, apart from the ordinary horses and wranglers of the movie company.

But before he reached his destination, a scream filled the air.

With a shout, he urged El Fuego to an all-out race to the tent that housed Annika Eriksson, Swedish star of stage and screen.

Chapter One

Orval Brown never liked the Christian name his parents gave him, so he came up with one of his own: Latigo.

Folks not in the know sometimes mispronounced it *luh-TEE-goh*, but those folks tended to know nothing of horses, or they rode pancake saddles with girths and billets, rather than stock saddles with cinches and latigo straps. Thus, everyone who mattered knew it was *LAT-i-goh*.

Just now he is occupied with a saddle of a different kind. In all its basics it is a typical western saddle. But it is not. It is a muley, a committee saddle, an association saddle—a bronc saddle, built for riding bucking horses in the rodeo. Its most notable feature at first glance is the absence of a saddle horn. Latigo Brown sits under a shade tree at the county fairgrounds, fiddling with the buckles and straps and leathers on said bronc saddle, readying it for this evening's contest under the lights.

Sitting beside him—reclining, to be accurate, hat plopped over his face to intensify the shade—is his *amigo* Harley Warren. Between the two of them, they are entered in every event in tonight's show, sometimes competing against one another, and cooperating in the team roping. Harley is not as fastidious about his gear as Latigo. The caked-on rosin on the tail of his bull rope is likely to be infested with bits of grass and sand and even pebbles, but he seems not to notice. His catch ropes are often limp and limber from exposure to the weather, whereas Latigo protects his lariats and pigging strings in a lidded metal can. Then there are the bareback riggings. The body of Latigo's is firm, the sheepskin underside clean and fluffy, the handhold powdered with dry rosin, the D-rings shiny, the latigos straight and lubricated with talcum powder. Harley's rigging, on the other hand, is a tangled and twisted mess of cinch and latigos and rusted D-rings, the wool padding so matted and scuffed as to be unrecognizable to the sheep that spawned it, the hand-hold itself gobbed with clumps of burned rosin, and the body as limp as raw bacon.

Still, Harley wins his share of prize money, and, to hear some tell it, more than his share. It all comes naturally to Harley. He has the balance of a mountain goat, house-fly reflexes, the strength of a grizzly bear, eyes like a barn owl, and his hands a wolf-jaw grip.

Latigo, on the other hand, works at it. Oh, he has talent and natural ability to spare, and likely could equal his friend without much effort. But, owing to his attention to equipment, study of the habits of broncs and bulls, and clean living, he cashes in more often than Harley, and stands his friend to more than a few meals and pays many an entry fee for the next rodeo when the animals in the arena get the best of him.

Harley raised up on his elbows and tipped his hat brim back with the touch of a finger. "Son, I swear you're goin' to wear that saddle plumb out 'fore it comes time to strap it to a bronc. Best let it rest up some."

Latigo kept at his work, Harley looking on with a wry smile. "Where we goin' next week, Latigo? There's two or three rodeos we could get to 'thout too much trouble. Which one you want to try?"

"Not me, brother. I'm headin' for the ranch come mornin'. There's hay to put up back home. Be a couple weeks. Give me a holler from wherever you're at Wednesday week, and we'll hook up somewheres."

Latigo made a few more adjustments to the quarter binds on the stirrup leathers of the bronc saddle, then set it next to his war bag, dusted off his pants legs, straightened the tuck of his shirttails, and settled his hat. "Let's wander on over to the arena and have a look at the stock."

Harley sat up, cocked one knee and extended the other leg and raised off the ground without using his hands for lift. Once on his feet, he stretched and yawned. The boys ambled over to the pens behind the bucking chutes, propped their elbows on a fence rail and studied the penned horses and bulls. The horses stood, some hipshot, others with bowed heads, flicking away flies with swishing tails or a shiver of hide. Bulls, most sitting on their bellies atop tucked legs, showed no more activity than the blink of an eye to shoo a fly, or lazy jaws working over a cud.

The cowboys pointed out the critters they had drawn to ride, and talked some about their proclivities once the chute gate swung open. But that was merely for the sake of discussion to fill the air with something more than the odor of animals and their leavings, for there is little a cowboy enjoys more than just watching horses and cattle, simply for the sake of it. No sooner had they taken up their third position along the fence than their woolgathering was disturbed by the slamming of a door.

They turned to see Walt Barlow, rodeo producer and stock contractor, standing just outside the wooden shack that served as rodeo office, muttering, removing his hat to rake fingers through his hair, replacing the hat, turning a circle, and repeating the activity, the muttering ever more intense.

"What's the matter, Walt? You look like somebody stole your best cowdog."

"Ah, hell, Harley. It's Juaquin. He's done took sick and he can't go tonight."

"Juaquin Garza? The Tampico Twister?"

"Yup. Don't know what to do. That boy draws a crowd with his trick and fancy ropin' and his ridin' tricks. Folks'll be downright disappointed if they come to the rodeo and he don't. Some may want their money back, and the committee damn sure ain't goin' to like that."

Latigo and Harley watched Barlow hem and haw, twist and turn, fidget and fuss, stew and stammer, whimper and whine.

Then Latigo removed his hat, held it against his chest, and stepped forward. "Mister Barlow, sir..."

"What is it, Latigo?"

"How 'bout if I do it?"

"Do what?"

"The act—I'll be the Tampico Twister tonight."

"Aw, Latigo, that's right kind of you, but—"

"—Don't you worry none, Mister Barlow. I've seen the Tampico Twister go through his paces so many times I could do it in my sleep."

Barlow drew back and studied Latigo with wrinkled brow. "You can rope like he does?"

"Sure. Shucks, there ain't nothin' to it. I been doin' them same rope tricks since I was a kid."

"What about his trick ridin'?"

"That, too. Well, not all of it. There's some of the things he does I ain't never thought of tryin', but I reckon I could pull it off. My brother and me, we used to do all that kind of stuff just for the heck of it, ridin' around the pasture back home."

They talked it over. The specialty act would have to be shifted in the program so it would not conflict with Latigo's competitive events. The substitute entertainer would be announced as "The Tampico Twister's Twin" so as not to mislead the audience. And, of course, the idea would have to be cleared with the head of the rodeo committee and with Juaquin Garza.

All of which was accomplished in short order.

Latigo saddled up Garza's horse and rode him around the arena some so they could get familiar with the feel and smell of one another. And he worked a little with the trick roper's sixty-foot lariat, the rope near twice as long as those Latigo used to rope calves and to heel steers in the team roping.

The sun went down, the arena lights came up, and Latigo and Harley hauled all their rough-stock gear behind the bucking chutes and tied their roping horses outside the other end of the arena. Despite having drawn the pick of the pen in the bareback riding, Latigo only managed a score that earned him third-place money. He wrote off the poor showing to butterflies fluttering about his innards in anticipation of his role as the Tampico Twister's Twin. But the flutter bugs took roost by the time the team roping rolled around, and he took his dallies on his heel loop and he and Harley stretched their steer for first place. His saddle bronc decided to take the night off, and, despite Latigo giving it all he had, he placed out of the money.

Again at the other end of the arena, Latigo's loop had eyes and he caught and tied down his calf in a jiffy, topping all other times in the event. And that completed his competitive events for the evening, and not a bad showing. (For the record, Harley did not place in the bareback riding, broke the barrier and lost out in the steer wrestling, won first place with Latigo in Team Roping, finished third in calf roping, and would win the bull riding to finish up the rodeo with a bang.)

Following the calf roping, and while the cowgirls were running the barrel race, Latigo changed into the Tampico Twister's costumer. He felt a bit silly in the spangled sombrero, the britches with silver conchos down the outer seams, the bright white shirt with ruffled front, and the short-waisted jacket with contrasting piping and embroidered cactus flowers. Still and all, despite the garish garments, he knew full well he had never been as well dressed. He checked the rigging on Garza's horse and led the animal to the entry gate and handed it off to the arena worker there for the task.

The last barrel racer pounded out of the far end of the arena. The announcer read off her time. The audience cheered. The lights went down. A spotlight projected a bright circle in the center of the arena. The public address system blared music rich with mariachi trumpets. The announcer bloviated about the treat in store for the audience, finally urging the spectators to welcome with their applause the Tampico Twister's Twin.

Latigo took a deep breath as the gate attendant squeaked the hinges to allow him entry. He took a deep breath and found himself unable to expel it, or to put his legs into motion. After what seemed to him an eternity, but, in reality, was only the time it took for the announcer to once again urge the audience to cheer him on, Latigo's motor functions returned and he strode into the dark arena toward the spotlight. Just before reaching the bright circle, he shook out a small loop in his lariat and whipped up a butterfly loop, the rope spinning to the left, then the right in front of him. He stepped out of the shadows, rolling the loop across his shoulders as he did, eliciting applause from the audience. The loop rolled off his hand and, before reaching the ground, spun flat. Latigo let it build for a couple of rotations then skipped in and out of the loop. He let the loop grow and jumped inside, a trick called the wedding ring, and lifted it aloft and let it float down a time or two before stepping out from under it and spinning a merry-go-round loop around and around his body, then standing the loop upright in front of him and jumping back and forth through it in the ever-popular Texas skip.

Although he heard not a word of it, the announcer, accompanied by the mariachi music, kept up a constant patter throughout, interrupted only by outbursts of applause, explaining the moves and stirring excitement in the crowd.

The Tampico Twister's Twin took a bow, and coiled his rope. The circle of light widened to reveal Garza's saddled horse standing nearby. Latigo passed the short rope off to the attendant and leapt into the saddle without benefit of stirrup, taking up the sixty-foot lariat from the saddle horn. He built a loop and started it spinning, feeding more rope down the spoke and into the loop as he flipped butterfly loops around the horse, then switched to a merry-go-round flat loop. With a touch of a spur, he set the horse spinning as the loop spun around it in the opposite direction. The horse walked backward, as Latigo lifted loops over and around, in front of and behind the moving horse.

The audience cheered.

Latigo stopped the horse, but never the loop, and stood on the saddle, spinning a wedding ring loop around the horse, then dropped into the saddle and spurred the horse into a lope around the arena, the spotlight following and crowd cheering as the wedding ring continued. The horse came to a sliding stop near the entry gate and the lights came up as Latigo handed off the long lariat. He turned the horse in a quick pivot and set off down the arena at speed. Latigo grasped the horn, kicked out of the stirrups, and swung out of the saddle, his feet striking ground and propelling him into a vault over the running horse's back to land on the opposite side, only to vault again over the saddle.

He took a seat, and immediately dropped to the side of the running horse in a move called the Indian layout, and followed it by lifting himself and spinning around to ride backward, then frontward, then backward, then frontward again. Hearing, as if at a distance, the announcer's comments and the cheering crowd, he hefted one leg, then the other, and stood in the saddle. After a lap around the arena, in a move he and Harley worked out that afternoon, Harley rode into the arena on Latigo's roping horse and matched Latigo's speed to ride beside him. When the speed and stride of the horses synchronized, Harley passed the reins to Latigo and stepped out of the saddle and ran alongside until he found his balance and stopped.

As soon as he cleared the seat, Latigo stepped onto it with one foot and he rode Roman style, standing with one foot on each horse's back. After a lap around the arena, he slowed the horses and stopped in the center of the arena, swept off his sombrero and took a deep bow. Only now did the enthusiastic applause of the audience break through his concentration. He bowed again, dropped into the saddle on Garza's horse and rode out of the arena, followed by his roping horse and the cheers of the crowd.

So ended Latigo Brown's first experience in show business.

Chapter Two

Sunbeams trickled through aspen leaves, stippling the ground and undergrowth and softening the air with a gauzy shade. Latigo rode a palomino colt new to the saddle; a horse taken in payment for training others. He liked the feel of this horse he called Nugget. Its flashy palomino looks definitely stood out in the pastures and pens of the Brown ranch, where sorrels, bays, and browns were the order of the day. But Latigo Brown did not object to a little flash.

Latigo followed his father along a trail through the forest lease on the mountain, where they ran the cow herd during the summer months. With a hackamore rein in each hand, Latigo watched his horse's ears as the attentive colt looked from side to side, snorting occasionally at a brush or limb disturbed by the horse in the lead. Still, the rider's attention to his mount did not interfere with his scanning the ridges and draws and clearings for cattle, watching the animals watch him as he and his father looked for signs of illness, swollen udders, or other untoward omens and portents.

The ride to the cattle was a welcome relief from haying. For days, Latigo had all but wore out his neck driving forward and looking backward, raking hay in the meadow. His brother, Raymond, was doing much the same thing today, dragging the baler around as it gobbled up the windrows and spat bales of hay out its backside. Tomorrow, the brothers would each walk the day away beside the hay wagon, bucking bales onto its bed for their father to stack into a load while little sister Penny—short for Penelope—steered the tractor and wagon through the meadow. Haying was not to Latigo's liking, but it was a job to do, that must be done, to keep the cows fed through the cold and blowing winter months.

But the monotony and discomfort of bucking bales would not commence until tomorrow, and Latigo was determined to enjoy his horseback day in the cool on the mountain. The horses topped out in a grassy park where cattle watered at a pond fed by a spring. They reined up to study the scattered cows and calves.

"That black bally calf yonder—he look all right to you?"

Latigo followed his father's gaze across the clearing to the calf in question. It lay on its belly, neck stretched and jaw on the ground. "Can't say. Could be he's just takin' a snooze."

"We had best go see."

They rode, separating as they approached, toward the white-faced black calf. The calf stood on its hind legs and struggled to get its front end off the ground. Its head hung low even as it stood and watched the horses through wary eyes crusted with matter. The calf's tongue crept out and licked discharge from its muzzle.

Latigo said, "Don't look so good, does he?"

"Nope." His father unhitched his lariat from the saddle and built a loop. "We'll give 'im a shot. Best tie up that colt of yours."

By the time Latigo dismounted and hitched a tie rope around an aspen sapling, his father had tossed a soft loop around the calf's neck. He held the rope taut as Latigo approached the calf, but it made only a half-hearted attempt to elude the cowboy's grasp. Latigo grabbed the rope on the calf's neck, reached over its back with his other hand to grab the flank, then tipped and lifted the calf with both hands and a knee to lay it on its side. He knelt, one knee on the calf's neck and the other on its ribs, and grabbed the shank of the foreleg and bent the leg back, lifting enough to roll the calf slightly toward him.

After probing around in his saddlebags for a time, Latigo's father filled a hefty metal and glass syringe from a bottle of antibiotic. "Watch the cow," he said, with a nod toward the calf's mother, standing nearby snuffling and looking nervous, with its eyes on the creature abusing her weakly bawling baby. Father walked over and straddled the rear end of the calf, and with practiced ease, inserted the needle, pushed the plunger, and injected the medicine into the calf's rump. He rubbed the injection site briskly with his fingers and stood upright. "That ought to do it. Let 'im up."

Latigo released the calf and stood, but the animal did not care. He grabbed it by the tail and with a twist and a lift, helped the calf to its feet. It stood spraddle-legged for a bit, then shook its head, streaming snot. Latigo stepped away and by the time he and his father were horseback again, the cow had taken over, licking the calf while still watching the cowboys with suspicion.

After watering the horses at the pond, Latigo and his father drank from the spring and sat in the shade to eat sandwiches wrapped in wax paper. Between bites, his father asked if Latigo thought the palomino would amount to anything.

"I think so. He rides easy. Don't seem like nothin' much bothers him any."

"Sometimes them stud horses get a little ringey. You thought of cuttin' 'im?"

"Thought about it. Don't believe I will. Like I said, he's pretty calm."

His father thought for a time. "Well, you best keep an eye on 'im. Don't let 'im go crazy on you." He wadded his sandwich wrapper and stuffed it back into the canvas sack from his saddlebag. "We had best be ridin' if we expect to get home by supper."

They made it with time to spare, after doctoring a few more claves on the way. As Latigo pushed back from the table, Penny said, "Say, Orval, you and Raymond want to go the picture show tonight? They got a new cowboy movie this week."

"I don't know, Penny. Them cowboy movies ain't but a lot of nonsense."

"Whatever do you mean? They're good!"

Latigo laughed. "Oh, c'mon girly—when was the last time you saw one of them movie cowboys give a snotty-nosed calf a shot of antibiotic like me and Dad did today? That's the kind of thing cowboys do—not ridin' all over the country at a high lope firin' off them six-guns that hold lots more than six bullets. Heck, most of them cowboy movies ain't even got a single cow in 'em! And most of them movie cowboys wouldn't know which end of a cow gets up first anyway."

"Oh, Orval! They ain't supposed to be real! Everybody knows that. Movies is just for fun."

"You think so? There's probably folks all over the place in them cities back East that thinks them movie cowboys is the real thing."

"Well, who cares? They're fun to watch." She turned to her other brother. "What do you say, Raymond? You want to go?"

"Sure, Penny. I'll come along. I don't mind a little make believe. Beats the heck out of balin' hay."

As she cleared the table, Mother encouraged them to have a good time and begged them to be careful. Father reminded them they had a long day's work ahead of them come the morning, and said not to stay out too late. Latigo relented and agreed to go along and keep an eye on the other two.

Sitting in the dark munching popcorn, Latigo dozed off. But gunfire on the screen awakened him, and he watched as the "cowboy" in the white hat on the pinto pony with a tail so long it dragged the ground chased after four riders dressed in black. He did not count the shots the hero fired from the revolvers he held in each hand, but he suspected it surpassed the dozen the cylinders held—and that assuming the hammers had not rested on empty chambers for safety's sake.

A bullet must have found its mark, for one of the retreating riders tumbled out of the saddle, bouncing and rolling when he struck the earth. Somehow, he kept his grip on a bridle rein as he fell, pulling the horse down to fall with him. The hero reined up to determine the fate of his victim. He dismounted and found him stunned, but alive. With a heft on the miscreant's collar he lifted him to his feet and shoved him along to a trailside tree, where he tied him up with the scapegrace's own lariat. The outlaw's horse stood by, watching.

Meanwhile, the surviving trio of nefarious riders had veered off into the shelter of a cluster of rocks and boulders to discuss the situation. The leader, spitting venom through a thick black moustache, ordered his compadres to reverse course and overwhelm the hero with their superior numbers and firepower. The villainous men were reluctant, but obeyed the boss's orders at gunpoint.

The hero, hot on their trail, heard them coming. He holstered his twin six-shooters, and without his racing horse even breaking stride, he stood in the saddle. The overhanging limb of a tree offered refuge, and he grabbed hold, and spun once around the branch like a gymnast before hoisting himself to sit upon the limb. A sharp whistle sent his pinto horse off the trail to wait, concealed in a clump of trees.

Soon, the rascals appeared, racing along the trail, guns drawn. The leader was not leading the charge, however, choosing to take the fight to our hero from a position well behind his henchmen. As he passed beneath the tree concealing the hero, the man in the white hat dropped from his limb in a move perfectly timed to knock his adversary from the saddle.

The bad guy gained his feet, six-gun in hand, but was no match for the cowboy hero, who snapped off a shot that knocked the revolver from the vile hoodlum's hand without even drawing blood. The outlaw looked around for aid from his thugs, but they had ridden on after assessing the hopelessness of challenging the hero in the white hat.

"Give it up, Slocum!" the beau ideal said. "I've got you fair and square."

The villain sagged, at the same time raising his hands above his head in the classic sign of surrender.

The hero bound the hands of his two captives and followed them into town, annoying them along the way with a sermon on the importance of right living. The movie ended with the clang of the cell door in the local jail, the prisoners glaring out through iron bars.

On the ride back to the ranch in Latigo's battered 1948 pickup truck, Penny's delight bubbled over, spilling from her place on the middle of the bench seat onto the brothers who flanked her. "How'd you like the show, Raymond?

"I thought it was pretty good."

"How 'bout you, Orval?"

"Oh, I don't know—usual bunch of malarkey, I guess."

"You slept through half of it! How do you know?"

Latigo laughed. "Well, Sis, the half I did see looked about like all the others I've seen. Different color horse for the hero, maybe. Different crease in his hat. Still, there ain't much difference from one of them movie shows to the next."

They rode in silence for a time—if you don't count Penny's chatter, which did not require much listening to. Then Raymond said, "Heck, Orval, you got to admit them movie cowboys ride some pretty good horses."

Raymond and Penny saw in the weak glow of the dashboard lights Latigo nod in agreement.

"And most of them boys can flat-out ride."

"I reckon you're right, Ray. They do get up to some pretty good tricks—like that feller grabbin' onto that tree like he did."

Penny pitched in. "Some of 'em can handle a rope, too!"

Again, Latigo laughed. "Sure. They can put a loop around another horseback man. And I seen 'em throw a loop to rescue someone drownin' in a pond or sinkin' in quicksand. But I don't know as they could catch a steer hightailin' it through the timber. Come to that, I don't know as they could put a loop on a calf in a corral."

"Some could," Raymond said. "I read where some of them boys in the movies are sure-enough hands, gone off to Hollywood to get rich by bein' movie stars."

Latigo thought about that for a time. "Maybe so."

"Heck, Orval, that's what you should do! You and Raymond! You two can ride anything with hair on it, and you can rope as good as most anybody. Heck, you can even do some of that fancy ridin' you see in the picture shows—I seen you doin' some of them tricks right out there in the horse pasture, when Papa ain't around."

Both boys laughed. "And you better not be tellin' no tales on us, girl," Latigo said.

"I won't! You know I won't! Still, you should go off and be in the movies. Heck, that name you hung on yourself—'Latigo' Brown—even sounds like a movie star."

Latigo did not reply. Soon, Raymond snored softly, chin on his chest. Penny appeared to have wound down, staring out the windshield through eyes that focused on nothing. Latigo cranked down his driver's side window a few inches, needing the fresh air to keep him alert as he steered the truck down the lonely road toward home.

Chapter Three

The haying was a day away from done. Latigo, Raymond, Penny, and their father brushed dust and chaff from their clothes in the dark and washed up for supper.

"That Harley Warren friend of yours called a while ago, Orval. Long distance," Mother said, once the edge was off Latigo's hunger and he was eating at what looked to be an interruptible pace.

Latigo laid down his fork and looked up from his supper. "Oh? What did ol' Harley have to say?"

Mother refilled the gravy bowl and set out another plate of biscuits. "Said he won big at the rodeo up in Blackfoot. Wants you to meet up with him over to Oakley on Friday. Said he already got you entered, and paid your entry fees."

Latigo smiled and turned his attention back to the meal.

The family ate in silence for a time, Mother looking on from her station near the stove. She enjoyed watching hungry men eat. Even watching Penny feed her appetite after a long day driving the tractor pulling the hay wagon was satisfying.

Then, Father swallowed his last bite, emptied his milk glass to wash it down, and pushed his plate away. "One of these days, that rodeo business will be the death of you, Orval."

"Aw, heck, Dad, ain't hardly nobody gets killed rodeoin'."

"That may be so. But there's sure as hell a lot of cowboys get hurt by them broncs and bulls. Even ropers'll lose a finger now and then. You'll end up all stove up, one way or another, if you ain't careful."

"Yessir. I'll watch myself."

Mother let loose a long sigh. "I worry too, Orval. At least you've got better sense than to ride them bulls."

"Yes'm." Latigo pushed back from the table. "If it's okay, I think I'll take me a bath now. Then I'll maybe do a little readin' and get to bed early. The last of that hay ain't goin' to jump on the wagon by itself."

The hay did not haul itself. It took another long day of Latigo and Raymond plodding along beside the crawling wagon, hefting bales and lifting them with a push and shove of the knee onto the wagon bed, where father collected the bales bucked up by the boys to stack into a load. The stagnant air and stifling heat of unloading the wagon in the stackyard made the monotony of loading the wagon seem almost restful. But there was little about haying that any of the crew found enjoyable—save, perhaps, father, who saw in every bale he lifted the full stomachs of his cows come winter.

Latigo took satisfaction only in the fact that the job was done, freeing him to get back on the road to the summer rodeos. The drive to Oakley ended when he found Harley right where he expected to—napping in the shade of a tree at the fairgrounds. Latigo pulled his rusty tin trailer next to where Harley had unhitched his, dropped the tailgate and unloaded his horses.

The racket awakened Harley and he raised up on his elbows and tipped his hat back, watching his friend.

Latigo said, "C'mon sleepyhead. Let's go water these horses and have a look at the draw."

Harley made his way to his feet and stretched and yawned. He took the lead rope of the horse Latigo roped calves on and followed Latigo and his heeling horse over to the arena. While the horses sucked water from the trough, Harley told Latigo about his success last weekend in Blackfoot. They led the horses over to the wood building with its peeling paint that housed the rodeo office in the rear and the concession stand up front. Tacked to the outer wall in a constellation of tack holes from years past were sheets of paper for each rodeo performance, listing the events, the competing cowboys, and the livestock drawn for each.

"That bareback horse you got tonight might be good for some money," Latigo said.

"Yeah. But you got a better one tomorrow. You'll likely knock me out of the money—if I'm even in it. There's way better horses. Don't know 'bout some of these riders."

"I could win somethin' if I can get by that horse. He ain't too easy to ride. Bucks off most guys when he blasts out of the gate like he does."

Harley lamented a similar prospect in the bull riding. He had drawn an animal that got the better of most cowboys most times. Latigo's draw in the saddle bronc riding was a horse, relatively speaking, easy to ride but hard to win money on.

Unlike the colorful names given most of the bucking stock, the calves and steers in the timed events were designated only by numbers, mostly meaningless, unless you had seen the stock run. Unlike rough stock, timed even cattle came and went, and did not carry with them lasting reputations.

"Hey, Brown, what's that you got on your head?"

The voice came from behind the two cowboys, their attention yet fixed on the sheets tacked to the rodeo office wall. Latigo turned around and saw Danny Wickham, a bareback and bull rider who often showed up at the same rodeos as he and Harley. Flanking Wickham were two people unfamiliar to Latigo.

Instinctively, Latigo's eyes turned upward, as if to assure himself he still wore the hat he put on that morning when he left home.

Wickham Laughed. "I heard you wore one of them Mexican sombreros these days. Didn't expect to see you in no ordinary cowboy hat." The statement elicited a laugh from Wickham's friends. He tried for another. "I'm surprised to see you lookin' at the stock draw. What I hear is, you're a specialty act nowadays—dressin' up like a greaser and spinnin' ropes. Yessiree. Heard you gave up on cowboyin' to be a showman."

Wickham's friends laughed, despite his comments turning mean-spirited and away from friendly banter. On more than one occasion, Latigo had bested Wickham in the bareback riding, taking money from his pocket, and the fact irritated him like a bur under a saddle blanket.

"I bet you wish he would give up ridin' them bareback broncs, Danny," Harley said. "That way, you may be able to win some money."

Wickham laughed. "Harley, you're so full of shit your eyes are brown. I can ride circles around Latigo—or whatever the hell he's callin' himself now he's a performer—any day of the week."

"Like hell. Not only can Latigo outride you, he could do them rope tricks you're so all-fired excited about while he does it."

Latigo stood by, watching the argument.

"How about it, Latigo? What you got to say for yourself?"

"Not much I can think of, Danny. Only reason I did that trick ropin' and ridin' was to help out ol' Walt Barlow. That Mexican boy was sick and Mister Barlow worried about disappointin' the spectators." He shrugged. "Just helpin' out, that's all."

Harley said, "C'mon Danny. Go on and mind your own business. You've had your fun."

Wickham looked from friend to friend with a malicious grin. He reached out with a finger and ran it down Latigo's cheek.

Latigo grabbed his wrist. "What're you doin', Danny?"

The grin stayed put. "Just checkin' for grease. Wanted to see if you'd turned sure-enough greaser, or if it was just play actin'."

Latigo pushed Wickham's wrist away, shoving the cowboy a step backward as he did. Wickham bristled, and shoved back with both hands on Latigo's chest. He followed up with a sweeping roundhouse punch. But the blow did not land, as Latigo knocked it aside with a forearm.

"Knock it off, Danny!"

"I'll knock it off, all right," Wickham hissed through clenched teeth. "I'll knock your damn head off!"

Wickham's jab went wide when Latigo sidestepped. His uppercut did not miss. The fist hit Wickham on the point of the chin, snapping his head back and rattling his brain. He fell backward, the fall broken only when he bumped against one of his friends, who caught him under the arms and lowered him to the ground. The other of Wickham's sidekicks, a tall, skinny kid who looked unsure of what he was getting into, started toward Latigo, but stopped when Harley stepped in front of him.

"Stay out of it, you," Harley said. "Get Danny gathered up and get the hell out of here."

The two friends helped Wickham, whose senses were coming back to him slowly, standing him up and half-walking, half-carrying him away, slung between their shoulders.

"Well, hell," Latigo said as he watched. "I never thought a few rope tricks would lead to somethin' like that."

Harley snorted. "Aw, to hell with 'em. Let's go feed these horses and find ourselves somethin' to eat. All this excitement's got me hungry."

The cowboys had no trouble finding a table at the local café. It would have been a different story that—or any—morning, as it was the kind of establishment found in most Western towns, where farmers and ranchers and loafers congregated for morning coffee. The food was uniformly plain, good, and aplenty in most such places.

Back at the fairgrounds, Latigo went through his usual routine checking and adjusting his bronc saddle. Harley, too, followed his usual custom of laying back, tipping his hat over his face, and napping the afternoon away. Latigo let him sleep when he saddled his team roping horse and rode to the arena to stretch the horse's legs, familiarize it with the arena and the roping box. Latigo built and rebuilt and spun loops as they rounded the arena, limbering up his arm and testing the condition of the grass rope he carried.

Other cowboys did the same, or similar, things. One, Willard Smith, rode up to ride beside Latigo.

"How y'doin' Latigo?"

"I'm all right, Willard. How 'bout yourself?"

"Oh, I'm doin' okay. You up in the ropin' tonight?"

"Yup. Team ropin' tonight with Harley. Got a calf tomorrow night. Drawed up in the saddle bronc ridin' tonight, too."

Willard smiled at Latigo and said, "Heard you cold-cocked Danny Wickham a while ago."

Latigo shook his head and sighed. "Didn't mean to. He come at me. That boy don't like me. Don't know why. I ain't never had much to do with him."

"What I hear, he ain't too happy about you beatin' him in the bareback ridin' so much lately. He fancies himself a top hand, Danny does."

"He can ride 'em, that's for sure. But you pay your money and you take your chances—ain't no different for him than what it is for every other cowboy entered up in a rodeo."

Willard rode along in silence for a time. "Heard he was funnin' you about fillin' in for that trick roper a couple weeks back."

"Yeah, he mentioned it. But there wasn't no fun in it."

"I saw what you did at that rodeo. Hell, I thought you did good. You could take up fancy ropin' and ridin' regular, and put ol' Juaquin out of a job."

Latigo laughed. "Not me. Playin' with a rope's a way to pass the time, but that's all. And those ridin' tricks—well, I'd lots rather work on stayin' in the saddle, 'stead of jumpin' in and out of one, or standin' on it, or hangin' out of it—a feller could get hurt doin' that stuff."

Willard warned Latigo to keep an eye on Wickham—said he was known to bear a grudge and did not care much about fighting fair. He wished Latigo luck, then spurred his horse into a gentle lope and rode away.

Latigo rode around the arena visiting with other cowboys and cowgirls until the announcer, working up in the crow's nest preparing for the evening performance, came over the public address system. He asked the riders to clear the arena so the crew could bring in a tractor and harrow to work the ground.

Harley was stirring when Latigo got back to the trucks and trailers. His team roping horse stood soaking in the sun, saddled and ready to go, as was his bulldogging horse. Harley had put out a bale of hay and stuck a set of mounted steer horns in it, and was throwing loops to practice his head catch for tonight's team roping.

Latigo watched while he unsaddled his horse and scrubbed its sweaty back with a gunnysack. "How's it goin' Harley? Looks like your accuracy's up to about what, forty percent?"

Harley laughed. "Don't you worry none about me, son. You just have your heel loop ready when I nod for the steer—and make damn sure you get all four toes and all the dewclaws in it."

"That would be pure pleasure. Thing is, heelin' for you, a man don't get too many chances to throw his rope, so I might be a little bit out of practice."

Harley laughed again, and flung his loop into a flat overhead spin and snaked it through the air to drop over Latigo. He jerked in the slack as it settled around his ankles and pulled it snug. "See that, boy? You ain't the only one what can make a rope do tricks. You'll see I got both legs, too—you ought to try that, come team-ropin' time."

Latigo kicked loose the loop and stepped out of it, and Harley coiled his rope. "Well, son, it looks like the sun is sinkin' slowly in the west.

It's rodeo time!" He opened the cab of his pickup and tossed the rope onto the seat and fetched his gear bag with his bareback rigging from the back. Latigo put the saddle back on his heeling horse and worked over his feet with a hoof pick. He balanced his bronc saddle to ride atop the other, fetched his lariat, slung his war bag over his shoulder and led his horse toward the arena, joshing with Harley along the way.

From the front seat of his car, parked across the way, Danny Wickham watched them go. Given the soreness of his jaw and the ache in his head, he was glad he did not ride tonight.

But he had work to do behind the bucking chutes, and he would be there to do it.

Chapter Four

Moths darted about in the glow of the arena lights on their tall poles as the beams spread through dust stirred up by the Grand Entry. Latigo tied his roping horse to a fence rail after participating in the parade, as everyone who is mounted is encouraged to do, and hustled to the bucking chutes where Harley readied for his trip aboard his bareback bronc. Latigo grabbed the top of the highest chute board and jumped up to land on the plank to stand next to one of the arena crew, who was bent over into the chute latching and adjusting the flank strap around the horse.

Harley's rigging already sat on the bronc's withers, the latigo wound through the cinch ring and D-ring, ready to be tightened. Harley slid the rigging back and forth, feeling for the best seat. "Pull."

Latigo bent over into the chute and grabbed the leather latigo and stood, pulling the looped strap taut as he did. Harley rocked the rigging up and down, and pushed and pulled it side to side.

"More."

Latigo pulled harder on the leather, paused while Harley tested its position, then pulled again. Harley was satisfied, so Latigo pulled tight the tail end of the latigo where it threaded back through its top loop and handed it to Harley. He twisted the strap around and around to shorten its length before laying it across the horse's neck and threading it through the D-ring on the opposite side, then snugged it back against the front of the rigging, out of the way.

Out in the arena, the pickup men hazed a bronc along the fence toward the catch pen as its former rider stood near the chutes, watching the horse that had just bucked him off trot through the gate, waving him goodbye with its upheld, sweeping tail.

"Okay, Harley. Arena's clear. You're up," Latigo said. "Now, bear down and try! Kick the hair off this sumbitch!"

The gate men rattled the chute, the flank man readied to pull the strap tight when the bronc turned into the arena, and the chute boss hectored Harley to hurry. But Harley took his time as he set the grip of his leather glove in the handhold of the rigging, then slid up under his arm. He leaned back and hunched his shoulders, then slid his feet off the sideboards of the chute and hugged his knees against the horse's neck. He cocked his free arm and nodded.

With a rattle and clatter, the chute gate flung open. The flank man leaned back, pulling the strap and releasing it when the tension was right. The judges in the arena watched the position of Harley's feet to make sure he obeyed the mark-out rule, with his spurs over the point of the horse's shoulders when the horse turned out and its forefeet hit the ground.

Through it all, the announcer up in his booth had carried on a line of talk about Harley, about the bronc, and all manner of other patter, of which neither Harley nor Latigo had heard a word.

The horse turned out flat, and took a couple of long strides. Harley sat firm, almost upright, well-balanced, and held his feet in the front end. Then the bronc leapt into the air, jerking Harley's feet loose. The rider rocked back with the motion, and when the horse kicked its hind legs and started back down to the ground, that motion, and his grip on the rigging, pushed Harley back upright, threatening to jerk him over the front end. But he fought the momentum, keeping his seat, and finding a new hold between the bronc's neck and shoulders with his spurs. The same action, more or less, continued through the eight-second ride, except the horse, feeling respect for the balance of the cowboy on its back, started ducking and diving, reaching out with its front legs in one direction while tossing its head in the other, and kicking out sideways

28

with its hind legs. The movement created a jarring zig and zag to the forward motion, as well as a rock and roll to the up and down.

Harley weathered the storm, regaining his balance each time it was jolted loose, and finding new spur holds with every leap of the horse. It was the kind of ride that makes it both difficult to stay aboard, and hard to make the kind of showy ride that results in a high score. But the pair of judges on duty were experienced, and saw Harley's performance for what it was, rewarding him with a score that put him in second place, where he stayed for the duration of the night's bareback competition.

The pickup men rode in, one keeping the bucking horse on course while the other raced up next to the bronc. He reached down and pulled the latch on the flank strap, which fell away, then urged his mount to move ahead and past the bronc. The pickup man grabbed Harley under the arm as the rider let loose of his rigging and grabbed his rescuer around the waist and let himself be pulled and lifted off the bronc, then lowered safely to the ground.

Rather than walking back to the bucking chutes, as most riders did, Harley hurried along the fence to the other end of the arena and the timed-event chute, where he would soon be up in the steer wrestling. Latigo would fetch his rigging from the stripping chutes, where arena helpers removed it from the bronc, then he would venture to the other end of the arena for the team roping, which followed the steer wrestling.

Harley asked Everett Parker, the cowboy who would haze for him, if he knew anything about the steer drawn for him, but he did not, saying most of the steers in the pen were new, and had only been run a few times for training and practice. Everett was an old friend of Harley's and could always be counted on to do his job—keep the steer running straight down the arena, pushed near enough to the bulldogger's horse to allow him to drop off his mount onto the steer, grabbing it by the horns. When competing at a rodeo where Everett wasn't present, Latigo would take on the job of hazer—but he preferred not to, as he would rather keep his horse's mind on roping.

The steer they ran into the chute with Harley's number glued to its back turned out to be a good one. When Harley nodded for the gate, the steer came out clean, ran down the arena at a good pace, in a straight line. Harley leaned out and fell onto its shoulders, grabbing the left horn in his hand and tucking the right one in the crook of his elbow. As his bulldogging horse ran on by, Harley's feet pulled away, hitting the ground ahead of the steer. He slid along on the soles and heels of his boots, friction and strength slowing the steer as he lifted its head and twisted its neck, his left hand releasing the horn and wrapping his wrist beneath the steer's muzzle, continuing to lift and turn as the animal's rear end swung around. Harley laid back, pulling the steer down with him to land on its side. The horseback judge, flag held in the air, dropped the flag when the steer lit, stopping the clock on a time that put Harley in first place.

"Damn!" Latigo said when Harley walked through the gate out of the arena. "That was a heck of a run, Harley! Ought to hold up pretty good; keep you in the money."

"I hope so."

Everett trotted out through the gate leading Harley's bulldogging horse, smiling at Harley as he handed him the reins. "Nice job, son. That steer laid down like a pup for you."

"Sure did. Thanks for your help."

The hazer smiled again and rode away, contemplating a cut of the winnings for his work on what looked to be a winning run.

Harley unsaddled his bulldogging horse and tied it to the fence, then saddled and mounted his heading horse for the team roping, He and Latigo waited their turn outside the arena gate, watching the teams ahead of them go about their business. Between broken barriers, missed loops and single-leg catches with the resulting five-second penalty, the team stood a good chance of winning some money—if they could manage a quick, clean, run.

Which they did. Harley's horse pushed the barrier that guaranteed the steer a head start, but did not break it. As if it had eyes, his loop encircled the steer's horns. Latigo was ready when Harley dallied his rope around the saddle horn and turned sharply to the left, forcing the caught steer to follow. The heeling horse positioned Latigo for the throw, and his heel loop stood up under the steer's belly, the next hop landing both hind legs in the trap. Latigo reined up as he took his wraps, and his horse stepped backward, as Harley's did as well, after spinning around to face the steer. When the ropes drew taut, the flag judge signaled time, and the boys moved into the lead with the fastest time of the night.

Latigo was up next in the saddle bronc riding. But even though it was the next event, there was no rush. It was time for the rodeo clown and his trained dog to entertain the audience with tricks and jokes and a comedy routine. With rope horses tied and cinches loosened, they walked behind the bleachers to the other end of the arena and the bucking chutes.

The saddle broncs were already in the chutes, with bronc riders on the planks setting their saddles. Latigo picked up his gear, found his bronc, and threaded his buck rein through the ring on the halter. He dropped his saddle onto the horse and Harley hooked the cinch below. He looped the latigo through the ring and handed it up to Latigo, then hooked the back cinch and buckled it. Latigo set the saddle and drew the cinch tight enough to keep it in place for now, and positioned the back cinch and pulled it snug. Then, with Harley's help, he slowly tightened the latigo until the saddle had just enough play to absorb some of the shock from the horse's bucking, while still staying in place.

Stretching the buck rein back along the horse's neck and over the fork of the saddle, he measured the length of a fist and an extended thumb behind the pommel, snatched a few mane hairs loose, and threaded them through the loose weave of the rein to mark the spot. On most horses, the measure provided the proper length of rein for the rider to maintain balance—too short, and you could get pulled down over the front end; too loose, you could find yourself launched out of the saddle to the rear.

When it came time, Latigo stepped across the chute, straddled the bronc, and eased himself down into the saddle. He reached down to either side to ensure the stirrups were snug against the heels of his boots. Finding the mane hairs marking the buck rein, he slid it between his little finger and the others, laid it across the palm of his hand, closed his fist, and tucked his thumb over his fingers. Grabbing the front of the saddle fork for leverage, he squirmed into a deep seat in the saddle, clinched the swells with his thighs, held the buck rein out ahead of him, and nodded his head.

The gate swung open, but the horse stood, quivering, as if struck with stage fright. Harley, standing on the plank behind the chute, pulled off his hat and swatted the horse on the side of its head. That woke up the horse, and it turned out of the chute. As it did, Latigo's legs swung forward, planting his spurs over the point of the shoulders to meet the test of the mark-out rule. The horse lunged forward, feinted a move to the left, then ducked to the right. Completing a circle, the bronc again jumped forward, then sucked back to leap nearly straight up, landing on all fours, the force of the landing radiating up Latigo's spine. Still searching for some rhythm in the horse's movements, Latigo raked his spurs from above the shoulders to the cantle of the saddle, but, like the horse, his movements were jerky and erratic.

The horse again lunged forward. Latigo's eyes widened and his stomach turned over when the front of the saddle lifted as if on hinges, rising up and tipping him backward. The bronc hit the ground with its hind legs tucked, and lunged forward again, ducking to the right. The loose saddle, flopping in the front and sliding toward the horse's rump, slipped sideways. Latigo looked for a place to land, but the right stirrup lay across the saddle seat, his boot stuck tight. The horse ducked back to the left, the saddle, held only by the slack back cinch, slid farther down the side and almost under the horse, now upset and confused. Flapping like hanging laundry in the wind, Latigo tried to avoid the bronc's churning rear hooves. One of the pickup men rode into the storm and grabbed the loose buck rein and dallied it around his saddle horn, stifling, if not stopping the bronc's panicked thrashing.

Whether by chance or through effort, Latigo's foot slid out of the stirrup and his legs fell to the ground. He rolled away from the bronc and stopped on his hands and knees, trying to exhale. The rodeo clown and one of the chute helpers reached him in an instant, and knelt beside him.

"You all right, Brown?"

He turned to see the painted face of the clown inches from his own. While he could not catch a breath, the wind knocked out of him, he knew he was not seriously injured, so nodded his head.

"Here, help me out," the clown said to the other man. "Let's sit him up."

Each took an arm and helped Latigo to a seated position. The clown pounded on his back, which did not seem to Latigo to do anything but make it harder to breathe. He raised a hand and shook his head. The clown stopped. Latigo strained and his lungs started working again, his breathing rapid and shallow.

"Help me up, boys, I'm fine." The crowd broke into applause at the behest of the announcer when Latigo found his feet. One of the arena workers handed him his hat. He looked it over, and pushed the collapsed crown somewhat back into its normal shape and put it on his head. The men tried to steady him as they walked toward the bucking chutes, but Latigo shook them off.

While all this went on, the pickup men had stopped the bronc and unlatched the flank strap, then unbuckled the back cinch on the bronc saddle and let it fall to the ground. Harley, seeing that Latigo looked to be uninjured, fetched the saddle and carried it out of the arena and behind the bucking chutes, where Latigo sat, back against the board fence at the back of the alley, still catching his breath.

"What the hell happened?"

Latigo shook his head. "Don't know, Harley. Saddle just come loose all of a sudden."

Harley tipped the saddle up to check the rings, latigos, and cinch. "Sonofabitch! Would you look at that!"

Chapter Five

Harley swore again. He turned the saddle toward Latigo. "Look at that!"

Latigo followed the point of Harley's finger to the D-ring on the opposite side from where they had tightened the cinch. The end of the latigo strap was wrapped around the D-ring as it should be, secured there by a length of whang leather looped and tied through a pair of punched holes. But, instead of several feet of strap dangling, only a little more than a foot hung below.

"Where the hell d'you suppose the rest of it is, Latigo?"

The cowboy could only shake his head. He studied the end of the latigo. Most of the width of the inch-and-a-half-wide leather strap was sliced clean; the remnant rough and ragged, as if pulled and torn apart.

Harley stormed off, watched for a break in the action, and found the rest of the latigo strap in the dirt where the pickup men had dropped the underslung saddle off the frightened horse. Back behind the chutes, he and Latigo looked it over, seeing that the cut and tear matched the end secured to the saddle.

"Damn it all to hell!" Harley spouted. "Somebody done cut the damn thing!"

Latigo could only nod his head.

"You coulda been killed! Darn lucky you wasn't!"

Barely above a whisper, Latigo said, "Who would've done such a thing?"

Harley tipped over the saddle in disgust and stood, fists doubled at the ends of arms hanging at his sides. His eyes swept back and forth, watching the throng of cowboys going about their business behind the chutes. "I don't know. But I've got a pretty damn good idea."

Latigo unbuckled, removed, and rolled his chaps and stuffed the bundle into his war bag. A kid from the stripping chutes came by with his buck rein, and he coiled it and put it in the bag.

"You okay, Mister Brown?"

Latigo looked up at the boy. He guessed him to be thirteen or fourteen years old, likely looking for a start in rodeo. The kid, thumbs hooked in his pants pockets, shuffled his feet as he watched the older cowboy.

Latigo stood. "Yeah, I'm all right. That horse never wanted to hurt me. They won't stomp on you if they can help it." He patted the thigh of his right leg. "This here leg that got hung up is a few inches longer'n the other one now—but it'll shrink up in time." He smiled and extended a hand to the boy. "Thanks for bringin' my bronc rein by. I'd've got over there to the strippin' chute to fetch it sometime—but I'm honored you saved me the trip."

The kid, a flush creeping up past his shirt collar, grinned and shook the offered hand. "You're sure welcome, Mister Brown."

"Please don't call me Mister Brown—that's what folks call my granddad. You can call me Latigo."

"Sure thing, Mist—Latigo." The kid grinned again and hustled back to his assignment at the stripping chute.

Latigo laid the stirrup leathers across the seat of his bronc saddle and threaded one stirrup through the other to hold them there, out of the way. He slung the gear bag over his shoulder, stuck a hand into the gullet on the saddle and picked it up. "C'mon, Harley. We had best go see to our horses."

"Yeah. Then we'll go huntin' that sonofabitch."

"What sonofabitch?"

"You know damn well what sonofabitch—Danny Wickham!"

"Wickham?" You think he done this?"

"Damn right I do!"

Latigo shook his head. "I don't know, Harley. Seems more likely he'd mess with my bareback riggin' if it was him—he don't even ride saddle broncs, so there ain't no profit for him to mess me up there."

"Except payback for you knockin' his block off. This is just the kind of thing that lowlife sonofabitch would get up to, you ask me," Harley said, shaking the cut-off latigo strap toward his friend's face.

Latigo stared at Harley for a time, his brow wrinkled. He shook his head slowly, shrugged, and turned away. "C'mon, Harley. Let's go."

The horses got their fill of water before the cowboys led them back to the trailer. Latigo poured out a measure of oats for each of his horses, and unsaddled his team roping horse while the animal lipped the grain from its pile on the ground. He curried and brushed the sweat marks from the horse's back, then pulled a flake from a bale of hay for each horse. He locked his bronc saddle and war bag in the cab of the pickup, put his roping saddle in the trailer compartment and fixed the padlock through the hasp and staple.

Harley finished his chores at the same time. He said, "Let's get on back and watch the bull ridin'."

They wandered into the alley behind the bucking chutes where bull riders were getting ready while the last of the barrel racers completed their runs in the arena. Latigo found a seat atop a fence panel at the end of the chutes from which to watch. Harley said he would join him later. He worked his way along through the dim light in the alley, talking with cowboys he knew. Some of them had seen Danny Wickham there earlier, but no one had paid any attention to what he was up to, or if he—or anyone—had been near Latigo's bronc saddle.

"Nobody seen nothin'," Harley said as he climbed the fence to sit beside Latigo.

"I didn't figure anybody would. A man low enough to do somethin' like that to another man's bronc saddle would likely be sneaky enough to do it on the sly."

"Wickham was around, though."

"That ain't no surprise. Where else would he be? He's got just as much business here as me or you or anyone else who's entered up."

"I guess that's so. But you know as well as I do it was him that done it."

"Maybe so."

"Ain't no maybe about it. If it wasn't him, I'll eat my hat. 'Course, he could've had one of them local yokels that's followin' him around do it. But one way or another, Wickham was behind it—I just know it."

"Well, we'll have a hell of a time provin' it."

"Far as I'm concerned, we don't have to prove it. All we got to do is kick his ass—and if you don't want to do it, I sure as hell will."

Latigo sighed. "We'll see."

The bull riding went off without a hitch. It was a tough pen of bulls, and only two cowboys managed to make the eight-second whistle. The clown turned a couple of surly bulls away when they attempted hook their fallen riders, but there were no accidents or injuries.

Latigo and Harley went back to the trucks, intending to drive into town for a late supper. Nothing looked amiss at first glance—the horses all stood quietly, tied to the trailers, paying little attention to the dust and noise and lights of cars leaving the fairgrounds.

But Latigo sensed something wrong and stopped. "What the hell—my truck ain't sittin' right."

Harley looked, and could see the front end of the pickup slouched lower than it ought to. "Somethin's sure as hell wrong."

Latigo walked to the truck to find the left front tire flat. He walked around the front end to see the right front wheel also sitting on the splayed rubber of a flattened tire. "Well, Harley, looks like you're drivin' into town."

"Guess so. What do you suppose happened? You run over somethin'?"

Latigo shook his head. "Couldn't be that. Truck's been sittin' there all afternoon. Tires would've gone flat long time ago if I picked up nails or somethin' on the way here." He unlocked the truck and rummaged around in the jockey box and found a flashlight. In the dim yellow light from the weak battery, he studied the tire.

"Damn—looky here at this."

Harley squatted next to the slumped truck and saw Latigo poke the point of his finger into a slit on the sidewall of the tire.

"Bet the other side's the same," Latigo said, and walked around the truck to find it so. "Well, hell. Them tires is done for—you can't patch a hole in the side like that."

Harley stood with his hands in his pants pockets. He spat on the ground. "Danny Wickham. Again."

Latigo switched off the flashlight and shoved it into the jockey box with more force than necessary, but said nothing.

"You want we should pull them wheels off?"

"No, Harley. We can't do nothin' about it tonight. There'll be time enough tomorrow." He sighed. "I hope to hell our time holds up in the team ropin' and I get somethin' done in the bareback ridin' and calf ropin'. I never counted on buyin' no two new tires."

Supper was a solemn affair. The café was crowded and noisy with the after-rodeo crowd, but Latigo and Harley sat quiet in a corner booth. Harley showed his usual fondness for food, but Latigo only picked at his hot beef sandwich, swirling his fork in the gravy as it congealed. A few acquaintances stopped by their table to exchange pleasantries, but Latigo did not get beyond "howdy" with any of the visitors.

Harley left to use the restroom and stopped on his way back to the booth to settle the bill. "C'mon Latigo. Let's get out of here." He dropped a few coins on the table to tip the waitress. "I could use me a cold beer."

Latigo looked up at his friend. "I don't know Harley—I got plenty to do tomorrow. Besides, I ain't much in the mood to party."

"I ain't talkin' about no party. We'll just have us a beer, then go on back to the fairgrounds."

"How old you got to be to drink a beer in this town?"

"Hell, Latigo, I don't know. Don't care, neither. The place'll be so full of rodeo folks they won't have time to ask about your birthday. C'mon."

Latigo followed Harley out the door, and they walked across the street and halfway down the block to the beer joint. Music and colored light spilled out the propped-open front door. Several cowboys were on the sidewalk, leaning against the brick wall of the bar, talking and laughing and sipping beer from bottles. Some of them knew Latigo or Harley or both, and offered greetings as they passed.

Inside, Latigo stepped aside to wait by the flashing, vibrating juke-box blaring out a popular song called "Rhumba Boogie" by Hank Snow. Harley elbowed his way back from the bar through the crowd, doing his best not to let any of the foam-topped beer tip out of the schooners. They stood, sipping their beer, watching the crush of people whooping and hollering. Now and then the pistol shot of billiard balls striking each other on unseen tables somewhere in the depths of the tavern broke through the clamor.

Latigo finished his beer and set the glass on a window sill. "Let's go."

"All right. Let me finish this," Harley said, lifting his glass. He tipped it up and took a swallow, his attention still on the crowd. "There's that sonofabitch!"

He slugged off that last of his drink and put the glass on top of the jukebox, where it hummed and jiggled to the throbbing heartbeat of "Always Late with your Kisses" by Lefty Frizzell.

"You go on outside, Latigo. Meet me around the side of the building."

Unsure of what his friend was up to, Latigo slipped out the door, glad to be out of the stifling darkness and air that had already been breathed too many times. Soon, Harley came around the corner and into the alley, half carrying and half dragging the much-smaller Danny Wickham by a fistful of the back of his shirt collar. He shoved Wickham into the wall as he turned loose of his shirt.

"Here he is, Latigo."

Wickham looked at Latigo, wide-eyed, and saw that he looked as surprised to be there as he was. "You got somethin' to say, Brown?" he said, stretching his neck and tugging his collar back to where it belonged.

"Well…" Latigo said, so surprised by the turn of events he did not know how to continue.

Harley reached out and shoved Wickham's shoulder, forcing him to step sideways to keep his balance. "I'll say it. You seen a black '48 Ford pickup truck lately? Up close?"

Wickham blanched, but did not lose his bluster. "I got no idea what the hell you're talkin' about."

"Don't bullshit me, Danny." Harley looked at Latigo.

Latigo cleared his throat. "I had a little accident in the bronc ridin' today, Donnie. You know anything about that?"

Wickham sneered. "I heard about it, Brown. That's too bad."

"Thing is, it wasn't no accident. Somebody messed with my bronc saddle. I got a pretty good suspicion it might have been you."

"Well, you arrogant bastard, you just go on ahead and 'suspicion' all you want. Unless you got proof, you stay the hell away from me."

Wickham tugged his hat down tight and took the first step toward leaving. But he got no farther, as Harley pushed him back against the wall.

"You got a knife, Danny?" Harley said as he patted him down. "Ah! What's this?" He shoved his fingers into the right front pocket of Wickham's jeans and pulled out a clasp knife. "What you been doin' with this here knife, Danny?"

Harley stepped back and opened the longest blade, testing its sharpness with his thumb. "What do you think, Latigo—this here knife look like it might've cut a latigo strap, or maybe poked a hole in a couple of pickup truck tires?"

Before Latigo could answer, Wickham squawked, "Oh come on, Harley—damn near everybody packs a pocketknife! Hell, I'll bet either one or both of you's got one on you right now!" He turned to Latigo. "I'm tellin' you, Latigo, I don't know what the hell he's talkin' about."

Latigo took a deep breath and let it out long and slow. "You might be right, Danny. But I don't think so. I ain't got no proof, so I'll let it slide. But I'll tell you this—anything else unexpected happens, I'll kick your ass six ways to Sunday. And then I'll prop you up and do it again. You understand what I'm tellin' you? You leave me the hell alone, or you'll get a beatin' you won't soon forget."

Danny looked from Latigo to Harley and back again. "I hear you. But, like I said, I ain't done nothin' to you." He turned back to Harley. "Now, give me back my pocketknife."

Harley stuck the open blade of the knife into the gap between the bricks on the wall, pried, and snapped it off. "Sure, Danny. Here you go."

He dropped the broken knife and it fell to the ground. Then he and Latigo walked away, leaving Wickham seething.

Chapter Six

Latigo sat on the ground next to the jacked-up truck, the wheel between his legs, tightening the lug nuts when Harley's hazer rode up on his hazing horse, leading a haltered horse. He sat horseback watching Latigo work. Harley stood by in front of the truck, ready to lower the bumper jack when Latigo finished with the jack handle that also served as the lug wrench.

"How you doin' this morning, Everett?"

"Doing fine, Harley. My momma always told me every new day was full of promise. Could be there's good things on the way."

"I hope that's so for ol' Latigo here. He's the proud owner of a pair of brand-new tires, but his checkbook ain't nearly as excited about it as he is. Fact is, I heard that checkbook whimper when he tore out the check to give to the man at the shop to pay for these tires."

Everett sat quiet for a time. Then, "I heard something about those tires."

Latigo and Harley perked up. Latigo stopped work, took off his hat, mopped the sweat wetting his forehead with a shirtsleeve, and asked what he had heard.

"Well, you know, I was at the beer joint last night having a few, and Danny Wickham and those two local yokels he's been hanging around with were there. Danny, he wasn't too drunk, but the others were. They were laughing and talking with some other local boys, bragging and telling lies and the like. I couldn't hear exactly what all they were saying. But one of those friends of Danny's—I don't know his name—was giggling and carrying on, and he made a motion like he was poking a hole in something with a knife, then he took to hissing, like he was losing air. This morning, when Willard Smith told me about your truck tires getting flattened, it put me in mind that they might be connected."

"You're sure?"

"No, Latigo, I can't be certain. Like I said, I couldn't hear what all they were saying. That bar was pretty noisy. But I saw him laughing, and doing like I said. He did it twice, too, so there ain't no doubt in me about that much of it."

"What'd that boy look like, the one who did that?"

"He's the tall one—skinny, pencil-necked fella been with Danny. He's got that eagle feather in his hat."

Latigo nodded. "I know the one you mean." Latigo thought for a minute. "Danny was there? When he did that?"

"Sure was. He was laughing right along with them."

Harley looked like a balloon about to burst. A red balloon. "Them sonsabitches!" he hissed. "You hear any of 'em say anything 'bout messin' with Latigo's bronc saddle?"

Everett shook his head. He watched Harley work the handle on the bumper jack, dropping the front end of the truck like he was gravity itself. He finished the job, drops of sweat falling from his nose and chin, and his breaths coming fast and shallow—whether from exertion or anger, Everett could not say.

"You sure you didn't hear nothin' 'bout the bronc saddle?"

Again, Everett shook his head.

"Don't worry about it, Harley," Latigo said. "Could be we won't never know for sure. But I'll damn sure be askin' that tall drink of water 'bout them tires."

Everett bid them good day and rode off toward the arena to exercise the horses. Harley seemed to calm down some as he and Latigo stowed the jack in the truck.

"Latigo, we never got no breakfast and my stomach thinks my throat's been cut. Sounds like they got that carnival cranked up yonder way. What say we go on over there? I'm bettin' we can get us a hot dog or some other gut bomb. I'd eat damn near anything 'bout now."

The cowboys walked across the fairgrounds and beyond the rodeo arena to the carnival midway. The closer they got, the more insistent came the monotonous faux-calliope music from the merry-go-round. Motors and chains and pistons and wheels on carnival rides clattered and rattled and groaned. Smells from oily machinery and cooking grease and unwashed bodies concocted a miasma that settled over the midway like a fog that refused to dissipate.

Town kids scampered from one carnival attraction to another, faces smeared and stained and sticky from cotton candy and candy apples, mustard and ketchup. Harried parents rode herd, as much as is possible in a stampede, some pushing baby buggies and strollers over the trampled dirt and grass, their streaming sweat not enough to settle the dust. Drifts of discarded food wrappers plastered tent walls and the fences around the rides like wallpaper, held there by a light but persistent wind heated in a furnace or kiln fired at whatever place weather originates.

Harley stepped up to the window of a food wagon on wheels and ordered half a dozen corn dogs. He was halfway through the haul, dunking the battered wieners on their sticks into puddles of mustard and ketchup, by the time Latigo sat down in the shade of a tent wall with a hamburger dripping grilled onions, and a paper boat of French-fried potatoes. Sweating bottles of root beer washed the food down both throats.

While the greasy food did not satisfy Harley's appetite, it did take the edge off it. Wiping his fingers one at a time on a flimsy paper napkin, he studied the parade of people tramping up and down the midway.

"You done eatin' yet, Latigo?"

"All but," Latigo said, licking his fingers and mopping a dribble from his chin.

"Well, get it in you. We got work to do."

Latigo swallowed a wad of French fries. "Oh—what's that?"

"I see Danny Wickham and his gunsels over yonder way," Harley said, nodding his head as a pointer.

Latigo guzzled the remaining root beer in his bottle. He and Harley gathered their food wrappers and piled them atop the heap on an overflowing trash barrel. They gave the empty root beer bottles to a boy pulling a red wagon, which clinked with a load of other glass bottles he had collected for the bounty they would earn upon return to a store.

Wickham and his cronies stood in passing shade and sunlight cast by the Ferris wheel turning around and around at the end of the midway. All three looked somewhat the worse for wear, eyes bloodshot and red-rimmed, clothes disheveled and shirts sweat-stained, and unkempt hanks of hair poking out from under hats.

"Say, Danny, you don't look so good today. You think you'll be in any shape to ride your bareback horse this evenin'?"

"To hell with you, Latigo. I'll be there. And I guarantee I'll beat your sorry ass."

Latigo smiled. "Maybe so. But I guess the judges'll have somethin' to say about it."

Harley said, "I heard you boys was whoopin' it up pretty good down at the bar last night."

Wickham's sidekicks mustered weak smiles and looked at one another. Danny said nothing.

"What was it that was so funny?"

Again, no response other than a giggle that escaped from the tall skinny one.

Latigo looked hard at him. "I don't believe I've had the pleasure of meetin' you. Seen you around here, but can't say as we've met. My name's Latigo Brown." He extended his hand.

The toady's long neck worked up and down as he swallowed hard. When he spoke, his voice cracked. "Alan. Alan Nicholson." He swallowed again, his narrow neck revealing a throat working overtime inside. "Folks call me Slim." He took the offered hand.

Latigo smiled and squeezed the hand, crushing it in his grip. Slim cringed.

"Slim, huh? Well, I'll tell you what you're goin' to do, Slim. Reach around with your other hand and fetch me the wallet out of your back pocket. And don't tell me you ain't got one, 'cause I can see where it's worn tracks on your pants."

Slim did as ordered, still wincing from the pressure on his hand. Latigo took the wallet, then released the hand. He opened it and pulled out three bills—a twenty and two ones, all well-worn, wrinkled, and damp.

"Twenty-two dollars. Hell, Slim, you're flush. But this ain't but about half of what you owe me."

Another hard swallow. "Owe you? What do I owe you for?"

"Just this morning I put two new tires on my truck. Had to, on account of somebody—I thought it was ol' Danny here, but word is, it was you—poked holes in the old ones."

"I never did no such thing! It was—" A poke in the side by Wickham's other bootlicker cut the answer short."

"Who? Who was it?"

No response. This time it was Latigo who poked him, just below the ribs, his finger sinking up to the second knuckle, nearly deep enough to reach the spine on Slim's narrow frame. Slim gasped and doubled over.

Harley pounded his back. "Take a breath, Slim. Take a breath."

Slim stood, crouched with both hands gripping his stomach. "It was Bucky. Bucky's the one what done it."

Latigo looked at the third member of the trio. The nickname fit the kid's prominent overbite and receding chin. "You Bucky?"

The kid took a step back, looking from side to side as if an avenue of escape might reveal itself. But his face sagged as he abandoned any hope of flight and nodded his head.

"Was it you who ruined the tires on my truck?"

Again, he nodded.

"Well, then, let's have a look in your wallet, Bucky."

He reached to his back pocket and pulled out a billfold. "There ain't nothin' in it. I'm flat broke. Spent ever' cent I had at the beer joint last night."

"How'd you intend to eat?" Harley said.

"I was goin' to borrow off of Slim. I knowed he had that twenty dollars."

Latigo smiled. "I guess you done borrowed it, then. You—or somebody—still owes me twenty-three bucks more." He looked at Wickham, then back at Bucky. "Where do you aim to get it?"

Bucky shrugged. "Maybe if Danny wins somethin' in the bares tonight, he'll give me the loan of it."

Harley laughed. "I wouldn't count on that. Danny looks like shit warmed over. I don't reckon he'll be up to much tonight."

"Like I told Latigo, don't you worry none about me. I'll be ready."

"I sure hope so," Latigo said. "You better hope you win somethin'. 'Cause if I don't get my money tonight, I'll take it out of ol' Bucky here's hide. Then I'll go to work on you. 'Cause I got me a sneakin' suspicion that even though one of your flunkies done the job, he did it on account of you said to."

49

Latigo folded the clammy bills and stuck them in his front pocket. Wickham turned to leave, his followers following.

"One more thing, Bucky."

Bucky stopped and turned around, as did the other two.

"Since you seem to be handy with a frog sticker, you know anything 'bout the latigo strap on my bronc saddle bein' cut?"

Bucky blanched, but only shook his head in reply.

"How 'bout you, Slim?"

He swallowed hard, his Adam's apple working in his throat like the sucker rod leathers on a windmill pump, but he, too, shook his head.

Harley said, "Well, Danny already denied doin' it, so one thing's for damn sure—one or all three of you sonsabitches is lyin' like a dog on a hot day. Sooner or later, we'll find out which one of you done it. Then, like I told Latigo, if he ain't in a mood to kick your ass, then I'll be standin' in line for the job. Hell, I might decide to beat the hell of all three of you anyway 'cause I know one of you done it." He glared at Wickham. "And I'll start with you, Danny. Even if one or the other of these gunsels did it, you're the one pullin' their chains."

Wickham stared at one, then the other, of the pair, then repeated the glare with a look that made the red in his bloodshot eyes seem to glow like fire. "I'll be goin' now, boys. I need to rest up for tonight." He started away, then stopped. "And don't you boys be thinkin' I'm dodgin' you. Hell, I'd take either one of you on right this minute if I wasn't feelin' so poorly."

Harley smiled. "Well, you go on along and get yourself feelin' better, Danny. We'll be waitin'—but I ain't got much patience, so don't keep me waitin' too long."

Chapter Seven

The Saturday night rodeo was over. Latigo survived his bareback bronc's initial jump out of the gate that bucked off most cowboys. The horse reared up until near vertical and lunged out of the chute as if blasted from a mortar. Latigo went on to complete the ride, topping Harley's score and that of another rider to win first-place money. Danny Wickham's horse, the best draw in the pen, performed up to expectations, but the rider did not. He weathered the storm, but without much style to his ride, to earn fourth-place money; a win he owed mostly to the strength of the horse.

Latigo caught his calf in the roping in good time, but the beefy critter ran back up the rope on him. Flanking the hefty calf without any help from his horse, despite the mount's scuttling backward as quickly as possible to take the slack out of the rope, proved a chore. Latigo finally tipped the calf over and completed the tie. But time lost in the struggle put him out of the money. Harley did not get past his bull, tossed out of a fast spin like a stone from a slingshot. Still, between the two of them, the weekend's winnings were sufficient to get them down the road to the next rodeo—in Las Vegas—on full stomachs and with full gas tanks.

After the bull riding, Harley and Latigo were in the alley behind the bucking chutes stowing gear in their war bags when Wickham's toady Bucky came along. Slim was with him, but he hung back, watching.

"Here you go, Latigo," Bucky said, holding out folded bills. "You said twenty-three dollars. It's all there. Go ahead and count it if you want."

Latigo eyed the boy and unfolded the wad. He peeled off a ten-dollar bill, a five, and eight ones. "Danny give this to you?"

Bucky shook his head. "Nah. I went home and got it off my old man. He weren't too happy about it. Kicked my ass good, if you want to know the truth. It ain't like we got a lot of money."

"Well, kid, you ought to keep that in mind next time you take a notion to flatten somebody else's tires."

Bucky nodded. "Yeah. I know. I ain't never done nothin' like that before. But Danny, well, he…."

Latigo folded the money and stuffed it into the front pocket of his jeans. "You might want to hang out with a better class of people, Bucky."

He stuffed his hands into the front pocket of his pants. He looked back at Slim. "Just so's you know it, it weren't me nor Slim that messed up your saddle."

Harley jumped into the conversation, asking if Wickham had been responsible. Bucky allowed that he did not know—Wickham had not said anything to them about it. At the same time, he did not doubt that he had done it.

"Well, boys, I'd like to say it's been a pleasure, but it sure as hell ain't," Latigo said. He slung his gear sack over his shoulder and he and Harley set out for the timed-event end of the arena to fetch Latigo's roping horse.

Latigo and Harley soon had most of their gear loaded and the trailers hitched, and were about to load horses when a car pulled up, its headlights piercing the dust hanging in the air. Through squinted eyes, Latigo looked at the car, unsure of what he was seeing. It was a long, low, wide convertible that looked to be about the size of a hay wagon. A set of steer horns, mounted on the front of the hood, stretched to nearly the width of the car. It looked like one of those cars he had heard about, but was not sure he believed the stories, driven by Texas oil men. And yet here was one, sitting not twenty feet away, the dust settling about it in the glow of the headlights.

The engine shut down, but the headlights stayed on. The door opened and a tall, broad man stepped out. Latigo could not make out the man's features in the dim light, but could see he was wearing a suit with a Western cut, a string tie at his throat, a cigar in his mouth, and a broad-brimmed, high-crowned hat. As he walked toward Latigo and Harley, polished steel caps on the toes of his boots glinted in the headlights.

"You would be Latigo Brown, if I am not mistaken," the man said, reaching out to shake Latigo's hand.

Latigo took the man's hand, and it closed around his with a vice-like grip. "Yessir. That's me. And who might you be?"

"I am Junior Blevins. I am pleased to make your acquaintance, Latigo Brown." He turned his attention to Harley. "And you must be Harley Warren."

"That's what my Momma calls me, so I guess I must be."

He turned back to Latigo. "Tough break in the calf roping, Latigo old son. But you looked right fine in the bareback riding. They say you two won the team roping, too. And placed in a couple other events, they tell me. Pretty good winnings, all in all, wouldn't you say?"

With furrowed brow, Latigo said, "I guess we did okay. What can we do for you, Mister...."

"Blevins. Call me Junior," he said, grasping the lapels of his suit jacket in his hands. "Here's the thing. I saw you boys perform tonight, and I am impressed. You look to be a couple of fine cowboys. Top hands. Last weekend, I was at a rodeo over in Evanston, put on by Walt Barlow. He speaks highly of you boys. He tells me, Latigo Brown, that you did a credible job for him filling in for the Tampico Twister."

Blevins could not see Latigo's blush in the dim light.

"Now, you boys have no doubt noticed that I travel with a good deal of flash. That is not by happenstance. While some mistake me for a Texas oil man—an impression that is erroneous, but not unwarranted—I hail from the great state of Wyoming. Sweetwater County, to be precise. My family has ranched there since territorial times. But it is not cattle upon which we have built the Blevins empire, but coal. Our land is rich with anthracite, and that richness has enriched generations of Blevinses."

After a silence, Latigo spoke. "That's a right fine story, Mister Blevins—Junior. But what's that got to do with us?"

"Glad you asked. Here's the thing, boys. You have heard of the town of Jackson, Wyoming?"

The boys allowed as they had.

"I am in the process of putting on a rodeo there. Not a once-a-year affair like this," he said with a wave of his hand around the fairgrounds. "I intend to put on a performance seven nights a week. You see, since the end of the war, tourists are pouring into the area. They come to see the National Parks—Yellowstone and Grand Teton. Most of those tourists come with pockets stuffed with cash. And I intend to deprive them of some of that cash—in exchange, of course, for some genuine Wild West entertainment in the form of a nightly rodeo."

Again, the silence stretched. Again, Latigo broke the silence. "That sounds right fine, Junior. But I still don't see what that's got to do with me and Harley."

"Don't you understand, boys? I am opportunity come knocking! I propose to employ you, Latigo—and you too, Harley—as star attractions of my nightly affair."

"Just how's that goin' to work?"

"The rodeo—the Grand Teton Stampede, it will be called—will run like any rodeo, open to any and all cowboys, come what may. There will be prize money paid—a modest amount, but prize money, nonetheless.

However—and this is where you come in, boys—attracting a sufficient number of contestants on a nightly basis to present a show for the tourists will not happen immediately, so I intend to, shall we say, stack the deck, or salt the mine. A prescribed number of cowboys will be on my payroll, their jobs being to show up every night and compete in their chosen events. In addition to what I pay them, any winnings will be theirs as well.

"Now, as for you, Latigo Brown, I will increase your salary significantly if you will perform for the crowds trick roping and trick riding, as you did for Walt Barlow."

Latigo laughed. "You got me all wrong, Junior. I'm just a cowboy, I ain't no performer. I only did that stuff to help Mister Barlow out of a tight."

"I don't care why you did it, Latigo Brown. Fact is, you've got the talent and the ability and that's what counts. And, don't forget, it's sure money. Now, I don't know how much you earn on the rodeo circuit, but this money is steady. And, of course, it will be supplemented by money won in the rodeo events, which I am confident you will continue to do well at."

Latigo turned to Harley. "What d'you think?"

Harley shrugged. "I ain't had time to think. I ain't against the idea right off, but I got to think on it some 'fore I can say anything."

This time, Junior Blevins broke the stretching silence. "Add this to your calculations. As I said before, many of those tourists are rich folks. Some of them come from Hollywood. Movie people. Good looking kid like you, Latigo Brown, you could end up in the movies once they see what you've got. Come to that, they make movies right there in Jackson Hole sometimes. You could easily work in those movies—doing horseback stunts, being extras. Like I said, a good-looking kid like you could end up with a speaking part—even become a regular actor, a movie star, a cowboy hero. But you'll never do that at rodeos like this," he said, again waving his arm across the fairgrounds. "You come to Wyoming and work for me, son, and there ain't no limit on what you can do."

"Well, Mis—Junior, like Harley says, it'll take some thinkin'. Fact is, bein' a cowboy movie star ain't exactly on my mind. Neither is bein' a rodeo performer like Juaquin Garza. Like I said, I'm just a cowboy."

Blevins reached into the inside pocket of his suit jacket and came out with a handful of cards printed with his name and address and telephone number and passed one to each cowboy. "Well, boys, you think on it. Here's my card. Tells you where you can get in touch with me. But don't wait too long—the Grand Teton Stampede is going to be a success with or without you. You may as well come along and share in that success. Like I said, you come to Jackson Hole and the sky's the limit." Junior Blevins again shook hands with Harley and Latigo. "By the way, boys, Danny Wickham—I'm confident you know him—has all but agreed to become a leading attraction at the Grand Teton Stampede."

Blevins climbed into his oversized automobile, started the big engine and revved it up a time or two, then drove away, stirring up a cloud of dust as he went.

As he drove away, Latigo looked at Harley and Harley looked at Latigo. "I guess he don't know that that last thing he said ain't goin' to work in his favor," Harley said.

"No, it ain't. I can't see no profit in spendin' that much time bein' around the likes of Danny Wickham."

Harley smiled. "Well, hell, Latigo—if we don't go, it could be you'd just be kissin' goodbye your chance for the fame and glory of bein' a cowboy movie star."

Latigo led the way down the lonely highway deep into the night. They reached the Brown Ranch in the wee hours of the morning and pulled in at the barn. After unloading the horses and turning them into a pen with water, Latigo broke open a bale of hay and spread it in the manger.

"C'mon, Harley. Let's get on over to the house and get to bed 'fore it's time to get up again."

"You go on ahead, Latigo. I'll just sleep in my truck. Don't want to disturb your folks and all, traipsin' around in the middle of the night."

Latigo laughed. "Look yonder at the house, ol' son. Mom's already got the kitchen light on, and unless I miss my bet, she'll have somethin' to eat on the table by the time we get there. Besides, you know Mom and Dad won't take kindly to you sleepin' out here when there's a perfectly good bed in the house. You know 'em better'n that."

"I suppose you're right."

The boys filled up on cold roast beef sandwiches and milk. No sooner had they crawled into bed than Latigo's brother Raymond started shaking shoulders. "Come on you two lazybones. Get up and piss—the world's on fire!"

Latigo rolled onto his back and pressed a pillow over his face. Harley sat up in the bed and scrubbed his face with the palms of his hands. "Good Lord, Ray—what time is it?"

"It's morning time. Sun's up. We're burnin' daylight. Chores is done. I already grained them nags of yours. They still had hay left over from whenever you fed them supper. More like breakfast, maybe."

"So what for would we want to get out of bed?" Latigo groaned from under his pillow.

"Dad wants to move the cows up on the mountain lease onto a new pasture. Says if we all go to help, it'll go lots easier. You too, Harley. Dad's got a horse already picked out for you—don't worry, it's a nice gentle old nag."

Harley took a half-hearted swipe at Raymond. He lifted his hat off the bedpost and put it on, then slung his legs over the side of the bed, found his pants and pulled them on. He reached back and gave Latigo a shove. "Remind me of this next time you invite me to sleep at your place."

Over breakfast with the rest of the family—Mom and Dad and Raymond and Penelope—Latigo told of their successes and failures at the rodeo. He left out the part about the cut latigo on the bronc saddle and slashed truck tires, hoping to spare his parents'—especially his mother's—concern for his safety.

Latigo took a deep breath and held it when Harley said, "There's somethin' else. Somethin' Latigo ain't told you."

Every eye around the table locked on Harley, except Latigo's, which were downturned, studying the faded pattern on the oilcloth covering the table. He exhaled in relief when Harley started talking.

"There was this rich feller, see. Rancher from out in Wyoming whose family got rich off of coal. He's startin' up a rodeo up in Jackson Hole. Every night, for tourists. He wants me and Latigo to go on up there and work for him. Says he'll pay us regular, plus whatever we can win in the rodeo."

Latigo's mother said, "Orval, is this something you think you might do? Jackson Hole's a long ways from home."

"Oh, I don't know Mom. It ain't likely."

"The thing is, that feller—Blevins is his name, Junior Blevins—he says he wants ol' Latigo here," Harley said, reaching out and clapping Latigo on the shoulder, "to do some fancy ropin' and trick ridin' too. Says there's sometimes movie folks up there in Jackson Hole. Says ol' Latigo here would catch their eye with his good looks and natural abilities, and they'd make him a cowboy movie star."

"I knew it!" Penny said. "Didn't I say so, Latigo? Didn't I say you ought to be in the movies?"

"Oh, Penny—it ain't nothin'. Just that old boy blowin' smoke is all. Ain't no way in hell you'll be seein' me in no picture show."

Chapter Eight

Once again, Latigo rode Nugget, his young palomino horse, onto the mountain. The day went without a hitch, the cattle soon gathered and moved onto a new section of the government lease. Latigo's father sat by the gate and kept count as he watched the cattle move through, pushed slowly by the other riders. He also noted any that looked to need attention, and the crew cared for them before coming down off the mountain.

Late afternoon and the evening after supper found Latigo in the round corral they used for training, working on the finer points of Nugget's education. Harley, Penny, and Latigo's father watched, and Raymond joined the crowd on the top rail after finishing his chores.

"Orval, he thinks the world of that palomino stud," Dad said. "Says he'll make a hell of a cow horse once he gets him schooled."

Harley said, "Looks to me like he might be right. He moves pretty good. And it looks like he's already keepin' up with what Latigo's got in mind—if not bein' ahead of him."

"That ain't hard to do," Raymond said with a laugh. "That old spotted dog asleep yonder by the barn is way ahead of Latigo when it comes to thinkin'. At least that dog's got better sense than to climb onto them rodeo broncs."

Harley reached out and punched Raymond lightly on the shoulder. "Ah, c'mon, Ray! Rodeoin's more fun than most anything else you can do that's legal! You ought to give it a try."

"Not me," Raymond said with a shake of his head. "I don't see no sense in gettin' on a horse that don't want me on him. I'll just fall down the stairs if I want to get busted up. And them bulls you get on—ain't no wonder your brain's addled, Harley."

Harley punched Raymond on the shoulder again, and turned his attention back to the horse. "What do you think, Mister Brown? You think Nugget'll make a horse?"

"Could do. He's pretty even-tempered for a stud horse. If that don't change as he gets older, he could be a good'n."

"I think he's pretty," Penelope said. "He's ever' bit as good lookin' as them horses on TV and in the movies."

"Well, honey," father said, "you best go on into the house and borrow that Brownie camera of your mother's and take a picture of Orval on that horse. That's likely the closest you'll ever come to seein' them two in a picture show."

Latigo unsaddled the tired horse in the gloaming, and was up again at dawn to start again. Harley saddled another horse and together they rode out through the pastures and meadows of the Brown Ranch. Latigo played with his lariat as they rode, to accustom Nugget to the presence of a spinning and thrown rope. Harley tossed a few loops out in front of and under the horse, again to help it overcome the oddity of a swirling and twisting and flying lariat.

The next day found them horseback again, this time after hauling the horses the few miles into town and the rodeo arena. Around and around Latigo rode Nugget, in circles and figure-eights, teaching the horse to change leads smoothly. He rode into the roping boxes while Harley rattled gates and latches. Nugget shot out of the box at Latigo's urging, streaking down the arena and sliding to a stop at his command. Nugget practiced spinning, his hind legs acting as a pivot as his front legs clawed a circle in the dust one way, then the other. He walked backward, spun around and walked backward the other way, and accomplished all manner of other maneuvers at Latigo's touch and commands.

"By damn, Latigo, I believe you've got yourself a horse there," Harley said.

"He's a quick learner, that's for sure."

"Why don't you try a few of them tricks of yours on him—y'know, jumpin' off and swingin' back on, and such."

"Oh, I don't know if he's ready for that, Harley."

"Aw, c'mon—give it a try. You and Nugget ain't never goin' to get in the movies if you don't know a few tricks."

Latigo shook his head. "Harley, I don't know who's worse when it comes to me bein' in the movies—you or Penny."

Harley smiled. "Don't forget ol' Junior Blevins."

Latigo urged Nugget into an easy trot down the arena. He grabbed the saddle horn and lifted a leg across the cantle and hung in one stirrup for a few strides, the horse craning its neck around to see what had appeared beside him. Latigo slid his foot out of the stirrup and dropped to the ground. Nugget shied, sidestepping away. Latigo lost his grip on the horn and stumbled to his knees. Nugget bolted, but stopped after a few strides, twisting his neck to look back at Latigo as if surprised to see him there on the ground.

Horseback again, Latigo repeated the moves. This time, Nugget knew what to expect, and kept trotting when Latigo stepped out of the saddle. Latigo ran along beside for a few strides, then, with the strength in his arms and the spring in his legs, swung into the saddle. On the way back down the arena, he tried the move again, this time off the opposite side. Nugget hesitated, but kept moving, and Latigo remounted on the go. A few more trips and Nugget allowed him to vault to either side at an easy lope.

"Ain't no doubt about it," Harley said when Latigo stopped to give Nugget a blow and to catch his own breath. "That horse is a good one."

"I believe you're right. He catches on quick. Can't believe he's so easy goin'. I don't think he'd get too upset if a bomb went off under him."

"Well, hell—we can sure try it, Latigo. I believe I got some old fire-crackers left over from last Fourth of July in the jockey box of my truck."

Latigo swatted at Harley with his hat. "No thanks, Harley—but it's nice of you to offer."

They talked some more about the finer points of the palomino horse. Then Latigo said, "We ought to be gettin' on home. If we're leavin' for Las Vegas in the mornin' we had best get our butts in gear and get things ready."

The rodeo-bound cowboys got an early start, caravanning down the two-lane desert highway, trailers hitched to pickup trucks. They traveled up and down cedar-stippled ridges and across sagebrush-carpeted flats, they flanked wide alkali playas and drove through narrow green valleys watered by meandering streams, they sometimes paralleled railroad tracks and occasionally slowed for small towns when the highway bent to follow a cardinal compass point to become Main Street.

Harley, leading the parade, pulled off the highway as they approached one such town and stopped at a dusty rodeo grounds on the outskirts of the likewise dusty burg. He walked back to Latigo's truck, propped his elbows on the door frame and leaned into the rolled-down window. "We can water the horses here and let 'em rest while we go on into town and get some dinner."

Latigo did not see the attraction of the place. "Why here? Don't look like much."

Harley smiled. "Whatever do you mean, son? This is a fine town! I won the bull ridin' and the bull doggin' last fall in this very arena. Ain't never won a dime in the next two places down the road—and once we pass them, there ain't nothin' but hungry for more'n a hundred miles. 'Sides, I know the old boy that owns the café here, and he'll feed us good."

The food was good, and Latigo pushed back from the table more than satisfied. The proprietor, leaning at the end of the counter reading a newspaper, a cigarette in danger of dropping a long inch of ash dangling from his lip, folded the paper and pushed it aside and asked the boys—the only patrons at the time—if he could get them anything else. Both cowboys refused, their hunger overcome by hot soup, pot roast, boiled vegetables, dinner rolls, and apple pie with ice cream.

Harley U-turned across main street and drove back out to the rodeo arena. They loaded the horses and pulled out, stopping to fill gas tanks and top off engine oil at the filling station and garage at the other end of town before taking to the highway for the last leg of the trip to Las Vegas.

While Harley was familiar with the desert boomtown, it was Latigo's first trip. He was not impressed when, in the late afternoon, they drove into the dingy town with its hot wind and the film of dust that seemed to coat everything in spite of it. Harley led him to the fairgrounds and its rodeo arena and racetrack. Rodeo contestants were assigned stalls at the track. Latigo allowed it would be the first time a horse carrying the Brown Ranch brand had ever spent a night under a roof. They stabled and fed the horses and parked the trailers and Harley's truck, and Latigo drove them to the motor court where they would share a cabin. Neither cowboy was accustomed to paying for lodging, sleeping out at the rodeo grounds being their customary—and preferred—way. But Las Vegas, with its thermometers reaching beyond the 100 mark in the daytime and not descending much at night, along with a dearth of shade, made the indoors more enticing than usual. Besides, the motor court featured a swimming pool. It was not much larger than a saddle blanket, but it was wet, and the water was cooler than the air.

With all the necessaries seen to, Harley suggested they visit a tavern he had heard about where cowboys congregated. Latigo relented, despite his wariness of the traffic. It only took four U-turns with varying stretches of backtracking, and two occasions of finding themselves where they had already been, before finally locating the place. Pulling into a spot among the few cars and pickup trucks parked at random on a big patch of gravel, Latigo sat for a time, both hands glued to the steering wheel.

Harley opened the passenger door and stepped out of the truck. "C'mon Latigo. You can't sit here any longer or you'll bake like a spud in the oven."

Latigo took in and let out a long breath, feeling the heat. "I guess so."

Stepping out of the desert sun, the beer joint seemed darker than night inside. Other than a jukebox crying "Cold, Cold Heart" by Hank Williams, the place was quiet. A few men sat along the bar, and three tables were surrounded by groups of men and a few women. A few occupants turned to study the new arrivals. A puddle of light near the far wall illuminated the green felt of a pool table, and lit the midsections of the men standing around it. Slot machines lined two of the walls, and a single card table and its tall stools stood empty in the corner.

As soon as they believed they could see to cross the room without crashing into anything that might be in the way, the cowboys found seats at the end of the bar. Looking around the dim room, they could see that a cowboy hat covered most every head.

"You boys in town for the rodeo?" the grizzled barman said, wiping down the bar in front of them, leaving a sheen of dampness.

"Yessir. I'm Harley Warren. This here's Latigo Brown."

"What can I get you?"

"A couple of beers. Whatever you got on tap."

"You boys old enough to be drinking?"

Harley and Latigo looked at each other, then back at the bartender. Harley smiled. "The police might not think so, but we've done it before."

The barkeeper shook his head and tried not to smile. "Well, I'll pretend you said you was of age. I'd ask to see some identification, but it's too dark in here to read it anyway." He swiped at the bar with his towel again before leaving, and came back with two glasses, foam streaking down the outsides. He walked with a limp.

Latigo sat and sipped for few minutes, then carried his beer around the end of the bar to study a collection of framed photographs on the wall. Some were portraits of movie cowboys going back years, and he strained his eyes to read the signatures and greetings written on many of them. Other pictures looked to be taken during the production of movies, nearly every one including horses and cowboys. There were a few action shots—horses falling, cowboys or Indians after stagecoaches, horses running and chasing, saloon fights, gun battles, and other scenes typical of Western movies and television shows.

Harley joined Latigo looking at the pictures. After a few minutes, the bartender brought two more glasses of beer, set them down, and leaned himself against the bar, watching the boys.

"You got quite a collection of pictures here. I seen some of these shows," Harley said. "You know these guys? Lots of them autographs is wrote to somebody named Clete. That you?"

The man nodded. "Yep. Clete Holman is my name."

"How'd you come to have all these pictures?"

"I know those boys. Used to work with them in moving pictures. I'm in some of those photographs." He hoisted himself upright and hobbled over to the boys, pointing to one action shot then another, telling what movie or television program it came from, and tapping the glass over a cowboy or an Indian in the picture, saying it was him.

A group had come in while they talked. The men were pushing a couple of tables together to accommodate their crowd, as their ladies stood back, watching. Once the chairs were arranged, they all sat. "I had best go see to these folks," the barman said. "If you-all are interested, come on back sometime and I'll tell you all the stories you can sit still for about my days as one of the Gower Gulch men."

They watched him limp away toward the thirsty new customers; bar towel slung over one shoulder.

Chapter Nine

The sun was gone, but the sky in the west burned red as Latigo and Harley scuffed across the gravel parking lot toward the pickup truck.

"Toss me your keys," Harley said.

Latigo reached into his pants pocket, fingered out the keyring, and lobbed it to Harley. "What for?"

"Somethin' I want to show you. Seein' as you ain't too fond of driving in the city, I'll take you there."

As Harley negotiated the streets, the western sky darkened, replaced by another glow; a halo of light that brightened as the sky dimmed. The truck turned to follow an empty street for a few blocks. Latigo read FREMONT on a street sign as Harley made another turn.

Neon lights cast a phantasm of colors up and down the road ahead. Cars cruised slowly, making way for pedestrians crossing the street any and every place. People crowded the sidewalks, moving in both directions up and down the street and in and out of wide-open doorways. The truck moved along, Latigo craning to see the strobing, pulsing, racing lights—some ornamental, others spelling out the names of casinos and hotels and other attractions within the buildings they covered. Glowing marquees shouted the names of singing stars and stage shows. The clatter and clanging of row upon row of slot machines visible through open fronts competed with the clamor of the crowds of people.

"Holy hell! I heard about gambling and such down here, but never thought of nothin' like this."

"You've led a sheltered life, Latigo."

"Looky there at that!"

"Seen it before."

"Stop!"

Harley pulled the truck to the curb and they watched across the angle of the street as the biggest cowboy they had ever seen went through his motions. The smiling cowboy, painted on sheet metal cut to shape, loomed above. He wore a broad-brimmed hat tipped at a jaunty angle, checked shirt with patch pockets, a wide belt with a big buckle holding up blue jeans rolled into cuffs over high-heeled boots and spurs, all outlined with bright neon. An upraised arm moved back and forth at its bent elbow, the hand with its cocked thumb pointing the way to the casino and hotel he oversaw. A cigarette, blowing actual smoke rings, dangled from the cowboy's mouth, and one eye winked with neon lights.

"He's a big sucker," Latigo said.

Then an amplified voice filled the air. "Howdy, pardner!"

Latigo laughed. "Hell, he even talks!" He stepped out of the truck door and stood on the running board, reading the signs up and down the street. "Most everything's named after somethin' Western, but there ain't none of it looks real."

Harley laughed. "It ain't meant to be real, son. It ain't nothin' but a make-believe place for all these city folks to play in. I guess the people that own these places figure made-up cowboy and Western stuff is as good a way to empty folks's pockets as any. Ever'body likes cowboys."

"I wonder if they like 'em so much once their pockets is empty."

"I reckon they like 'em fine. Lots of these folks'll be back to do it again next year."

"It always this crowded?"

"I ain't been here but a time or two, but it sure was then. And the people who come here don't never sleep, near as I can tell. Leastways not at night."

What sounded like the bellow of a cow with a lost calf split the air. Latigo and Harley heard it again, and spotted its source in the traffic coming toward them. Junior Blevins's big boat of a roadster, mounted with its oversized steer horns, fit right in on the glitzy Las Vegas street. The convertible's top was down, Blevins behind the wheel with a big cigar poking out of his smile. He pushed the klaxon lever again, releasing another bovine bellow into the bright night. In the passenger seat, elbow cocked over the top of the door, sat Danny Wickham, eyes as wide as Latigo's as he took in the sights. Two underdressed women occupied the backseat, seated not on the bench but perched atop the seat back and folded convertible top. From their raised position, they raised drinks—one an oversized cocktail glass, the other a bottle of beer—in salute to the crowds along and in the street.

"What do you suppose them two's up to?" Harley said.

"Most likely ol' Junior'll be at the arena lookin' to attract more cowboys to his tourist rodeo."

"Probably so." Harley smiled. "Maybe he'll gamble away the family fortune in these casinos and have to call the whole thing off."

"Maybe. But I don't think so. Seems to me Junior Blevins knows just what he's doin'. I don't think he's near as flighty as he lets on."

Blevins hailed the boys with his cigar and Danny gave them a reluctant wave as they passed. Harley started up the truck and Latigo climbed back in. Harley drove them out along the highway that led to Los Angeles, down a stretch of the road called "the Strip." Popping up here and there along stretches of empty desert were yet more casinos and hotels, glowing with neon and sprawling across vast roofed-over spaces.

"This town looks a whole lot different at night than what it does in the daytime," Latigo said.

"Sure as hell. Looks right fancy in the dark."

An airliner roared overhead and the boys to ducked as it passed, the noise loud enough to rattle the fillings in their teeth. They watched it ease toward the ground and settle between rows of runway lights off to the left of the highway.

Harley shuddered. "I believe that's about enough for me for one night, old son. What say we go on back to the motel and get us some shut-eye?"

"Sounds good to me. Been a long day. And this place makes it seem like we're a lot farther from home than what we are."

The boys slept well and were up with the sun, splashing around in the pint-sized motor court swimming pool. Red lines in thermometers climbed faster than the sun, heat radiating from the pool deck and warming motel guests lounging there.

Once dried and dressed, Latigo let Harley pilot the pickup to the rodeo grounds and racetrack to tend to the horses, then to visit the rodeo office and check the rough-stock draw.

"Harley, looky there—that's Larry Bascom."

"Sure is. Let's say howdy."

Bascom was one of the leading cowboys on the professional circuit, as he had been for years, and Latigo and Harley encountered him from time to time at rodeos. He smiled when he saw them. "I do believe my eyes are seeing things that aren't there! Looks like Latigo Brown and Harley Warren! You boys are a long way from home."

Latigo shook his friend's hand. "Yessir. We thought we'd come on down here and see how the big boys rodeo."

Bascom laughed. "I don't believe you'll see much you haven't seen before. Fact of the matter is, I've wondered for a long time why I don't see you at more of these big rodeos."

Latigo hemmed and hawed and tried to stitch together some sense of a long list of lame-sounding reasons, from an inability to travel far afield, work to be done at the ranch, the expense involved, horses suffering from being hauled, uncertainty of his ability to compete, and other excuses that unraveled and trailed off into silence.

"First off, you need to cut yourself some slack, Latigo. I've seen you ride, and you can top off a bronc with the best of them. You could likely make a bull rider, too, if you'd get on the brutes. If I was wearing your boots, I'd put those roping horses out to pasture and concentrate on broncs and bares. Then I'd get to as many rodeos as I could, the bigger the better. You know, you're beating the same cowboys at those punkin-roller rodeos and winning hundred-dollar checks, when you could beat them just the same and win thousand-dollar checks at bigger shows."

"Oh, I don't know, Larry. Can't see givin' up ropin'. Me and Harley do all right in the team ropin', and I purely love to put a loop on a calf. It don't get much better than workin' with good ropin' horses."

Bascom shrugged. "Your call. But while you're spending two days here waiting your turn to ride and rope, I'll ride here tonight, drive on over to Flagstaff where I'm up tomorrow afternoon, then on down to Phoenix to ride tomorrow night. Bares, broncs, and bulls at all three rodeos. See, that gives me nine chances to win some money, while you lounge around in this burning hell of a city to compete in what? Four events? And in two of them—the ropings—it isn't even up to you whether you win or not. You've got to rely on your horses, and old Harley here—meaning no disrespect, Harley—to win anything. If you ask me, it just doesn't add up." He smiled. "Besides, you know full well that the only reason rodeos have those timed events is so the crowd has something to look at while the bucking chutes get filled back up with more rough stock."

Latigo laughed at the joke he had already heard a hundred times or more, and would hear another hundred times or more. They talked longer, swapping the usual rodeo cowboy array of re-ride stories, tales of wrecks, reports of winning rides, and the comings and goings and doings of cowboys of shared acquaintance.

"Say, do you boys know anything about a fellow named Junior Blevins? I ran across him downtown last night and he buttonholed me and carried on about putting together a rodeo up in Jackson Hole."

Harley said, "Oh, yes. We know Junior. Met him a while back. Heard all about his big plans. Says he intends to put on a rodeo every night of the week the rest of the summer and on into fall for all them tourists they got up there."

"I thought it was something like that. It was noisy where we were, and there were lots of other people wanting to talk, so I wasn't sure what all he was saying. Man talks a mile a minute."

"He offered me and Latigo jobs. Says he wants enough cowboys on his payroll to put on a rodeo in case he don't attract enough other entries. Says he'd pay us a wage, plus whatever money we could win. 'Course we'd have to help out working the stock and such."

"Well, he didn't offer me a job. But he did say he would pay me an appearance fee or some such if I would come to ride on big holiday weekends. I told him I would give it some thought, but those weeks are the ones where there are plenty of rodeos to get to, and that's when I win the most money. Do you think he can pull it off—put the whole deal together?"

Harley thought before replying, eventually giving up on a concrete answer. "Can't say. He's got no shortage of ideas, and claims he's got the money to do it. One thing's for damn sure—he's got plenty of big talk. He even half-way promised to get ol' Latigo here in the movies. Says movie stars and such like to come up to that country on vacation, and they even make some movies and TV shows there sometimes. Claims he knows those movie folks." Harley smiled and wrapped an arm around Latigo's shoulder and gave him a shake. "Says this boy's got what it takes to be a big star in them Westerns."

Latigo did not see Bascom's reaction, as he had bowed his head and drawn it in like a desert tortoise as he felt the heat rise up his neck and flush his cheeks.

But he did hear his laugh, and, after a moment, "You might want to give that a try, Latigo." Bascom reached out and patted him on the shoulder. "I don't know anything about making movies, but it must be an easier way to buy a bag of beans than climbing onto bucking horses."

With any thought of breakfast long since gone, Latigo and Harley bid Bascom goodbye as set off in search of dinner. After filling up on burgers and fries at a roadside drive in, and with hours to kill, they decided to pay a visit to Clete Holman's beer joint.

As before, it took their eyes a time to adjust to the inside of the tavern, lit only by neon beer signs, a few dim concealed lamps behind the bar, and the pools of light illuminating the green felt tops of the pool and card tables, empty at the time. Besides Clete behind the bar, the only other person in the place was a cowboy perched on a stool, hunched over a glass of beer and talking with the bartender. Once they could see well enough, Latigo and Harley made their way to the bar, steeping around the tables and chairs in their path. As before, they took up stools at the end of the bar near the wall displaying photographs of cowboy movie actors and movie stills.

Clete waited until they settled in, then asked what they were drinking. He drew each of them a beer from the tap and carried it to them, foam spilling down the sides of the glasses and puddling on the bar top. "How you boys doin' today?"

The cowboys allowed they were doing fine. Harley, with a nod toward the framed photographs, said, "Say, mister Holman, I'd like to know some more about these pictures you got there."

"Sure, boys. I got more stories than you got time for. But before I get rollin', there's a friend of mine here I'd like you-all to meet. He's got a few stories his own self." He hailed the man. "Say, John! Bring your beer and come on down here."

The man slid off his stool. He stood, bent a bit at the waist, put both hands in the small of his back and pressed himself upright. He picked up his glass and walked along the bar.

"Boys," Clete said, "this here is John Benson."

Chapter Ten

Harley hopped off his barstool so fast that he may as well have fallen off. He doffed his hat, put it back on, wiped his palm on his pants leg, and extended it to the cowboy.

"John Benson! Everybody knows who John Benson is," Harley said. "My name is Harley Warren and I'm honored to shake your hand!" He pumped the man's hand and arm as if he expected to draw water, his smile so wide it threatened to tear flesh. By now, Latigo had slid off his seat. Harley turned Benson's hand loose and reached back to grab Latigo by the arm and pulled him forward. "This here's my friend Latigo Brown. Latigo, say howdy to John Benson!"

Latigo nodded, offered his hand, and shook hands, but with much less vigor than Harley. "It's a pleasure to meet you, Mister Benson."

By name, if not acquaintance, John Benson was well known among rodeo cowboys. A tough competitor, he had once been named World Campion Steer Wrestler, and was runner-up All Around champion, as his winning ways covered more events than bulldogging. Now, he was even more widely known for his work as an actor in Western movies and television shows.

"Nice to know you gents. Just call me John. Ol' Clete here treating you right?"

The young cowboys looked at one another, looked at Clete, looked back at one another, looked at Benson, and nodded.

Benson said, "You know, this old boy is one of the best hands ever to saddle a horse. A few years back, he rode with the Gower Gulch men—most likely, he was the best of them."

Latigo said, "He mentioned that name when we was in here before. If you don't mind sayin', what's the Gower Gulch men?"

Benson smiled. "Boys, let's sit down and take a load off. Clete, grab yourself a drink and join us." He walked to a table, pulled back a chair, and sat.

Latigo and Harley followed suit, and Clete came along soon after, carrying a dripping bottle of soda pop from the cooler.

"You boys in town for the rodeo?" Benson said. Latigo and Harley nodded in unison. "Me too. No work on at the moment, so I thought I'd drive on up here for the rodeo."

Harley perked up. "Are you entered?"

Benson laughed. "No, son. I'm long past that. Just here to spectate. Guess you could call me a railbird." He sipped his beer. "You asked about the Gower Gulch men. Well, let me tell you."

John Benson, with the occasional interjection from Clete Holman, told the story of Gower Gulch—in effect, the story of Hollywood. For years, the area around Sunset Boulevard and Gower Street, called Gower Gulch, had been home to numerous movie studios and film production companies, most of them cranking out Westerns as fast as they could run film through a camera. From silents to shorts to B-movies to feature films to television serials, Westerns had been and were in demand, and that meant cowboys.

Cowboys—real cowboys—from ranches and small towns across the West and the country migrated to Hollywood to find work on the screen. They sought parts as extras, actors, and stars, and Gower Gulch was the place to find work. They hung around the intersection ready to ride, and producers and directors and casting agents sought out the men they needed for whatever they were shooting that day. While the dream died for many cowboys, who starved out and went back home, others made a living riding on the silver screen. Some worked their way into speaking parts, whether by design or happenstance, and a few became known to the public; if not stars, household names on the big screen or on television.

Among the elite of the movie cowboys were the stunt men—the Gower Gulch men, they came to be known. Members of the fraternity fought with fists and guns, battled against—and as—Indians, did horse falls, fell from buildings, drove stagecoaches and sometimes got dragged under them, crashed wagons, forded rushing rivers, braved fire, stampeded cattle, dropped dead, and did whatever else the screenwriters and directors dreamed up. The best of them stood in for the stars to perform the dangerous work, protecting the actors from injury while fooling the audience into believing it was their heroes who were surviving all manner of risk and danger.

"Like I said, Clete here was one of the best," Benson said. "He pulled off more dangerous stunts than anybody. Some of the stars made using Clete for stunts part of their contracts. He made more of those famous boys look good than you could shake a stick at. Even now, they tell stories about some of the stunts Clete pulled off. And some of the ways he figured out how to do things are still used today. I tell you boys, the man's a legend in Hollywood. It's a durn shame all those folks who saw him on the screen don't know who it was they were looking at."

The men sat silent for a time, Latigo and Harley soaking up what they had been told. Then Harley asked Clete how he came to be running a beer joint in Las Vegas.

"One stunt too many is what done it. See, boys, there used to be this rope and wire rig they used on a horse called a Running-W. They don't do it anymore—rightly so, on account of it hurt and killed too many horses. But what it did was trip up a running horse so he'd fall, sometimes flip ass over teakettle, do a somersault, you see. The horse never knew when the fall was coming, but the rider knew where the director wanted it, so he could kick free and the horse wouldn't land on him.

"But this one time—the last time—the horse stumbled just before I sprung the trap, and it throwed me off balance just enough that I couldn't get out of the way when I tripped him up. Horse flipped all the way over and when the saddle hit the ground, my leg was under it. Horn, forks, seat, or cantle—hell, all of them maybe—bounced up and down on my leg and busted it all up. That was the end for me. Doctors operated on my leg enough times that I got scars that look like a street map of Los Angeles, but it ain't no good." He shrugged. "So I took what money I'd saved up and put it down on this place." He shrugged again. "It's a living."

Again, Harley and Latigo were quiet, lost in thought about what they had heard. Clete limped back over to the bar and came back carrying a tray loaded with glasses of beer for Benson and the boys and another bottle of pop for himself.

He sat down and said, "What John ain't told you is that doing stunts is how he got his start in the movies."

Harley sat up straight and looked at Benson. "That so?"

Benson nodded. "Did stunts and worked as an extra long before I got any speaking parts. Little bits, at first. Then I started getting cast as what they call a character actor, and that's what I still do. I ain't ever goin' to be a leading man or a big star, and that's fine with me. Wouldn't want it. Way it is now, I can still do all my own riding and stunts if I want to. Like it that way, for a fact."

Latigo, with furrowed brow and questioning eyes asked why.

Benson smiled. "If a man's going to fall off horses for a living, he can make a hell of a lot more money doing it in front of a movie camera than in a rodeo arena."

Following a good laugh, Benson asked the boys about rodeo—what events they worked, where they traveled, and the like. He promised to look them up that evening at the arena.

Latigo wondered if that would be the case as he sat horseback waiting for the Grand Entry. Word had gotten out about John Benson's presence, and he was deluged with admirers wanting to visit, stand for photographs, and asking for autographs. A rodeo committee member stood by with a saddled horse, as Benson had agreed to an introduction by the announcer and to lead the parade into the arena. When the gate opened and the flag bearer entered the arena, Benson mounted up and rode over to where Latigo sat.

"Evening Latigo. Where's that Harley fellow?"

"Ah, he's up in the bareback ridin' tonight, so he's behind the chutes gettin' ready."

Benson nodded. "I'll try to get back there and wish him luck." He looked around at people still standing by and hoping to catch his attention when circumstances permitted. "As you can see, it ain't always easy."

He did make it, barely. Latigo had just finished pulling down Harley's rigging when Benson leaned over the chute and clapped the rider on the shoulder and told him to bear down and make a ride. Harley smiled and sat astraddle of the horse with his feet propped on the chute boards, fiddling with his grip on the handhold. There was one rider ahead of him, and it was Larry Bascom. Bascom had a decent horse and rode him for as many points as possible.

"That'll be the score to beat," Latigo said. "You lift on that riggin' and get good holts with your spurs and you'll be all right."

When the pickup men cleared Bascom's horse from the arena, Harley gave the brim of his hat a final tug and slid up his bronc's back. The horse reared up, pawing at the slide gate at the front of the chute. Latigo and Benson each grabbed ahold of Harley. The bronc dropped back to the ground, then squatted, his rump against the rear slide gate. The flank man used the tail end of the flank strap to slap the horse on the rump a time or two to encourage it to stand, which it did. Harley checked his rigging and regained his seat and nodded his head.

The gate men flung the chute open wide, but the horse only stood. Latigo put a hand to the side of the bronc's head and pushed. Seeing daylight, the horse turned and darted out of the chute. After running a few strides, the bronc planted its front feet, jolting to a stop and instantly leaping upright. Harley kept his seat, showing a little air between his backside and the horse's back as it dropped to land on all four feet. The shock of the landing gave his brain a jolt on its way to knocking his hat loose.

With a lunge to the right, the horse bucked in a tight circle, almost a spin. The force got Harley hanging off-center away from the turn, but he managed to find a new hold with inside leg to keep his seat. The eight-second whistle hadn't finished its burst before Harley opened his hand and let the horse fling him away. He hit the ground on his shoulder and rolled, then raised to his knees to watch the pickup men haze the bronc out of its circle. As it bucked straight away, one of the outriders pulled the latch on the flank strap while the other cut off the path of the now trotting horse to turn it back toward the catch pen gate and out of the arena.

Harley's senses returned to normal in time to hear the announcer say, "That score puts Harley Warren in second place in the bareback riding, just a few points shy of tonight's leader, world champion cowboy Larry Bascom!"

He picked up his hat and brushed the dirt off it and left the arena. Latigo and Benson met him at the top of the steps on the platform behind the chutes. Latigo grabbed Harley by both shoulders and gave him a shaking. "It weren't pretty, Harley, but you got the job done!"

"Hell of a ride, son," Benson said. "That was one rank horse." The cowboy actor said he would see them later, but, for now, felt obligated to mingle with the crowd.

"Well, I suppose we ought to get on down to the other end and get ready to rope us a steer," Harley said.

"You reckon you can spin a rope? That horse stretched your arm pretty good."

"Don't worry none about me—you just make sure you're ready to put your twine around some toes."

They sat horseback and watched the steer wrestlers. They were third up in the team roping when the bulldogging finished. Harley's confidence overreached his ability that night, and his head loop caught only one horn and the boys rode out of the arena with no time. But they did not stop to worry about what went wrong, as Latigo's presence was required at the bucking chutes for the saddle bronc riding.

As Latigo found his bronc in the chute, he saw Danny Wickham perched on the top rail of the fence. He double-checked the latigos and cinches on his saddle, as well as his bronc rein. All looked to be in order. The bronc stood quiet when Latigo dropped his saddle onto its back, and the horse stayed that way, as if uninterested in the goings-on, while they positioned the saddle and pulled the cinches snug.

But the bronc, a tall, heavy, thick-legged bay with four white socks and a blaze face, came to life when Latigo nodded for the gate. It leapt out of the chute and kicked high over its head, and kept up the high jumps and kicks as it turned in a wide arc across the arena, offering the judges a perfect view of the ride. In time with the horse's rhythm, Latigo made a snappy ride, using his free arm to emphasize the horse's action as his spurs raked from the mane line to the cantle. After the whistle, the pickup men rode by. He handed off the bronc rein and leaned over the pickup horse's rump as he grabbed the rider's waist, then slid across to lower himself to his feet on the opposite side, taking a few strides to catch his balance and slow the momentum. The judges scored the ride generously, putting Latigo well into the lead.

As the bronc riders gathered their gear behind the chutes, Larry Bascom, whose saddle bronc ride had him in third place, squatted down facing Harley and Latigo, who sat on the planks stowing their gear.

"You boys rode good tonight."

Both cowboys nodded their thanks.

"If your scores hold up, and I'm guessing they will, you'll earn a pretty good paycheck for your work. I hope you do as well tomorrow. What are you up in?"

Latigo said he was up in the calf roping and Harley had a bull in the afternoon performance, then he had a bareback bronc in the night show, and Harley was up then in the bulldogging.

"Well, good luck to you boys. I'm off to Arizona as soon as I get off my bull. Latigo, you ought to think about what I said. Now that you've seen you can shine in these bigger rodeos, you ought to get serious about it and go down the road."

"I'll sure give it some thought, Mister Bascom."

"You do that." Bascom said as he stood up. "I mean it. You could win some big money. You need any help, you let me know." He turned and walked away.

Danny Wickham stepped up to fill the space Bascom had left. "Hell of a bronc ride, Latigo."

"Thanks."

"What do you think, Harley? You goin' to win anything with that bareback ride?"

"I don't know, Danny. If they was to pay by the bruises and loose teeth, I sure would."

Wickham stuffed his hands in his pockets. "You boys figurin' on goin' to work for Junior Blevins?"

Latigo said, "Don't know. Haven't thought on it much. Looks like you and him is gettin' pretty thick."

Wickham shrugged. "Oh, he's a good ol' boy. I might take him up on it. But if I do and you don't, I'll sure miss kickin' your ass in the bareback ridin'."

Latigo smiled. "When you up, Danny?"

"Tomorrow afternoon."

"You draw good?"

"Can't say," he said with a shrug. "Don't know much about these horses down here. Some of the boys say he's pretty good."

"Well, good luck to you. Bascom's score'll be hard to beat."

"Oh, I'll beat it all right. Don't you concern yourself none about me—you're the one who'll need the luck."

The boys latched their gear bags shut and found a place on the top rail to watch the calf ropers, the barrel racing, and the bull riding.

"Well, hell, Latigo," Harley said, rotating his shoulders and stretching to straighten out the kinks in his spine, "I say we put the horses up and get on back to the motel. After a good long time in a hot shower, I aim to sleep the night and half the day away. If I ain't up in time for the afternoon show, you wake me up."

Chapter Eleven

The boys hung around behind the bucking chutes through most of Saturday afternoon's rodeo. Latigo, especially, liked watching cowboys he knew only by reputation ready themselves for their bronc rides. There were a few contestants he knew from his travels, and he met others whose names consistently appeared on the list of top money winners. The same was true at the other end of the arena, where cowboys from around the region competed against the full-time professionals to win a share of the prize money.

Danny Wickham's hopes to take the top prize in the bareback riding were dashed when his bronc stumbled and fell, briefly trapping him under its bulk. The horse clawed its way to its feet, pulling Wickham up with him. He found himself off the side of the horse opposite his riding hand, the rosined glove rolled over in the handhold, binding his fingers beneath, making his efforts to open the hand and pull loose futile. The crazed horse lunged and jumped to free itself of the cowboy, kicking out at him with its hind leg. After what seemed an eternity to the horrified onlookers, a solid blow to Wickham's hip applied enough force to pull his hand loose, and, as he fell, another strike of the hoof hit his shoulder, then glanced off and raked the side of his head.

He spun a circle when falling through the air and landed in the dirt like a bale of hay thrown from a wagon. The rodeo clown and an arena worker dropped to the ground beside him and immediately waved in the ambulance parked outside the gate. As the ambulance attendants and the on-call doctor examined the fallen cowboy, careful not to worsen his injuries with their poking and prodding and palpations, Junior Blevins trotted into the arena and, hat in hand, watched them load Wickham into the ambulance. He followed it out the gate and kept walking to his car and trailed the flashing lights to the hospital.

The wreck put something of a damper on the rest of the rodeo, but the cowboys tried to go about their business as usual. Latigo's run in the calf roping put him in good position to place in the money, sitting a close second the fastest roper. The bull riding went well for Harley, his sore arm strong enough to last the eight seconds atop a rank animal that wanted him off its back. As in the bareback riding, he ended up just behind Larry Bascom on the score sheet. Depending on how riders in the evening performance fared, he was well positioned for another paycheck.

Many of the contestants hung around at the arena and racetrack after the rodeo, waiting for the night show. They congregated in groups in the shade of the bleachers, swapping stories and tall tales, laughing and joking, filling their stomachs with greasy burgers and cold soda pop from the concession stand. Now and then, the humor would subside when someone wondered aloud how Danny Wickham was doing.

The answer came with the tinny and amplified bellow of cow. As one, the cowboys turned to watch Junior Blevins drive up in his decked-out convertible roadster. Junior sat at the wheel, a cigar of a size to match the automobile poking out of his mouth. Behind him, propped sideways in the backseat, sat Wickham. He wore his hat, but all could see the head beneath it was wrapped with bandages. With a crutch retrieved from the floor of the vehicle, he hoisted himself up to sit on top of the seatback. He swung his legs over the side and eased himself to the ground, using the crutch for balance. His riding arm—his left—was in a sling. The protruding hand showed fingers poking out of a plaster cast, the other end of which was visible at the other end of the sling, stopping just short of his elbow. His right foot was without a boot, wrapped in thick bandages.

"Well, hell, Wickham—it looks like you ain't dead," someone said.

"Not yet."

"What ails you?"

"Broke some bones in the wrist of my ridin' arm. Ankle got smashed up a little and my hip's all bruised up but it ain't broke. Collar bone's busted, and a few ribs is cracked. Got a few stitches and a knot on my head. All in all, I guess I'm okay."

While cowboys questioned Wickham further and engaged in other conversation, Blevins worked the crowd, buttonholing the men singly and in groups, pitching his plans to put on the tourist rodeo in Jackson Hole. He invited them to come, as contestants or employed participants, passing out his cards.

"C'mon, Danny," Blevins said after a time. "That sawbones at the hospital said you needed rest. Let's get you back to the hotel." He helped Wickham back into the car. Before stepping into the driver's seat, he turned to the shaded-up cowboys. "Gentlemen, I believe you all know now who I am and what I am about. The Grand Teton Stampede is goin' to be a big deal—entertainment for folks from all over the country who come to see the splendor of Yellowstone Park and the Tetons. You're welcome, one and all, to help make a go of it. I predict it will grow to be a rodeo without equal in the West."

With that, he slid into the seat, started the rumbling engine of the big car, levered a pair of cow calls from the claxon, and backed away, negotiating a Y-turn at the end of the bleachers and roaring away with the rear wheels spitting gravel.

A few minutes after Junior Blevins left, a more welcome visitor arrived in the person of John Benson. He backslapped and hobnobbed with cowboys he knew, and welcomed introductions to those he did not, moving from cluster to cluster of cowboys.

Latigo and Harley were in a small circle comprised mostly of rodeo hands who, like them, stayed closer to home, competing primarily in small-town rodeos. To pass the time, Latigo fiddled with one of his lariats, spinning butterfly loops as they talked, bouncing flat loops up and down and spinning them away to land around the shoulders or wrap around the legs of the cowboys in the group.

Unbeknownst to Latigo, John Benson had his eyes on him, keeping watch as he visited and made his way through the relaxing rodeo hands. And though his course meandered like that of a honeybee, he was, like the bee, sure of his destination and determined in his arrival.

Benson stopped on the fringe of the group of cowboys that included Harley and Latigo. He stood, unobtrusively, listening to the talk but mostly watching Latigo spin his rope. At a lull in the conversation, he cleared his throat and said, "That's some mighty fine roping, Latigo."

Latigo's arm froze, the loop falling to the ground as he turned and saw Benson. "Aw, it ain't nothin'—just foolin' around."

"You're a ropin' fool all right. That's what Will rogers called himself. You know who Will Rogers was?"

"Sure. Everyone knows who Will Rogers was. But I ain't no roper like he was."

Benson smiled. "Nobody is. Most likely nobody ever will be. Man was one of a kind. But what I've seen you do ain't easy. Not many can do it. I've thrown enough ropes to know that."

Harley jumped into the conversation, telling Benson and the others— much to Latigo's dismay—about his friend's brief tenure stepping into the boots of "The Tampico Twister" at a rodeo weeks ago. His account included the trick riding demonstration as well as the rope tricks. A few of the hands, who had been at that rodeo, bore witness to the performance.

Benson listened, his eyes shifting from Harley to Latigo, his interest in the report reflected in the intensity of his gaze. When Harley finished, Benson asked what the boys' plans were once the rodeo was over.

"Just goin' back home," Latigo said.

"When will you be pulling out?"

"No special time. Just when we get up and around in the mornin'. Maybe have us a swim first. Then get the horses loaded and hit the road."

"Think you-all will have time to come have breakfast with me?"

Harley jumped in with, "Why sure! Hell, we ain't in no real hurry. Ain't a thing back home that won't wait till we get to it."

Benson looked to Latigo, who nodded his assent. "Well, then, you boys come on by. How about, let's say, ten o'clock, if that works for you-all?" The boys nodded their agreement. "Come on by my hotel—they've got me put up in a suite downtown in that place with the big cowboy sign. You know the one I mean?"

"Sure thing," Harley said. "We'll be there. You can count on it. Ten o'clock, sharp."

*****

A thin veil of dust drifted above the rodeo arena, illuminated, almost incandescent, in the light from the low-hanging sun. Harley and Latigo rode from the racetrack stables to the arena, Harley on his bulldogging horse and Latigo on his team roping horse, which he would use to haze for his friend in the steer wrestling. Latigo, up in the bareback riding, stowed his gear bag behind the bucking chutes then the two cowboys joined others in the arena warming up and exercising horses that would compete in the timed events.

The announcer called out to clear the arena. Latigo and Harley tied their horses to a fence rail, out of the way behind the pens that held the roping calves and the steers for team roping and steer wrestling, then made their way to the bucking chutes. Neither cowboy would participate in tonight's Grand Entry parade.

"You heard anything 'bout this horse?" Harley said as they stood above the bronc Latigo had drawn.

"Nope. Nobody seems to know much about him."

The stock contractor came by, checking the flank straps to make sure his helper had put them on properly, and making fine adjustments based on his knowledge of each of his horses. When he arrived at Latigo's chute, the cowboy asked about the horse.

"Oh, he's a good one. He'll go out there and jump and kick a little."

The boys were unfamiliar with the contractor, and did not know that what they had heard was his standard response to any inquiry about his bucking horses.

Quivering and shivering as if nervous or cold, the bronc was otherwise quiet in the chute while they set the rigging. As his turn neared, Latigo sat on the horse and worked his hand in the handhold, warming up the rosin. He was ready when the chute boss told him to go, and he pulled down his hat, slid up behind the rigging, set his knees against the horse's neck and nodded his head.

The gate crashed open and the horse leaped out. As it turned, Latigo swung his feet forward and set his spurs for the mark out. Like his saddle bronc the day before, the bareback horse bucked with an easy rhythm, and Latigo settled into it, grabbing new holds in the neck with his spurs with each jump, his backside keeping its balance atop the horse's spine. The judges rewarded the ride with a score just one point shy of Larry Bascom's high mark.

By the time Latigo retrieved his rigging from the stripping chute and peeled of his chaps, Harley was mounted and ready for the steer wrestling, holding Latigo's horse by the reins. Latigo double-checked the snugness of the cinch and stepped into the stirrup. When his turn came, Harley rode his horse into the box. The mount was nervous and flighty, as he often was, and it took a few tries to get him backed into the corner of the box and settled down. Harley lifted his chin to signal the gate man.

The double doors of the narrow gate flipped open and the pusher shoved the steer out the gap. The steer took a lazy step or two, but refused to run. It had not even tripped the barrier when Harley's horse sped by. Latigo was beside him, both cowboys looking back helplessly at the lazy steer. Bad luck in the draw meant no time for Harley, and that meant no chance to earn a paycheck in the bulldogging.

The announcer's voice rang through the public address system. "No time for Harley Warren in the steer wrestling. Let's give that cowboy a round of applause, because that's all he'll get tonight."

The clapping followed the cowboys out of the arena. They tied their horses and walked back down to the bucking chutes. Their work finished, they would be spectators for the rest of the rodeo. But their work had paid off. Latigo ended up first-place in the saddle bronc riding. A second-place finish to Larry Bascom in the bareback riding fattened Latigo's wallet even more, and Harley's wild ride held on for a fifth-place finish and a small share of the payout. Just as Latigo had done in the bareback riding, Harley placed second to Bascom in the bull riding. Latigo's third-place time in the calf roping rounded out the winnings for the cowboys.

All in all, the long drive to Las Vegas to compete against some of the top cowboys on the professional circuit had been well worth the effort.

Paychecks snapped into shirt pockets, Latigo and Harley rode back to the racehorse stalls and stabled their horses and drove back to the motel.

Neither cowboy even thought of celebrating in the bright lights of the city. It had been a long day, and what was left of the night would not last long.

Chapter Twelve

The casino on the ground floor of the hotel under the smiling cowboy sign was not as busy as it had been the night before. But even at ten o'clock in the morning there was no shortage of bleary-eyed gamblers rolling dice at the craps tables, watching roulette wheels spin, propping elbows on blackjack tables trying through the haze to make cards add up to twenty-one, and shaking hands with one-armed bandits, hoping—and betting—the whirring, spinning wheels would clatter to a stop on a winning combination of colorful fruits, numbers, bells, bars, and other symbols.

Latigo and Harley inquired at the at the hotel desk, and the clerk informed them they were to go on up to John Benson's suite on the top floor where breakfast would be provided by room service. Benson hailed them to come in when they knocked on the door.

The room looked to the boys more like a living room than a hotel room. Two sofas formed a corner in which sat a low table. Two overstuffed chairs defined the other sides of the square. A window covered the full length of the wall opposite the door. An open door in another wall revealed a bedroom beyond, the bedclothes rumpled. Tucked against the other wall stood a kitchen-type table, set with more plates and saucers and cups and glasses than either Harley or Latigo had ever seen laid for one meal. A wheeled cart beside held silver domes which they assumed kept food beneath warm, along with other serving dishes, a pitcher of orange juice, another of water afloat with ice cubes, a tall coffee pot, and a squat teapot.

With a smile, Benson watched the wide-eyed boys study the room. "Ain't no sense in you two standing around with your mouths hanging open. Pull up a chair at yonder table and we'll put some food in them mouths and see if your jaws work."

Their host saw to filling their plates and glasses, covering with more food any empty spot that appeared on a plate. Sausage, ham, bacon, scrambled eggs, fried potatoes, biscuits and gravy, buttered toast, pancakes and syrup, strawberries, sliced melon, and tiny orange sections filled plates of various sizes and stomachs in turn.

Latigo pushed his chair back from the table and raised his palms in surrender. "If I take one more bite, I'm liable to bloat up like a heifer in an alfalfa field."

"I ain't far behind you," Harley said as he drenched another pancake with syrup.

When the boys finished eating, Benson herded them over to the sofas and seated himself in a soft chair. He sipped from the cup of coffee he carried with him. "What is it that you two have got in mind to do?"

Latigo and Harley looked at one another, then at their host. "What do you mean, Mister Benso—I mean, John?" Latigo said.

"Well, I mean your future, son. What is it you intend to do with it? Not only down the road, but right now."

Latigo thought it over.

Harley yawned.

Latigo said, "I don't rightly know, sir. For now, I guess I'll go on home and help out on the ranch for a while. There'll be hay to put up. I got a horse I'm workin' on. And Harley and me'll likely find a rodeo or two to go to. Larry Bascom, he says I ought to rodeo full time. Thinks I could make my way at them bigger rodeos. I'm wonderin' about that."

"You give any thought to what that Blevins fellow with the fancy car is offering?"

Latigo shrugged. "Not much—not that I ain't tempted. It just don't seem like the thing to do, is all."

Benson nodded. "What about you, Harley?"

Stifling another yawn, Harley said he, too, would spend a few days at home. There was a job at the auction yard in the town he lived in, if he wanted it. But getting to some more rodeos was on his mind. "Fact is, I might even head on up to Wyoming and see if this deal Blevins is puttin' together pans out. Gettin' paid to help put a rodeo on don't sound so bad. And the notion of a shot at some prize money ever' night of the week sounds even better."

Benson let their responses percolate while he filled and delivered coffee cups to his guests, then refilled his own. He sat back down. "I got a proposition for you, Latigo—by the way, Latigo Brown is what you go by, but I don't guess it's what your momma and daddy named you...."

"No, sir. Orval is what they hung on me. After my mother's grandpa. They call me that at home when they want me to come to supper, but mostly I go by Latigo. Orval's okay, I guess, but I don't prefer it."

Harley said, "I always tell him 'Latigo' sounds like a cowboy singer. Maybe somebody in a Western novel, or one of them movie cowboys."

"Movie cowboy, huh? Well, you might be right," Benson said with a smile. "Which brings me to my proposition." He fixed his gaze on Latigo, locking eyes long enough before speaking, to mean he meant business. "There's a movie that starts shooting two weeks from tomorrow. I've got a part in it—a pretty good part. The studio that's doing it is a good one, and I've worked before for the man who'll direct the picture. He knows his stuff."

Latigo listened, his brow furrowing as he wondered what the man's words had to do with him. Benson said nothing. Latigo arched his eyebrows. "Sir?"

"How would you like to be in it?"

Harley gasped.

Latigo swallowed hard, shuddered, and said, "I ain't sure what you mean—I don't know nothin' about bein' in movies. Don't even like 'em all that much, to tell you the truth."

"Why's that?"

Latigo thought for a moment. "Oh, I don't know. They always seem kind of silly to me. Same with them Western shows on TV. What them cowboys do ain't got nothin' to do with what real cowboys did in the old days, or even now."

"That's true enough. They're just stories—entertainment. Everything is overdone because it makes for a better story." Benson thought for a time. "Movies are kind of like rodeo, you know."

Latigo sat up straight, his eyes wide open. "What do you mean?"

Benson smiled. "You ever put a bareback riggin' on a ranch horse? Bulldog a steer in the pasture? Climb aboard the herd bull? I'm guessing you don't urge a saddle horse to go on bucking when it bogs it head, like you do in the bronc riding. And I'm willing to bet your daddy would tan your hide if you were to run down a calf and rope and throw it the same way you do at a rodeo. You see, son, it's a show. Entertainment. Just like a movie."

Latigo sagged against the sofa back, thinking about what Benson said. After a time, "I guess I ain't never thought of it that way." And then he sat silent, his thoughts drifting.

Harley reached out and gave his friend's shoulder a push. "Come on, Latigo! Don't be dumb! Hell, there's cowboys that'd line up from here to hell and back for a chance to be in a picture show. Here's a man offerin' you a chance in a million, and you're settin' there like a old hen on a nest—and if that sounds like I'm callin' you chicken, it's 'cause I am!"

Latigo bowed his head, interlacing his fingers, pulling his hands apart to set them on his knees, then clasping his hands together. He looked up at Benson and tipped his hat back. "What would I have to do? Like I said, I don't know nothin' about bein' in a movie."

"Can't say for sure. There's no doubt I can get you on as an extra—that would be like the herd of cowboys riding in a posse, or hanging around in a saloon, or standing in the streets while the main actors go about their business. Could be, you could do some stunt work, if you've a mind to."

"I wouldn't know how to go about it."

"Harley here says you can do some trick riding."

Latigo shrugged. "Some. Nothin' too serious. Just stuff my brother and me learned to do foolin' around."

"Well, if you can do that, you can do horseback stunts. I imagine you get bucked off from time to time at rodeos, so you already know how to land in the dirt without it hurting you too much, and that's the most of it. They wouldn't start you off with the real dangerous stuff—but you could learn that too, if you wanted to."

Latigo had no answer.

"But I've got something else in mind for you. There's no guarantee I can make it work, but I believe I can."

"What's that?"

"See, this movie script has a dance in it. After a barn raising, the rancher throws a party for all the folks who helped, and the ranch hands, and all his neighbors in his big, new barn. There'll be food and drink, and a little band playing music for dancing."

Latigo paled. "Dance? I can't hardly dance a step without trippin' over myself."

Benson laughed. "That's all right, son—although the director might want to do a little funny business with something like that. But what I've got in mind is maybe you doing a few rope tricks for the folks at that party. Nothing too complicated; just a few little tricks like you were doing yesterday afternoon at the rodeo grounds."

Latigo could only stare.

"Now, like I said, there's no guarantee it will happen. It isn't in the script, but that won't make any difference with this director. I think it's a good idea, and I'm betting he will do it. You don't see a lot of that kind of thing much in movies these days, so I think it will appeal to him."

"I don't know...."

Harley said, "Aw, come on, Latigo! If for no other reason, do it for Penny—she's always sayin' you ought to be in picture shows." He told Benson Penny was Latigo's younger sister, and that she was crazy about Western movies and TV shows.

They talked some more, Benson mentioning the pay that might be involved should things work out as he hoped for Latigo—again, with no promises or guarantees. He offered his thoughts on what Latigo could earn in the future, should he take up acting and be cast as a character actor on a regular basis, as he was. And he threw out dollar amounts paid to the stars who got top billing in movies and on television series—wealth the boys could not even fathom.

"I don't see any reason why you couldn't make it, son—with a little hard work and a whole lot of luck," Benson said. "You're a good-looking kid, you can ride better than most, and the way you handle a rope, well, that could set you apart."

Benson pulled a notebook and a pencil from his shirt pocket and wrote something down. He tore out the page, folded it in half and passed it across to Latigo. "Take this. It's got my telephone number and address on it. You think about what I said, and let me know. Call collect. But let me know by the end of the week. If you're of a mind to give it a shot, load up and drive on down to Los Angeles over the weekend. That'll put you there a week before shooting starts on that movie, but it'll give me time to introduce you around and show you how things get done."

He stood up and raked his fingers through his hair. "Now, you boys get the hell out of here. I've got to use the bathroom." He smiled and shook hands with each of them. "Take any of that food that's left with you to eat on the road. Hate to see it go to waste."

Benson stopped again in the bedroom doorway. "You call me, Latigo Brown. I mean it."

The door closed.

Latigo and Harley hardly spoke on the way to the rodeo grounds and racetrack. They hitched the trailers and loaded the horses in silence and set out on the road, Harley leading the way out of the town and onto the two-lane highway leading north toward home. He pulled off the road hours later, into a roadside park beside a lazy little creek in a small town. After unloading the horses for water and to let them rest their legs on solid ground, they sat at a wooden picnic table in the shade of a stand of tall cottonwood trees.

They still did not talk much as they ate cold pancakes rolled around cold sausages, and cold bacon and ham stuffed into in cold biscuits. But once his belly was full, Harley's talker fired up, and he harangued Latigo about taking Benson up on his offer. He reiterated all the things the cowboy actor had said, then launched into a litany of his own of reasons why Latigo would be a fool not to head to Hollywood and give it a try.

Latigo let him talk, sitting quietly and sipping from a bottle of soft drink, warm from the long ride in the pickup truck. Eventually, Harley wound down somewhat and asked Latigo what he thought.

"I can't say as yet, Harley. It's an idea too big for me to fit into my head. I'd be walkin' away from everything I know to a place where I don't know nothin' about nothin'."

"You're a-scared, ain't you."

"Darn right I am. California's a long ways away, and Los Angeles is a big city—and I don't know a single soul out of all them thousands—hell, millions, maybe—that live out there."

"Sure you do! You know John Benson! He's *asked* you to come out there and all but guaranteed you a job in a movie. And it ain't like he's just some big-talkin' gunsel like that Junior Blevins. He's a genuine movie actor, and he knows the ropes. It sounds to me like about as sure a thing as there is—hell of a lot better odds than climbin' down onto the back of a bronc, and you don't even so much as blink at doin' that."

Latigo swallowed off the last of the soda pop. He stood and tucked in his shirt tail and walked away, leaving the empty bottle standing on the table, where he knew some local kid would find it and redeem it for penny candy at the local store. He opened the trailer door and loaded the horses, tying their halter ropes through the rings in the manger at the front. He stepped up into the seat of the pickup, closed the door, hung his elbow over the window frame and leaned out.

"Well, Harley, I guess the thing to do is get on home and see what Mom and Dad think about it."

Harley smiled. "There's a service station out on the edge of town that'll be open. We'll stop there for some go-juice and head on up the highway. Keep up."

Chapter Thirteen

John Benson accepted the charges on long distance collect calls from the Brown ranch three times in as many days. He talked with every member of the family save Latigo's brother, Raymond, who shrugged off the whole situation as yet another evidence of the oddity of Orval Brown; another deviation from the ordinary life of a ranch kid of the day. He could only shake his head at the things his brother got up to, from excelling at rodeo, to his ease with horses, to his trick roping, to the riding tricks they tried in the back pasture, which seemed to come naturally to Latigo.

For his part, Latigo harangued Benson with questions about where he might live, how he might learn to navigate the big city, what would happen if he froze up in front of the cameras, how he would be accepted by the people who made movies, especially the cowboy actors and stuntmen, against whom he feared he would not measure up.

Latigo's father wondered about job security for extras and bit players and stunt men and movie actors, Benson's answers serving to prompt yet more questions about the future his son might face.

Mother worried about her boy's safety, not only in the city but on the movie set. She expressed concern about a young man of Orval's tender years eating regularly and properly. And about exposure to temptation, citing the stories she had heard and read concerning the wild and depraved lives of movie actors.

Penny asked about the possibility of Latigo meeting her favorite movie and television stars, and if he could get autographs from them for her. And she asked that if she were to come to Hollywood on a visit, if she could meet them, too.

Benson understood their concerns. He did his best to assure them that he had come to Hollywood a raw ranch and rodeo kid just like Latigo, more familiar with horses and cattle than people. He told them that, for many, movie and television jobs were sporadic and uncertain—but that people who proved their reliability and willingness to work could make a better-than-good living. And he assured them that while there was temptation at every hand, Latigo seemed to have his head on straight and was unlikely to be lured into that kind of life. He won Penny over to his side with a little name dropping, mentioning stars and actors of his acquaintance, many of whom he counted as friends.

The final collect call to Benson came Friday evening. Latigo advised him he would be leaving the ranch in the morning, retracing his route of the week before to Las Vegas, and continuing on to Los Angeles. Benson told him which highways to take to get him to the right part of the city, then the roads and streets that would get him to his house.

"Now, son, you mind your manners," his father said as he tossed a battered suitcase and a cardboard box bound with twine, filled with clothing and such, into the bed of the pickup truck. "And don't forget—if things don't work out, the highway runs both directions."

His mother wrapped him in a tight hug. "Be careful," she whispered, then gave him a paper sack filled with sandwiches and apples and other foodstuff for the road.

Penelope handed him a stack of writing paper she had cut into squares and stitched together into a small booklet between covers cut from an old roll of flowered wallpaper. Tucked inside was a list of movie stars he was to track down and ask for autographs.

Raymond shook his hand and told him not to worry about the ranch work—that with Latigo being a sorry hand to begin with, his absence would not be any kind of burden. "Drive careful," he advised. "Don't forget that for every mile of road, there's two miles of ditch."

Latigo tossed the cut-down industrial-size lard can that held his ropes, his war bag full of rodeo gear, and his bronc saddle—just in case—into the back of the truck, as well as his regular saddle. He stepped into the driver's seat, turned the key and stepped on the starter switch, pumping the gas pedal to urge the pickup truck to life. The engine coughed, sputtered, and smoothed out. Latigo revved the motor a few times, stepped on the clutch and winced when the gears ground as he levered the floor shifter into position. He dared not look at his family as he pulled away, and instead waved out the open window.

"Don't forget to check the oil!" his father shouted as he bounced down the rutted ranch road toward the county road that would take him to the highway going south.

It seemed odd to Latigo to drive the highway without a horse trailer in tow. He had asked Benson about horses, and whether he would be expected to provide his own.

"Some do," Benson said. "Me, I've got a favorite horse I use when I can. He's steady and smart, and I can trust him not to do anything stupid. And I've got a couple others I use from time to time. But, for now, I think you ought to rely on the mounts the production companies provide. There are a bunch of outfits that raise and train movie horses out here, and they've got some pretty good ones, especially when it comes to doing stunts. Some of these wrangler outfits can teach a horse to do everything but tap dance—hell, I reckon they could do that, too, if there was a call for it. Once you get to working regular, start getting bigger parts, you might want to bring one of your horses out. I wouldn't do it just now, though."

Passing through Las Vegas for the second time in less than a week, Latigo noticed again how dingy and dusty the city looked in daylight, compared to the artificial gleam and glitter of neon after dark. From the look of things, the city lived a tenuous existence on the desert, the barren landscape and bare-skinned and bony mountains refusing to surrender to the sprawl. The desolate terrain appeared even more parched as the highway lost elevation, weaving through mountain passes to drop into broad valleys where vegetation consisted solely of scrawny, brushy plants scattered across otherwise empty terrain like ground pepper spill-sprinkled on a tabletop. The only evidence Latigo could see of water was eroded washes and dry lakebeds, neither of which looked to have been wet for ages.

He pulled off the highway at what passed for a town; a gas station hooked to a café attached to a short row of motel rooms, the same shade of pale green paint peeling off every wall and window frame and door. A few ramshackle houses, placed hodgepodge along dirt streets beyond the business, were the only other manmade things in sight.

The gas station attendant, as dry and wrinkled as the rest of the place, shuffled out of the uplifted door of the cluttered service bay. He stared at Latigo through the truck window. "Well, cowboy, what'll it be?"

"Fill it up and check the oil, please."

"Wash that windshield?"

"Sure. If you would. Gas is pretty high out here."

The attendant looked up the road the direction Latigo had come from, then slowly turned to look down the road the way he would go. He shrugged. "You're sure welcome to do business across the road. But as you can see, there ain't nothin' over there. Ain't no place else for many a mile, far as that goes."

The man stepped out of the way as Latigo opened the pickup door and stepped out. "Got anything cold to drink in there?" he said, nodding toward the café.

The attendant only nodded, and Latigo went on into the café as the man went about his work. A screen door squeaked on its spring and slammed shut behind him. A female counterpart of the old man sat perched on a tall chair behind a counter lined with four stools, the padding on the seats showing through rips and tears in the worn plastic upholstery. Two tables, shoved against the wall under filmy windows, flanked by mismatched chairs, confined salt and pepper shakers and bottles of mustard and ketchup in little wire cages. The pattern on the oilcloth covering the tables had been wiped off from scrubbing where plates would sit.

"If you please, ma'am, I'd like a bottle of root beer if it's cold."

The woman slid off her perch and ambled to an insulated chest, painted bright red and emblazoned with the name of a soft drink. She lifted the lid and pawed around in the water underneath until coming up with a bottle. She set it on the counter without wiping it off, and water puddled around it.

"Got an opener?"

The woman retrieved a bottle opener from under the counter and it dropped with a clink onto the countertop next to the bottle. Latigo pried the lid off the drink and took a sip. While the sweet liquid was several degrees lower than the ambient temperature, calling it cold would stretch the imagination of any thermometer. He took another sip.

"Five-cent deposit on the bottle if you take it with you."

"No, ma'am. I'll drink it right here."

He watched through the veil of grease on the windows as the old man finished washing the windshield and pumping gas. He lifted the truck hood and pulled the oil dipstick out, wiped it clean on a rag from his hind pocket, stuck it back down the hole then checked it again. He used the rag to twist off the radiator cap, stared down the mouth, picked up a bucket with a spout and poured in some water. He let the hood drop and it slammed shut.

He sauntered toward the café, stuffing the rag into a back pocket as he came. Sticking his head through the doorway, he told the woman how much to charge for the gasoline. "Oil's down a bit on the dipstick, cowboy, but it ain't low enough to worry about. She'll be fine, but keep an eye on 'er."

The man let the screen door slam and walked back toward the garage. The door banged shut again a minute or so later after Latigo settled his bill, and then left whatever place he was in to continue on his way to the City of Angels.

As the sun lowered toward the horizon, Latigo's eyes mimicked the movement, and he struggled to stay awake. Ahead, off the side of the highway, he spied a long, tall heap of gravel, most likely piled there by the highway department for one thing or another. He slowed the truck, pulled off, and maneuvered behind the pile, so it stood between him and the highway. He sat in the seat and ate the remainder of the food his mother had sent, save one apple he set aside, washing the meal down with water from a canteen; the tepid liquid flavored with the metallic taste of the aluminum container. As darkness fell, he rearranged the load in the truck bed to make space to unfurl his bedroll. He sat on the bed and tugged off his boots, set them aside and stuffed his socks inside, pulled off his shirt and draped it over the truck's side panel, then wormed his way into the bedroll and lay down, using the seat of his saddle for a pillow.

He did not know if it was the arrival of dawn lightening the sky or the increasing noise of traffic on the road that woke him. Latigo lay still for a moment, waiting for awareness to return and tell him where he was and why. Before long, he sat up and scoured the sleep from his face with the palms of his hands. He felt around for his hat and plopped it on his head, then dressed, the order of it mirroring his disrobing the night before. He passed water beside the gravel pile, and added to the wet stain with a mouthful of canteen water swished and spat out. He swallowed some of the water, ate the saved apple, then hit the road that seemed to disappear into a mountain range ahead.

Once he wound down through Cajon Pass to reach the Los Angeles Basin and the outskirts of the city proper, it took Latigo two more calls from roadside pay telephone booths to John Benson to sort his way through the labyrinth of city pavement; particularly the serpentine streets in the hills and canyons, where, somewhere, Benson lived.

Latigo pulled into a narrow driveway, its entrance barely visible through shrubs and bushes, at the end of which he believed—hoped—he would find the proper residence. He stopped at the end of the drive, next to a parked car, and sat, hands gripping the steering wheel, breaths coming shallow and rapid, heart pounding. He believed he had seen more automobiles in the few hours he had been in the city than he had seen before in all the years of his life. And, he thought, he had dodged a good many of them, which effort served only to create additional hazards with other vehicles. Had he thought he could find the way, he may well have pointed the truck toward home and put the quietus on his new life even before it began.

He meant to sit for a time, hoping to catch his breath. But, soon, the front door of the house opened and Benson stepped out onto the porch, positioning his hat and then tucking in his shirttails. Benson looked at Latigo, and Latigo looked back at him. The boy opened the door and slid off the truck seat, swinging his legs out and dropping to the ground, steadying himself with a hand on the doorframe.

"Come on in, son. Unless you intend to stay out here permanently."

"No, sir. Just gettin' used to what it feels like not to be movin'. Can't remember if I was born first or drivin' this here truck first."

He closed the truck door and stepped up the one step onto the porch. Shaded by an overhang and bordered by an outer wall that was more airy arches than solid material, the porch stretched across the width of the house. Thick leaves growing on some kind of green vines clung to the arch supports, climbing all the way to the overhang of the roof, some creeping above and out of sight. Painted white, the stucco walls of the house covered thick adobe bricks, the outer surfaces of some of which were visible where chunks of the coating had sloughed off.

"Sit down," Benson said, nodding toward a pair of low-slung redwood chairs with flared backs, flanking a small table, its round glass top balanced on a tripod of thin metal rods. "I know you're probably tired of sitting, but these chairs are sitting still. The stillness will help you unwind and relax. Can I offer you something to drink?"

"Well, sir, if you could spare a glass of cold water, I would surely appreciate it. What I've been drinkin' ain't been much, and it's been warm and tastes like tin."

"I'll do it—if you'll quit calling me sir."

"Yessir—I mean Mister Benson—John."

Benson returned after a few minutes, carrying a tray carrying a glass pitcher of water tinkling with ice cubes, and a tall glass. Also on the tray was an identical tall glass, the ice cubes inside swimming in a pale golden-brown liquid the color of a light sorrel horse; whether some kind of liquor or iced tea, Latigo could not say. Whatever it was, he doubted it would be as refreshing as the water, cold enough to hurt his teeth, that he poured down his throat in long gulps.

Benson sat and sipped his drink slowly, as Latigo did with the water once his thirst was satisfied. Neither man talked much, content to sit in the cool shade of the porch through the late afternoon.

After a good, long time, Benson said, "If you don't mind Latigo, we'll sit right here and you can rest this afternoon and evening. The wife will stir us up some supper after a while, then we'll get you settled. That sound good to you?"

Latigo nodded. He drew in a long, slow, deep breath and let it out just as slowly, fighting against the breath turning into a yawn.

"Tomorrow, I'll haul you on out to Slim Jones's place and let you have a look at what passes for horseflesh in these parts."

Chapter Fourteen

Slim Jones was a horseman. He understood horses. Some said he spoke their language; that he knew what a horse was thinking before the horse knew. He was an accomplished trainer and teacher. In his younger days, he could ride with the best of them. He encouraged horses to negotiate any kind of terrain. Handled them at any speed or gait. Stuck with them when recalcitrant, spooky, balky, or bucky. He could ride any kind of saddle or ride bareback. He was still an expert driver. He could drive a single horse hitched to a buggy, or any number of teams hitched to carriages, coaches, and wagons, in hand or on a jerk line.

Slim Jones was also a horse man. He owned horses. He bred horses. He raised horses. He traded horses. He bought and sold horses. He supplied horses—over the years he had provided remounts to the army, sent the unruly and obstinate to rodeo rough strings, the fleet to race-tracks, the agile to polo fields, working stock to farmers and freighters, riding horses to stables and pens and pastures.

Of late, and for years, most of his work had consisted of providing stock for movie and television production companies. Riding horses in quantity, driving horses, specially trained horses for stunt work, and any other horse required. If what was wanted wasn't available, he would teach and train a horse for a specific job. He supplied saddles and tack of all kinds—Western stock saddles for cowboys, McClellan cavalry saddles, sidesaddles, riding rigs more-or-less authentic to horseback Indian tribes, stock saddles rigged for stunt falls. He stocked harnesses and hitches. Covered wagons. Farm wagons. Delivery wagons. Conestoga wagons. Freight wagons. Chuck wagons. Mud wagons. Concord coaches. Passenger wagons. Medicine show wagons. Ore wagons. Army ambulances. Buggies and carriages of every description. Wagons that would fall to pieces and crash on command.

He even provided riding and driving lessons for actors unfamiliar with the arts, and worked with stunt riders to help them accomplish their work with minimal danger.

In short, if it was a horse, or anything that belonged in, on, around, under, ahead of, or behind a horse, Slim Jones was your man.

Latigo could not begin to keep up with where they had been or how they got to where they were when Benson drove him through the gate to Slim Jones's place. He knew only that they were in some place called The Valley, the San Fernando Valley. They had driven through canyons and hills, past neighborhoods old and new, past movie studios, business-es, citrus orchards, farm fields, and wooded and chaparral-covered hillsides to get where they were now.

Benson stopped the car in front of one of several barns. Latigo stepped out of the car and looked around. He could see horses grazing in pastures, confined in pens, and with necks hanging over stable doors to watch him. Pastured with the horses were mules and burros as well. Most of the horses were inconspicuous browns, bays, sorrels, and duns. But here and there were flashier horses with more distinctive coloration and markings—pintos, palominos, appaloosas, buckskins, grays, and whites.

Riders and trainers were horseback everywhere. Some rode up and down a long, straight track, others in a pair of large arenas, and some in smaller enclosures. Still others were afoot working with horses in round pens. Two men walked behind harnessed teams, the horses hitched to dragging logs, learning to pull a load.

Long rows of wagons were backed against a fence line, some under shed roofs, others in the open air. The line of horse-drawn conveyances gave way to trucks and trailers for hauling stock, as well as flatbed trailers used, Latigo assumed, for carrying wagons to filming locations.

He could not imagine what might be seen in the other barns and buildings around the place. Benson told him the horses here were only a fraction of what Slim owned—others were pastured elsewhere; brought in only when needed. Latigo also learned that Jones was in the cattle business, in partnership with a rancher out on the high desert. They kept, mainly, old-time Mexican and Texas cattle, as well as oxen, and rented them out in any numbers required for movie and television use.

Benson was known to many, if not most, of the cowboys in Jones's employ. Some "howdied" as they rode by, others dismounted for a short visit before getting back to their work. After a time, a loud, high-pitched voice from somewhere behind hollered, "John Benson! Get your sorry behind off my place! You've got ten seconds to get in that car and haul your butt out of here or I swear I'll shoot you where you stand!"

Latigo spun around to find the source of the threat. He looked at Benson, who had not reacted, still leaning against the fender of the car, a faint smile tracing his lips. Latigo looked again and saw the shouting man framed in a doorway on the wing of the large barn. A small, hand-painted sign reading office hung above the door.

The man started toward them, in no hurry, his histrionic hollering and threats continuing. He was a tall man, Latigo guessed him to be around six feet. His shoulders may have been broad, but looked narrow compared to the rest of the body between armpits and knees. His barrel chest joined a protruding belly which rounded into broad hips which narrowed to knees and shanks that looked too thin to support the weight they carried.

Benson finally turned around to face the threat, his smile now wide. The man stopped a few steps shy of reaching Benson and burst out laughing. Then, "John, you old so-and-so, what brings you way out here?"

Latigo looked from one man to the other.

Benson reached out and clapped Latigo on the shoulder. "Slim, I'd like you to meet a friend of mine, Latigo Brown. Latigo, this waste of hide—and a lot of it—is Slim Jones."

Slim reached out a hand. "Latigo Brown, is it?" Latigo grasped the hand, and Slim took a firm grip and shook it vigorously. "Any friend of John Benson probably ain't worth knowing, but it's a pleasure to make your acquaintance all the same."

Slim turned to Benson, offered a handshake, and when their hands clasped, the men drew each other close, into a back-slapping hug. Then Slim grasped Benson's shoulders and held him at arm's length. "Now, what's the deal with this unfortunate boy you dragged out here, John?"

"Well, I'm of a mind to get young Latigo here some movie work. He sits a pretty good horse from what I've seen. Hell of a bronc rider. And I'm told he does some trick riding."

"Trick riding, eh?" Slim said. "You any good at it?"

Latigo ducked his head and replied from under his hat brim. "Oh, no, Sir. Me and my brother, we used to fool around some back home. Nothin' special."

Slim thought for a moment, then hitched up his pants. "Let's see what you've got, boy. I'll get you a trick saddle," he said, then hollered out a name that got the attention of a cowboy in the alleyway of the barn.

"Hold on a minute," Latigo said.

"What's the matter?"

Latigo ducked his head again. "I—I—well, I wouldn't know what to do with a trick ridin' saddle. Ain't never sat in one. Fact is, I ain't seen one up close."

"What do you ride when you do your tricks?"

"Oh, just my regular ol' saddle."

"You got it with you?"

"No sir—well, it ain't here, anyway. It's back at Mister Benson's place."

Slim allowed that he had plenty of saddles and could fix him up. The cowboy he had hailed, waiting there for instructions from the boss, was sent away to fetch a horse Slim named, and to put a saddle on him. The cowboy returned several minutes later, leading the saddled horse, a bay gelding with three white socks and a star on its forehead. He handed the bridle reins to Slim, who refused them, telling the hand to give them to Latigo.

Latigo took the reins, then stepped in front of the horse, took its face in both hands and looked into its eyes. He rubbed and patted it on the neck, then stepped to the side and checked the stirrups, deciding with a look that they were probably set too long, and made an adjustment to one, then the other. He snugged up the front and back cinches, then led the horse out a few steps, turned a tight circle, and walked back. He spoke softly to the gelding, stepped into the stirrup and swung aboard, shifting back and forth in the seat and testing the length of the stirrups. He dismounted and raised the stirrup leathers another notch, climbed back on, and found them good.

"What would you like to see, Mister Jones?"

"Don't make no never mind to me. Do whatever you want, just so's I can get an idea what you got."

Latigo rode to the straightaway track, turned onto it, and urged the horse into a trot, then an easy lope, then into an all-out run. A good ways down the track he stopped, turned the horse around and started back toward the barn where Benson and Slim waited. Several of the men working stopped to watch.

He leaned forward in the saddle, tapped his heels into the horse's belly, and made a kissing sound with his lips. The horse, well-trained, lunged ahead, and reached a full gallop within a few strides, Latigo urging it along. Latigo pulled his feet from the stirrups, grasped the saddle horn with both hands, and lifted his right leg across the horse's rump. He swung it, along with the left leg, forward as he lowered—dropped—himself, both feet striking the ground and flying upward and back, his right leg swinging over the rump and landing him back in the seat. He instantly repeated the move off the opposite side, then again off the left side of the running horse. But this time, rather than landing in the saddle, he let the momentum carry him all the way across to land on the right side, vault over the horse again to land on the left, then up and into the saddle seat.

Latigo slowed the gelding, turned in a tight arc and started back down the track. His right leg came across again, but this time his left foot stayed in the stirrup and he laid out along the side of the horse, all but invisible to the spectators on the right, in a move called the Apache, or Indian, hideaway. He let the horse take the reins and climbed back into the saddle, this time facing rearward, and wrapped his hands in the long leather strings on the jockey of the saddle. He slid to the rear until his head hung below the dock, pressed down with his elbows on the horse's rump and raised his feet and legs into a stand. He held position for a few strides, lowered himself, and slid back into the saddle seat, still facing to the rear. With a hand on the cantle, he reached behind to place the other on the horn, raised himself and spun around to face forward, then spun again and again, getting back in the proper direction in time to slow the horse as it neared the end of the track.

Latigo patted the horse on the neck as he turned around and again spoke to it. Urging the gelding once more into an easy lope, he raised his right knee onto the seat, then his left, got his feet under him and pushed upright to stand in the saddle, absorbing the up-and-down motion of the horse with slightly flexed knees. He reined up the horse and turned off the track toward where Slim and Benson waited and watched by the car. Latigo kicked out and spread his legs, dropping into the seat. He stopped a few yards from Benson's car and stepped down, handing the reins to Slim. "That's a hell of a horse you got there, Mister Jones. He never batted an eye no matter what I did."

Slim nodded. "He's a good'n all right. Been plenty a trick rider and stunt man use him at one time or another. But I'll say this—there ain't been many of 'em much better'n you. 'Specially on a horse you don't know—and without even losin' your hat."

Latigo ducked his head, but did not reply.

Benson said, "I told you he was a hand, Slim. Think what he could do with you and your folks here to teach him."

Slim looked at Latigo. "You ride pretty good, son. But how are you at fallin' off?"

Latigo looked up, surprised at the question. Slim did not elaborate, his eyes locked on Latigo's, wrinkled at the corners as if they wanted to laugh.

"Well, sir, I got to say I ain't never done it on purpose. But I rodeo some and I've been on a good many buckin' horses, both barebacks and saddle broncs, so I've been pitched a good many times—not as much as I used to, I'm glad to say—but I ain't never been hurt much from eatin' all that dirt."

"What would you think of doin' stunt work for the movies and TV? Learnin' to fall properly off a horse is all part of it. But there's also jumpin' horses over and off of things, ridin' hell bent over some pretty dicey ground, and such. But it ain't all horseback. You'd learn how to wreck a wagon, fall off a building when you got shot, how to pull off a fist fight without gettin' the tar beat out of you, or beatin' the hell out of the other guy, how to dress up like the star of the show and do all the dangerous stuff he's supposed to do. There's a lot to it—John here, he's done it all, and still does it some."

Latigo swallowed hard. "Truth is, sir—"

"Stop callin' me sir. The name's Slim!"

"Yessir—I mean, Slim. Like I was sayin', I never knew there was any such of a thing until a couple weeks ago when I met a feller name of Clete Holman up in Las Vegas. First I ever heard of it."

"Aah, Clete—he was one of the best. Don't know none better. So, what do you think? Want to give it a shot?"

"I guess so. Mister Benson here thinks he can get me some work. Like I said, I don't know nothin' about it, but I'm sure willin' to learn."

Benson told Slim about the movie that started shooting next week—which he already knew about, as he was providing stock for it—and his plans to get Latigo on as an extra. And he told about Latigo's ability with a rope, and that he intended to cajole the director into including some rope tricks in a scene.

"You mean the boy ropes, too?"

"Yes, he does, Slim. I've seen him do it. The boy's a regular Will Rogers."

Slim looked at Latigo. "That so, son?"

Latigo looked down, scratching at the dirt with the toe of his boot, thumbs hitched in his pants pockets. He looked up at Slim. "No, Slim, it ain't—meanin' no disrespect to John. I can fool around with a rope some, but I darn sure ain't no Will Rogers."

Benson laughed. "Sure you are, Latigo. This is the movies we're talking about here, and like I told you, everything in the movies is exaggerated!"

Slim and Benson both laughed. Latigo managed a smile; unseen because, again, his head was bowed, watching the toe of his boot scrape and erase lines in the dirt.

Chapter Fifteen

Latigo sat on the bed in his sock feet, back propped against the rails of the headboard. On his lap was a cardboard box taken from a shelf in the room. Since the box had no lid, he felt no compunction about looking in, as it did not seem a violation of privacy.

John Benson had offered Latigo the use of a small apartment of sorts atop the garage behind the house. The upstairs rooms were sparsely furnished, used by the Bensons mostly for storage. The box held old rodeo programs, posters, back numbers, trophies, ribbons, belt buckles, and photographs from Benson's time on the rodeo circuit. Someone had marked the score sheets in some of the programs, and Benson's times in the steer wrestling and roping events were often the fastest listed. He also showed high marks in saddle bronc riding at many of the shows. There were several eight-by-ten action photographs taken at rodeos across the country, and a photo of Benson being awarded the trophy saddle and belt buckle as World Champion Steer Wrestler.

Other rodeo photos hung on the walls in frames, as well as movie posters and pictures of Benson with the stars of Western movies and television shows, some of which Latigo recognized, but others unfamiliar.

Latigo heard footsteps coming up the stairs, then a knock on the door. "Just a minute," he said, and slid off the bed, stepped to the door and pulled it open.

"Got a minute?" Benson said.

Latigo stepped out of the way to allow him into the room. Benson looked around the room as if he had not seen it for some time, noting Latigo's few belongings stowed here and there. He saw the box on the bed, and some of its contents scattered on the bed.

"Settling in all right?"

Latigo nodded that he was, a little worried that Benson had noticed the box on the bed.

Benson walked over and picked up a rodeo program off the bed, pulled a stack of photographs from the box and riffled through them. "I see where you're looking into my past."

Latigo swallowed hard. "Yessir. I hope you don't mind—I don't mean no harm—the box was just there on the shelf."

Benson shook his head. "No, son, I don't mind. No harm done at all." He looked through the photographs again, spending more time studying them. "Those were the days. I was rough as a cob back then."

"You were a hell of a hand—still are, I reckon. Why'd you give it up?"

Benson dropped the photos back into the box. He shrugged. "I dearly love rodeo. Can't think of a thing that feels as good as catching the horns of a fast steer and taking my dallies and turning the critter, watching the heeler snag both hind legs as my horse spins around keeping the rope taut, and seeing the judge whip that flag down." He sighed. "Unless maybe it's dropping down off a good horse onto the back of a steer and laying him down before he knows what hit him."

Benson slid some of the memories on the bed into a pile and sat down. "Still, it was time to hang up that particular pair of spurs. For one thing, I got married and Elaine never liked to travel much—and, the fact is, I wanted to be with her. Missed her like the dickens when I was on the road. Then one winter between rodeos, I delivered a load of horses out here to Slim Jones for a neighbor back in Oklahoma. I was curious about what he did with all those horses he had at his place—you saw what it's like—and why the hell he needed more.

"One thing led to another, and Slim got me to doing stunt work in some of the pictures. I moved Elaine out here, and we've been here since. Not here at this place—for years, we lived in a rundown apartment in a neighborhood most folks avoid. But when I started getting bigger productions, some speaking parts, then bigger roles, we were doing well enough to move up here." He picked up another rodeo program and thumbed through the pages. He looked up at Latigo and smiled. "And, like I told you before, if a man is going to make his living falling and jumping off horses, doing it in front of a movie camera pays a whole lot better."

Benson set the program aside, lifted his backside off the bed and pulled a thick sheaf of papers, folded in half, out of his hind pocket. He opened the fold, and Latigo could see the papers were punched along the side and held together top and bottom with brass fasteners. The top sheet was light blue, with a few words typed on it.

"Sit down," Benson said, flexing the fold out of the book.

Latigo dragged the one chair in the room over and sat, facing Benson on the bed.

"This is the script for the movie we start shooting next week. I wanted you to take a look at it; get some idea of how a movie gets made."

Benson opened the script and turned it to face Latigo. The words were typed in chunks, or blocks, spaced and indented on the page in various ways. Benson explained what it all meant; the slug lines at the head of each new scene telling where and what time of day the scene is set, the screen direction telling who is in the scene and what action occurs and the transitions, with the dialogue the actors speak in a narrow column down the center of the page.

"Now, son, you read through this and you'll get a sense of the story. It's not like reading a book, but you'll get the idea."

"I will, Mister Benson—John." He took the script and thumbed the pages, fanning from front to back. Some pages showed underlined passages and notes penciled in the margins in what Latigo assumed was Benson's handwriting.

"You have any questions, don't be afraid to ask. You can't learn a thing otherwise. Right now, you don't know what you don't know. Once you figure that out, you'll know what questions to ask."

Benson stood up and put a hand on Latigo's shoulder. "Elaine says supper will be ready in about an hour. Don't bother to knock when you come down, you just come on in."

Latigo spent the hour reading the screenplay. As Benson said, it was not like reading a book. The descriptions were concise, even sketchy. Outside of the actors' lines, everything hinted at what would be seen on the screen—there was no explanation of what the characters were thinking, no hint of how they saw things, nothing to tell what those thoughts and points of view might lead them to do. The words described only what was happening at that moment, as if seen and heard from the outside.

The back door of the Benson house opened into the kitchen. Latigo, out of habit rather than necessity, wiped his feet on the mat on the step and walked in. He took off his hat and hung it on an empty wall peg on a row beside the door. John sat at the table reading a newspaper, a pair of glasses perched on his nose and a tall glass of some kind of iced drink in front of him.

Elaine, reaching a stack of plates from a cupboard, said, "Come in, Latigo. Pull up a chair. Can I get you something to drink?"

"Oh, no, Ma'am—go on with what you're doing. I don't want to be a nuisance."

Elaine laughed; John looked over the top of his reading glasses and smiled. He folded the paper and tossed it onto a small side table against the wall, which held a pile of other newspapers and magazines along with a few whiskey and wine bottles.

"Have a seat, son. We don't stand on ceremony here. There's nothing fancy or formal about supper at the Benson *hacienda*. Now, what are you drinking?"

"Well, sir, if it ain't no trouble, a glass of milk would sure taste good."

Elaine dealt the dinner plates around the table, along with a drinking glass at Latigo's place and one filled with ice cubes at her own. She brought a bottle of milk from the refrigerator and poured Latigo's glass full and left the bottle. She was back in an instant with a wicker basket holding sliced bread nested in a cloth napkin, and a butter dish.

"Help yourself to bread and butter," Elaine said. "You might just as well have something to wash down with that milk." She wiped her hands on the lap of her apron. "It's all store-bought, I'm afraid. It has been years since I milked a cow or churned butter, and I confess I don't miss either chore one bit. And I've given up on baking bread—we eat so little of it, between the two of us."

She bustled off to the stove and returned with a serving bowl in one hand and a baking dish in the other, one holding string beans and the other sliced potatoes in some kind of sauce, glazed golden brown on the edges and ridges. She was back again in an instant with a tray of roasted chicken. One more trip across the kitchen resulted in a pitcher of iced tea. Elaine topped off John's glass, then poured some for herself, the liquid splashing over and swirling through the floating ice cubes in the glass.

No one spoke as they ate, helping themselves to the food and drink as needed. When they finished, little was left of the meal beyond clean chicken bones and dirty dishes. Elaine stood and stacked plates. "Did you get enough to eat, Latigo?"

"Yes Ma'am. I sure did. I'm 'bout as full as a tick. Can I help clean up?"

"Oh, no thank you. If it weren't for keeping busy in the kitchen, I wouldn't have a thing else to do. You and John sit and visit."

With the dishes out of the way, save the drinking glasses and the bottle of milk, Elaine wiped the table and put out a plate of cookies. John got up and got himself a fresh glass and filled it with milk, then sat and dipped a cookie in the milk and ate it.

"You look over that script?"

"Yessir, I did."

"What do you think?"

"Well, Mist—John, it's like you said. It ain't like readin' a book, but I think I got the gist of it."

"What do you think it's about?"

Latigo thought for a time. "It's about this rancher who's only got a daughter, and she's grown up. She's sweet on one of the cowboys who works on the ranch, and they're fixin' to get married. But he ain't honest—he's stealin' cattle on the sly from the old man. The foreman—that's you—he finds out what's goin' on, and tells the rancher, who don't believe it. But he catches the kid red-handed, proves it to the old man. There's a shoot-out where the foreman kills the thief. The girl hates him for it, but when he tells her why he done it, she's ashamed, but he's so understanding she ends up falling in love with him and the old man offers them the ranch for a wedding present."

John nodded. "That's the story of it, all right. But if you was to ask the director, he'd tell you it's about something altogether different."

Latigo's brow furrowed. "How's that?"

"Most directors, the good ones, anyway, are always looking for something deeper; things going on underneath the story. Mostly, they turn everything into questions."

"I don't know what you mean."

"Well, for instance," John said, dipping another cookie, "will the rancher's daughter realize on her own that the cowboy ain't no good? Will the rancher see that the kid is only interested in what he can get for himself and doesn't care about the girl? Will the girl see that the foreman, even though he's older, is in love with her? Will the kid get away with it? Will he break the girl's heart, or keep playing her along until he leaves? And, finally, will the good guy win out over the bad guy?" John paused to dip another cookie and let Latigo think on what he had said. "That one—will the good guy win and the bad guy get his comeuppance?—is always the big question in a Western movie, and most everyone knows the answer before the movie starts. But a good director will make it so it isn't so obvious, and plant just enough doubt that the audience can believe it might not come out that way."

Latigo shook his head. "I got to admit I never thought of none of that."

Benson shrugged. "Most people don't. But that's what makes the difference between a good movie and your everyday horse opera. Give that same script to a different director, and he might just shoot what's on the page without giving a thought to the things I talked about. Everything's straightforward and predictable—just your typical oater. People enjoy those kinds of movies, and they're entertaining, all right—but they forget everything about them by the time they get out of bed the next morning. The better movies, they stick with you. Even though the answer might be the same, the questions are more complicated."

Again, Latigo shook his head. "I guess I must be dumb as a bowl of oatmeal. I never thought anything like that. I thought a movie was a movie, and they was all about the same."

"It's easy enough to think that way—most movies are all about the same, no matter if the story is different. There are only a few that stand out. Think of it this way—it's like bronc riders. There are plenty of guys who will get on a bronc. Some of them, a few, are just plain awful, and they'll be looking for a place to land as soon as the gate opens. Others, the top hands, can put on a ride no matter the bronc they draw. They can make the tough ones look easy, and the easy ones look tough. Those cowboys are as few and far between as the bad ones. Most bronc riders, like most movies, aren't all that good or all that bad. They're just there. Sometimes they'll bite the dust, and sometimes they'll make a passable ride. But, mostly, they pay their money and take their chances and there isn't any more to it."

"I guess I sort of see what you mean. But how come there ain't none of the stuff you talked about written down in the script?"

Benson smiled and consumed another soggy cookie. "Well, if it's a good script by a good writer—and screen writers are just like bronc riders—it's there for them that can read between the lines. For some reason, the real stuff, I guess what you'd call the *art*, is always subtle. I've read scripts, even acted in movies, where the writer tried too hard. It all comes off kind of corny. They beat the folks who watch the movie over the head with what they're trying to say, and it just don't work that way. It works better if you feed it to them with a spoon instead of a scoop shovel."

Latigo considered what Benson said. He swallowed the last of the milk in his glass. "I think I need to read that script again. See if I can see more of what you're talkin' about."

Benson smiled and drank the milk in his glass. "You do that, Latigo. But don't be too concerned if it doesn't jump off the pages at you. The fact is, this town is full of people who make their living one way or another making movies and don't know the first thing about it."

Chapter Sixteen

The movie production got underway Monday. John Benson's "call"—the when and where he was required to be at work—was not until the next day, but he wanted to introduce Latigo to some of the players and the crew, and let him watch them at work.

Latigo assumed they would drive out in the country somewhere to a ranch, as the story takes place on a ranch. Instead, Benson turned off a city street into a driveway with an imposing arch created from big metal letters spelling out the name of a movie studio. A guard in a tan uniform holding a clipboard stepped out of a booth under the arch, greeted Benson by name, and signaled him through. Latigo watched over his shoulder as the guard marked something on the papers on his clipboard.

They drove for a time past tree-shaded rows of what looked like small houses. Benson said they were the offices for the various production executives and directors and the like. They drove past and down alleys between long, tall, plain-looking buildings with no markings on them save a big number identifying each one. They parked near one of the buildings.

"Well, son," Benson said, "let's go make a movie."

Latigo followed him to one of the nondescript buildings. Benson ignored the ordinary door, and instead passed under a tall, wide, partially raised overhead door. The light was dim inside the building, and the two cowboys stopped to let their eyes adjust. Latigo looked around at the ladders and scaffolds and frameworks of other kinds, and watched workers scurrying around carrying big light fixtures, framed squares of cloth, household-looking furniture, and all manner of things he could not identify. Light glowed deeper into the building, creating an island of sorts in the dimness. He followed Benson toward it.

They reached a wall, tall but falling far short of the building's ceiling. It looked like the wall of an unfinished house—a skeleton of raw lumber, backed by unpainted plywood, but was propped upright by wooden braces or buttresses. Benson led Latigo around the end of the wall, exposing the source of the brightness.

Spread before them was the interior of a house; a ranch house of an earlier time. Latigo's eyes darted from one part of the house to another—a large table cut from rough-hewn lumber, handmade wooden chairs along one side and at each end, a wooden plank bench along the other side. The table was set with plain, old-fashioned dishes. Overhead, a chandelier made from a wagon wheel flickered with what looked like lit candles. Pictures hung on the walls. A mortared rock fireplace covered most of one wall of the room, logs blazing within its cavernous maw. A sofa and chairs and small tables were grouped in front of the fireplace. A stairway climbed another wall, reaching a railed balcony along a row of doors on the upper floor. Beneath the stairway was an alcove with a shelf of books, a rolltop desk, and an upholstered chair beside a small end table. The other side of the room opened into a kitchen with a big cast-iron stove and old-fashioned cupboards and shelves stocked with supplies. The house looked lived in; tidy, but cluttered enough to suggest use.

Latigo studied the place, wide-eyed. It looked as real as any house he had ever set foot in, yet none of it was real. It was, Benson told him, called a "set."

"Those doors up there," Latigo said, pointing to the balcony. "What's behind 'em?"

"Nothing. Nothing but air."

"It all looks so real."

"Well, that's the point, son—to fool people sittin' in those movie houses into believing all this make-believe is real."

"I never imagined any such of a thing," Latigo said, his eyes trying to take in everything, trying to see beyond the apparent reality to the artifice underneath.

At the edge of the set, near where they stood, was a cart of sorts, with the movie camera on a pedestal, and a built-in stool for sitting. Atop a tall, wheeled stand balanced a long arm with a big microphone on the end, hanging above the set. The brightness in the room came not from the chandelier, or the fireplace, or the glowing lamps scattered here and there in the rooms, but from huge lights hanging from the building's ceiling and on stands and scaffolds positioned around the set. Workers bustled around shifting the lights, fiddling with the camera equipment, and adjusting furniture and fixtures.

"It sure takes a lot of people to make a movie," Latigo said, overwhelmed by all the activity. "How do they all know what they're supposed to do? It don't look line anybody's runnin' things."

Benson laughed. "Most all these folks have done this for a long time. They know most of what needs doing without being told. But there are people in charge. Once a production gets underway, it's in the hands of the director. But it's too much for one man to keep track of, so they have what's called 'Departments' responsible for different things that need doing.

"You may have seen a desk we passed out by the door. That's for the Production Manager. He keeps track of all the people and equipment and schedules—he makes sure the director doesn't spend too much money. They don't always get along. He's got production assistants to do all the running around. They're usually young people wanting to get into the business. Then there are Assistant Directors who work with the director who make sure the right actors and other people show up at the right time and the set is ready, and such like that.

"All these lights and where to put them are the responsibility of the Director of Photography. He's the one who makes sure everything looks nice on film, the way the Director wants it. He's got a Gaffer, who puts up the lights with his helpers. All these men lifting and toting and moving things around and building the scaffolds and putting up stands for the lights are called Grips.

"And there are sound men who deal with the microphones you see, and record what the actors say.

"Then there were designers and artists and carpenters and painters who figured out how all this was supposed to look, and build it so the camera could get around in it. And folks who provided all the furniture and other stuff they call 'props.' There's a whole bunch of other people, too. You'll see some of them soon enough. This movie has a pretty good budget. On a smaller production, there aren't as many to do the work, so they'll do more than one job, and the sets and such aren't as fancy."

While Benson and Latigo talked, a group of people had assembled near the set. Some of them Latigo took to be actors—people dressed in costumes not much different from what he wore, but from an older time. He recognized one of the men from programs he had seen on television, or from the rare occasions he sat through a movie. A young woman—whose beauty prompted a second, then third look—seemed vaguely familiar. Most of the talking was done by an ordinary-looking man Benson said was the director, Howard Walsh. He and the actors talked and laughed; other people came and went, passing information to, asking questions of, and getting instructions from the director.

Benson stood silent, save for answering questions from Latigo, letting the young man take it all in. When there was a lull in activity, he took Latigo by the arm and led him toward Walsh. "Howard? Have you got a minute?"

Walsh turned away from the group. With a smile, he extended a hand. "John! It's good to see you! Do we need you today? I believe your call is tomorrow."

"Right you are, Howard. But I wanted to come by and introduce this young man to you. He's the one I told you about—the one who's handy with a rope."

"Ah, yes!" Walsh turned toward Latigo. "So, you are the cowboy who ropes and rides so well. I am sorry, but I do not recall your name."

"Orval Brown," Latigo said, thrusting out his hand and giving a firm shake to the director. "But most folks call me Latigo. Latigo Brown."

"Ah, yes! Latigo Brown. I remember now."

"It's sure a pleasure to meet you, Mister Walsh." Latigo looked toward the set. "Quite an outfit you got here. I ain't never seen nothin' like it before."

Walsh smiled. "It would seem a bit strange, I suppose. We grow accustomed to it all. Perhaps we do not appreciate the mystery of it as much as we should."

"If you don't mind, Howard," Benson said, "We'd like to hang around the set today. I'd like Latigo here to see how we do things."

"Sure! Absolutely! And, by the way, John, that bit of business you suggested with the rope tricks at the barn dance—I believe we'll shoot it. It will add a little extra to the celebration, I think. Stop by the production office and get young Latigo here on the payroll. Bring him along tomorrow. We'll use him as an extra as needed, and, of course, for the barn dance scene." Walsh turned to Latigo. "Bring your rope along tomorrow, Latigo. If we've a moment, I'd like to get an idea what you can do."

A member of the production staff walked up and asked Walsh a question, showing him something on the script or a schedule or other sheaf of papers.

Walsh studied the page. "You will have to excuse me, gentlemen. I have to see to this." With a smile, he walked away.

Benson clapped Latigo on the shoulder. "Well, there you go, son. Now you're in the movies."

Latigo did not know whether to laugh or cry.

"Come on over here. I'll show you something."

He followed Benson beyond the set, deeper into the cavernous building. They stopped after passing another propped-up wall. Latigo squinted into the dim light and the interior of a barn took shape. The rafters and beams of a high, pitched ceiling vaulted over an exposed loft extending part way out from the back wall of the barn, reached by a wooden ladder nailed to the wall. A row of stalls lined one side of the center alley, with other stalls and solid walls with doors, meant, perhaps, for feed storage of for tack rooms, along the other side.

Everything was raw, unpainted, rough-sawn lumber; the floor a layer of packed dirt over the concrete. In the center stood a low platform, perhaps a foot above the floor, also of raw lumber. A square post stood above each corner, connected by taut ropes. Dangling from the rope at intervals around the square and across the diagonal were lanterns.

"Well, there it is, son—the scene of your movie debut. This is where the dance will be, to celebrate the barn raising."

Latigo shook his head. "I can't believe it. I thought we'd be in a real barn somewhere. Out on a ranch, you know. I can't believe you can make a whole movie in a building like this, on these, what you call, sets."

Benson explained something of the expenses involved. As much as possible, the company would shoot interior scenes on sets on sound stages, then, for exterior scenes, the company would move to outdoor sets—some of which were entire streets reminiscent of an Old West town—on the studio's back lot, and in the open spaces among the hills and valleys even deeper into the studio property. Only when absolutely necessary, and only on films with sufficient budget, did the company pack up all the lights and equipment and haul it all, along with all the cast and crew, out to a location away from the studio lot.

Latigo asked what they were preparing to shoot at the ranch house interior set.

Benson pulled his dog-eared script from his back pocket and thumbed through the pages. "I don't have the shooting schedule, and you'll remember there are several scenes in the house. But I'm guessing, on account of the actors we saw, it will be this scene here," he said, pointing out the chosen page.

Latigo strained to read in the low light. "I don't get it. That's way back in the movie—nearly to the end. Don't they start at the beginning and go on from there, like in the script?"

Benson explained further the economies involved; of the production people in the background who figured out the cheapest way to shoot the scenes, with the least amount of moving around, and the most advantageous scheduling of actors and extras and crew people. Seldom, if ever, were the scenes of a movie filmed in the order in which they occur in the story.

"When do you suppose they'll be doin' that barn dance stuff here?"

"Oh, I don't know. Maybe next week. Week after, maybe."

"So we'll be havin' a dance party in a barn that ain't even been built yet? I know that barn raisin' comes later in your script."

Benson laughed. "I guess so. But don't you worry. In a few weeks, we'll be out on the back lot getting that barn built. When they cut the movie together, people in the theaters won't know the difference. It will surprise you, too, once you see it. All the confusion of jumping around to different times and places all gets sorted out, and the movie gets put together from beginning to end, pretty much like the script you read."

Benson let Latigo soak all that in for a time. Then, "Let's mosey on over to the office and get all the paperwork taken care of to get you on the payroll. Then we'll go over to the commissary and get some dinner. By then, Howard ought to have things whipped into shape and ready to roll."

Chapter Seventeen

By the time Benson and Latigo made it back to the sound stage, shooting was underway. The characters in the scene—the man playing the rancher, the young woman cast as his daughter, and the actor Latigo thought he recognized playing the cowboy the girl was sweet on, shared a meal served by an older woman, the cook and housekeeper, who bustled about between the kitchen and dining table.

The actors repeated the scene, in whole and in part, several times, carrying on the same conversation about the future of the ranch, the young cowboy offering a lot of advice, which the rancher listened to with good humor, but did not seem to pay much attention to.

During a lull in the shooting, Latigo asked why they did the same thing over and over.

"Oh, it could be any number of things," Benson said. "The director might not like the way some of the lines were delivered, or the reactions to those lines. He'll shoot different angles—wide shots to cover everything and everybody, then shots with only some of the actors in them, then close-ups of the actors while they say their lines or react to what's said."

"What do they do all that for?"

"Well, Son, think of seeing it in a movie. The film editors—the cutters—put it all together so that while the talk goes on you see it from different points of view. Seems normal enough when you see it—fact is, most people don't even notice it, but they know something doesn't seem right if it isn't done that way."

Through most of the shooting, Latigo had a hard time looking at anyone but the young woman playing the rancher's daughter. He learned her name was Annika Eriksson, a rising star of Swedish origin. Latigo had noticed her accent when the camera wasn't rolling, then was surprised she could suppress it and sound so ordinary when speaking her lines. Whether accented or not, he strained to hear her every word, his eyes riveted on her every move.

Wandering around the cavernous sound stage when standing around grew tiresome, Latigo tried to stay out of the way, visiting with people who did not look too busy at the time. He asked about their work, and how what they did fit into the production. A few were gruff and close-mouthed, but most were willing to talk, some going so far as to fill him in on gossip already spreading concerning members of the crew and, especially, the cast. When he asked Benson about that, he was told such prattle was typical, usually baseless, and always best ignored.

Benson went to work the next day. His scene, meant to happen in late evening, started with his knocking on the back door of the ranch house—a door on the wall of the kitchen that opened only to emptiness—talking there briefly with the rancher, then coming inside to sit at the table with his boss, drinking coffee while he warned the rancher that something was up with the cow herds, and that he suspected the cowboy who was courting the rancher's daughter was behind it. Shooting the sequence required several moves to re-set the camera and the lights, including what Latigo learned was a "dolly shot" to follow the rancher and Benson as they walked through the kitchen and to the dining table.

Latigo's film debut came that afternoon—but no one who would see the movie would ever know it. In the scene, the camera looked at the rancher standing in the front doorway of the ranch house with Benson beside him. The door had not been there until some grips wheeled it into position in front of the ranch house set. The door stood in a short wall that extended a few yards to either side. The wall looked for all the world like squared-up and mortared logs, but was only molded and painted plaster. Reaching out from the door and wall was a plank porch, painted to look worn, right up to the peeling paint on the rails and a broken and partly missing baluster.

The rancher stood in the doorway, with Benson beside him on the porch in morning light. The two men addressed an assemblage of cowboys standing in front of the porch about the coming day's work. Latigo stood among the cowboys, the camera seeing only his back. The wardrobe people fitted him out in clothing, but, since his face would not be seen, there was no need for a visit to the makeup artists.

When the crew went to work setting up the next scene, the director, Howard Walsh, led Latigo off into an empty area, not hard to find in the vast sound stage. One of Walsh's assistants, a young woman, went with them, carrying one of the company's ever-present clipboards.

"I see you have a rope there," Walsh said.

Latigo lifted the coiled lariat and looked at it as if unaware of its presence. He had carried the rope all day, his hand apparently becoming so accustomed to it he no longer noticed it. "Yessir. I guess so."

"If you will, please, show me what you can do with it."

Latigo dropped a coil of the rope, the honda eating the coil as it fell. He started jiggling the rope back and forth, the loop reappearing as he worked the rope. The loop grew as Latigo continued, feeding out more rope from the coils. Latigo kept building and spinning the butterfly, moving and twisting the loop from one side of his body to the other. He turned it into a vertical loop and let it spin and grow, then jumped back and forth through it. He changed the angle of the spin and turned the loop flat and stepped in and out of it with one foot several times, then jumped inside. After a few rotations, he bounced the loop a few times, raising it from brushing the floor to above his head. Finally, he spun the loop away and let it fall over the head of the young woman, pulling in the slack as it settled around her waist.

The move prompted a gasp, almost a scream, from the woman, and a smile from the director. "That is remarkable, Latigo Brown. You keep that rope handy." Without another word, he walked away.

His aide pulled slack into the loop, let it fall to the ground, and stepped out of it. She looked at Latigo, then averted her eyes and set off on the track of the director.

Shooting continued on the sound stage for several days, moving from one indoor set to another—a bunkhouse, a saloon, and a line shack. Latigo worked as an extra in the saloon scenes; a face in the crowd or a man standing at the bar or sitting at a table in the background. Eventually, the setup moved to the barn.

Latigo was surprised when they moved to the barn to see some of the interior structure had been removed. He soon learned why, as several scenes were part of the barn-raising, with actors and extras rebuilding what had been unbuilt—the task a simple one, as every piece of lumber was cut to fit and nail holes drilled, the work as easy as assembling a big wooden toy. Latigo worked in some of the barn-building scenes, his most demanding task sawing a board propped on sawhorses. He repeated the job several times in the background as the actors performed the foreground scene and the camera filmed it from various angles. Each time, the boards Latigo sawed were carried away and tossed onto a scrap heap. He could not help thinking what use it, and all the other lumber on the sets, could be put to back home on the ranch.

The barn-raising scenes concluded with the rough construction of the dance floor by the actors and extras. The carpenters on the crew would have at it afterward, adding reinforcement and ensuring it would be strong and stable enough to support the several actors and extras who would be twirling and tromping around on it during the barn dance scenes.

At the end of the day, the young woman with the clipboard who spent all day every day at Walsh's side, unless he sent her off on an errand, found Latigo and told him the boss wanted to see him. He followed her to Walsh, and found him talking with the production manager, Annika Eriksson, the young cowboy actor, and two other people Latigo did not recognize. All held copies of tomorrow's shooting script.

"Ah, Latigo Brown," Walsh said as he walked up, stopping at the edge of the group. "Come, come—we need you for this."

Latigo joined the circle and one of the men he did not know handed him a sheaf of papers.

Walsh said to the group, "I have been working with the writers and we have made an addition to the barn dance scenes we shoot tomorrow." He introduced Latigo to the others, not bothering to give him their names. "Latigo, we have included your roping display, but have expanded that beyond our original intentions."

*****

Benson noticed Latigo fidgeting on the drive to the studio. "What's the matter, Son? Nervous?"

"A little bit, I guess. It ain't been so bad hangin' around in the background when they shoot, when the most important thing you got to remember is not to look at the camera."

Benson smiled. "Hell, Latigo, you won't be doing anything you haven't done a thousand times already."

Latigo nodded. "That's so. But I ain't never done it in front of all these movie people and those bright lights and such. What if I mess up?"

"You wouldn't be the first one. And you wouldn't be the last. If you do, don't worry about it. You'll get it right on the next take."

Latigo shook his head and studied the coiled rope sitting on his lap. "I ain't so worried about the ropin'. But I don't know about sayin' those words. I never counted on doin' that."

Benson reached over and patted Latigo on the shoulder. "Don't worry. You'll be fine. Besides, having those lines moves you up on the pay scale."

Latigo laughed, sort of. "Thanks a lot, John. Like that's goin' to help. Only discombobulates me more to think of that."

Cast and crew worked through the morning, shooting scenes for the barn dance. Some involved speaking, as when the rancher stepped up and welcomed all his neighbors and their hands to the party, expressing his appreciation for their help in raising the barn, and inviting them to enjoy the food and drink and dancing.

Latigo paired up with a few different girls during the filming, dancing among several actors and extras on the platform. The camera watched, at various times, from above and below as dancers reeled around the stage, even moving among them on an extended arm as the camera dolly pushed ahead. Music came from a bunkhouse orchestra of sorts—a fiddler, squeezebox player, banjo plucker, guitar picker, and harmonica player. Many times during the filming and the breaks between, Latigo watched, stared at, even, Annika Eriksson, wondering and worrying how his coming encounter with the most beautiful woman he had ever seen would play out.

He blanched when the First Assistant Director called out the scene number corresponding to his roping display. But he swallowed hard, fetched his rope, and took up his position at the edge of the dance floor. The same voice yelled "Roll sound!" followed by a distant voice calling back, "Speed!" Walsh said, "Roll camera!" and the operator responding, "Rolling." The First Assistant Director called for "Sticks!" and another of the assistant directors answered the call, stepping in front of the camera with a slate board filled in with the scene and take numbers, written in the appropriate places among the other boxes identifying the production, the film roll number, date, and other information useful for the film processors and editors. He announced the scene number and "Take one," then said, "Mark!" and slapped down the hinged clapper on top of the slate and stepped out of the way. The First Assistant Director signaled the band to play. Walsh took a breath, then called out, "Action!"

The plan was to shoot the scene in one continuous take. The bunkhouse orchestra played a few bars then finished the number. The dancers stopped, applauding. Then the rancher stepped up onto the dance floor, arms raised, walking to the middle of the platform.

"Ladies and gentlemen!" he yelled. He lowered his arms. "And you cowboys, too!" When the laughter died down, he said, "We're in for a special treat. There's a cowboy from one of the neighboring ranches they say is handy with a rope. He has agreed—reluctantly, I might add—to give us a demonstration of some trick and fancy roping!"

That was Latigo's cue. Among light applause, he stepped onto the platform and moved through the dancers as they moved away from the center of the dance floor. Some, including Annika Eriksson, stopped in a circle around the edge, leaving a gap for the camera to see through. Others stepped down to watch from the dirt floor, or walked away as if going for food or drink, as did the cowboy courting Annika.

Latigo, just as he had done for Walsh, dropped the coil and the honda and started jerking back and forth to build his butterfly loop. As the loop grew and he moved it from side to side, the band stuck up a tune and the dancers clapped in time. He performed the other tricks—the "Texas Skip" through a vertical loop, stepping in and out of a flat loop "spoke jumping," jumping inside the spinning loop for the "wedding ring," then bouncing the big loop up and down.

Then, as in his demonstration for the director, he let the loop fly away and guided it to settle around and capture a young woman. But this time, he captured a surprised Annika Eriksson.

He pulled in the slack as gently as possible to settle the loop around her waist. The onlookers' clapping turned to applause and the band, with a flourish, stopped playing. As the ovation wound down, Latigo pulled in his rope as delicately as he could, drawing Annika forward until she stood before him.

"Pardon me, Miss, but would you care to dance with me?" His hesitance and timidity in delivering the line required no acting.

Annika smiled, but before she could reply, the actor who played her love interest jumped onto the platform, dropping the cups of punch he carried and pushing dancers aside as he bulled his way through them. He grabbed Annika by the arm and pulled her aside, then pulled slack into the loop and lifted it over her head. He threw the rope at Latigo, then stepped forward and, with both hands in Latigo's chest, pushed. Latigo stepped back, and as he did, the cowboy threw a punch. As rehearsed, Latigo saw it coming and caught the flying fist as if it were a baseball. He held tight as the cowboy strained.

"She's my girl! You keep your stinkin' mitts off her!"

Latigo pushed back against the captured fist, forcing the cowboy to step back to retain his balance. He pushed the fist aside and let go.

"I'm sorry, Mister. I never meant nothin' by it."

Cast and crew held their breath. The camera kept rolling. During the altercation, the dolly had slowly moved forward, pushing the camera on its arm out over the platform, stopping behind and between Annika and the cowboy, their heads and shoulders framing Latigo's face.

"Cut!" Howard Walsh yelled.

Chapter Eighteen

The envelope trembled in his hand. Latigo stared at the movie studio's name and address in the corner, and his own name showing through the glassine window. He took a deep breath, turned the envelope over, stuck a finger under the flap, and tore it open. The amount on the check caused another intake of breath, this one sudden. He wondered if there had been a mistake, but was unsure who to ask. Finally, he showed the check to Benson, who said it looked about right.

The company was moving to the outdoor lot, so there was no work that day for the actors and extras. Benson drove to the imposing building where he did his banking, taking Latigo along so he could cash his paycheck. Latigo had an account at the local bank back home for his rodeo winnings and to pay entry fees, but decided to open an account here, uncomfortable with the amount of cash he would otherwise have to keep in a sock under his mattress.

When all the paperwork was wrapped up and the money on deposit, save some pocket money, Latigo asked Benson to take him to a post office. There, he purchased a money order with a good share of his pay and mailed it to his folks. Sending money home established a pattern Latigo would continue.

Shooting on the outdoor sets on the backlot continued for a couple of weeks. On the days Benson worked, Latigo rode to the studio with him. When extras or stunt riders were on call, but Benson was not, Latigo drove himself to the lot in his beat-up 1948 pickup truck. He managed the first solo trip without getting lost, and stopped worrying so much about the busy roads and streets. On some of the days when there was no work for extras, he found his way to Slim Jones's place. He helped out with horse training in trade for instruction in performing stunts.

He watched, he tried, he learned, and was soon able to perform a horse fall on cue, landing near enough the marked spot to suffice. He learned to execute jumps, both horseback and on the ground, watching the horse's hooves pass overhead near enough to stir the air. He needed no instruction in other horseback stunts, which consisted for the most part of fast riding and chasing, as his experience with horses and in the rodeo arena more than covered an apprenticeship.

The stunt men taught him how to fall off a porch roof, then a building top, and through stair rails and off balconies, landing on the pads properly to prevent injury. He learned the choreography behind fist fighting, surviving the lessons with only a few bruises, the result of dodging when he should have ducked, or ducking when he should have dodged.

He rode with the stunt men on the shoot from time to time, mostly going up and down hills at a high lope. During a break between takes, he asked Benson—doing his own stunt riding in the scene—if anyone in a movie ever rode at less than a lope.

Benson laughed, then tipped back his hat. "Not that I recall, son. I guess I have seen horses trot now and then, but only in town. Even then, you usually go at a lope, if not a dead run."

"Why is that? Hell's bells, nobody ever rides that way for real. You'd be wearin' out horses faster'n you could saddle 'em, else every one of them would be wind broke or get the thumps or end up stifled."

"You're right, Latigo. The only reason Slim's horses don't get hurt much is we spend most of the day doing what we're doing now—sitting around waiting. Of course, no one could hurry as much in real life as they do on the screen. But every director I ever worked with, and that's a whole lot of them, is of the opinion that people watching a movie or television show would fall asleep if they had to watch a horse *walk* across the street. Besides, you have to admit there isn't much in this world as pretty to look at as a horse on the run."

Latigo could only shake his head in wonder.

On one occasion, Latigo was asked to work as stunt double for the young cowboy star who was sweet on Annika in the story. The man who usually did the job had taken ill and was confined to his bed, and Latigo seemed the most likely replacement. The wardrobe department dressed Latigo in the same kind of clothing and hat the actor wore. Their hair color was similar, as was their body type, except Latigo was shorter than the actor. Walsh would explain what he wanted in the scene, and point out where the action should take place. He cautioned Latigo to keep his face away from the camera as much as possible, but not to worry too much as he would film the scene with a wide lens.

On cue, one of Slim's wranglers let a yearling heifer out of a trailer at the top of a brushy swale on the back lot and slapped it on the rump, sending it down the shallow gully. Latigo rode down the side of the swale, crashing through sage and chaparral and building a loop with his lariat. He broke out just as the heifer passed, and pursued it as his horse dodged boulders. At the bottom of the swale, he roped the animal by the horns and spurred his horse to run past it at an angle as he draped his rope along its opposite side and around its rump just above the hocks. The rope tightened, jerking the heifer's legs out from under it and tripping it to the ground.

Latigo was off in a shot, running down the taut lariat as he pulled a short rope from his belt. He stepped across the downed heifer, picked up a front leg and looped the string around it, then scooped up both hind legs and wrapped them all tight together, tying it off with a half hitch.

"Cut!" Walsh hollered. "Perfect, Latigo! Well done!"

Latigo walked away, passing the actor as he did. The camera crew set up the next scene, in which the actor would build a small brush fire and heat up a running iron to alter the brand on his boss's heifer. The actual branding would not be seen; the sequence would end with the actor horseback, watching the yearling bound back up the hill, then following along as he coiled his lariat.

The next scene Walsh filmed would fill the gap between the kindling of the branding fire and the release of the heifer. In the shot, John Benson's character watched the whole thing, concealed by the ridge top he peeked over, his horse ground-tied behind him, out of sight.

The final scenes on the backlot covered the barn raising. Both Benson and Latigo worked throughout the filming. Benson, as the foreman of a neighboring ranch, showed up with several cowboys and ranch hands to help with the work. He exchanged a few lines with the rancher, but mostly took part in the work. But while Benson was often in the foreground, Latigo was always in the background with the other extras, looking busy and moving from job to job as the scenes required.

When the shooting was complete, the barn looked for all the world like the real thing—at least from the camera's point of view. But all there was of the barn were two exterior walls—the front and one wing, propped up by sturdy braces hidden behind. When the sun dropped below the horizon and Walsh called it a wrap for the day, and the extras nailing up the roof and those on ladders brushing red paint on the walls walked away from the tenuous and temporary structure, the director knew it would fool viewers into believing what they saw was of a piece with the barn's interior, which stood inside the sound stage building on the other side of the studio lot.

Filming ceased for a few days while the company relocated to the Simi Valley to shoot scenes in the wide, western vistas familiar to movie and televisions watchers. Although Benson lived between the studio and the location, when it was time to go to work, he—along with Latigo, the other actors and extras, and crew members employed by the production company—was required to report to the studio to be driven to the site. The director and principal actors rode in limousines and cars; Latigo and everyone else filed into seats on buses.

Latigo's work on location could not have been easier. His job consisted of racing around on horseback. Sometimes he rode with one or two other riders, filmed at a distance as they followed the horizon at high speed. Sometimes he rode in a larger group; a vigilante posse of sorts searching for the cowboy sweetheart actor revealed to be a cattle thief. They raced across plains and valleys, up and down hills and ridges, along winding dry riverbeds, into and out of canyons, always in brief spurts for the camera, and always at breakneck speed. Occasionally Benson's character led the pursuit; sometimes the rancher was along.

In scenes leading up to the climax of the chase, Benson and the rancher led a group of a dozen or so riders on the heels of the thief. As always, they rode as fast as—or a little faster than—the terrain would allow. But, in these scenes, their quarry was in sight, and the posse left in its wake clouds of powder smoke belched from revolvers firing hopeless shots at the rustler.

The posse finally ran their prey to ground, and he surrendered after his horse stumbled and fell. The actor's regular stunt double was back at work, so Latigo only watched the wreck rather than being in it. Along with the rest of the posse, he raced up and skidded his mount to a hock-dragging halt, drawn pistol pointed at the thief as he found his feet after the fall. Benson dismounted, discouraged the cowboy from going for his gun, then tied his hands behind his back. After some quiet cajoling, and even quieter threats, Benson and the rancher pried the location of the stolen cattle from the whimpering rustler, all captured on film and tape.

Latigo captured the cowboy's horse—unhurt from the fall—and held it until Benson called for it. The foreman unceremoniously tossed the rustler belly down over the saddle as if he were already dead. The posse lit out on the run, the bound cowboy—in the form of his stunt double—bouncing tenuously atop the saddle.

Another scene found the posse riding into a blind canyon. Scattered along the narrow valley that followed a small stream were a few cattle grazing. Benson and the rancher rode from one animal to another, the foreman pointing out the altered brands.

Latigo sat in the shade during the scene, studying the grazing animals and wondering what the rustler might have had in mind for the stolen cattle. There were a few young heifers, like the one he had roped and tied in the scene on the studio lot, that would one day give birth to valuable calves, but not anytime soon. There were some steers that could be marketed for beef, but, again, they tended to be young and would require considerable time on grass to get their growth. The cowboy had rustled a few cows of breeding age, but there were no calves at their sides, nor a bull to encourage them to increase the size of the herd.

Just what intentions a rustler might have with such a selection escaped Latigo—but it clearly wasn't to make a quick buck in the meat market, or to build a herd to stock a ranch. He shook his head in wonder. *Movies*.

The extras were called back to work to hang the rustler. Latigo got the job of tossing the tail end of the rope with a hangman's noose tied in it over the limb of a handy tree. Another extra tied it off. The rancher himself fitted the noose around the neck of his daughter's sweetheart. Benson slapped the horse on which the cowboy sat on the rump with his coiled lariat, and all assembled watched the horse bolt and the cattle thief swing—again, the cattle thief replaced by his stunt double.

After Walsh hollered "Cut!" they lowered the stunt man and unlatched the safety harness he had dangled from. Then cast and crew alike sat and waited for the sun to reach the rim of the ridge on the west side of the canyon in order to get the director's final location shot.

When the time was nearly right, the crew strung up the stunt man again, the camera operator made some final adjustments to his camera, set up at ground level and downhill, some distance away from the hanging man. Walsh called for the camera to roll and one of his assistants held the slate in front of the lens, but did not employ the clappers as there was no sound to accompany the shot. Nor did Walsh call "Action," instead simply letting the stuntman and everyone else know he was shooting. Walsh squatted next to the camera and looked on as it reeled off and exposed several feet of film of the hanged rustler, in silhouette, dangling and slowly twisting in the wind, haloed against the blazing orange sun.

Chapter Nineteen

In the lazy days after the movie "wrapped," Latigo peppered Benson with questions. He learned there might be additional work to come for some, as certain scenes may have to be re-shot for any number of reasons. He was told there might be work in a recording studio, as sound recorded on sets or on location might be flawed by extraneous noise or other defects.

"One thing I wonder…" Latigo said as they sat over cool drinks on Benson's front porch. "That movie was all about cattle. It took place on a cow outfit, and the whole story was about cattle gettin' stole. But there weren't but two dozen cows in the whole show—that one I roped, and the ones out in that canyon where we did the hangin'."

"So?"

"So how come there's hardly any cattle in a movie all about cattle?"

Benson smiled, sipped his iced tea, and considered his reply. He set his glass on a side table, scooted forward in his seat, leaned forward toward Latigo, elbows on knees, fingers interlaced. He smiled again, and shook his head slightly. "To tell you the truth, Latigo, I've never once looked at it that way in all these years. But you're right. I've been in trail-drive movies where there were never more than a hundred steers at any one time. They just set up the shots so it looks like there's a thundering herd in a stampede, or thousands of cattle strung out on a trail.

"I can't say for certain, for I have never asked, but here is what I think." He sat back in his chair and sipped more tea. "We talked once before about how pretty a running horse looks. Directors love horses, and not just because they look good on film. Horses are easy to control. They will pretty much do what you want, when and where you want them to. Tie them up and they will wait there all day, if need be, without making a fuss.

"Now, cattle, on the other hand, are unpredictable, as you know. There is always a chance things won't happen the way you expect them to when you're relying on cows. Directors, they don't like it when things aren't under their control—won't take direction, in other words. Even when you're not using them, someone has to take care of cattle, or they're likely to wander off—maybe even walk into a scene where they are not wanted."

Benson sipped his tea again, then took in and let out a long breath. "Come to think of it, probably the worst hissy fit I have ever seen by a director was when a big old longhorn steer would not climb up a set of stairs. See, in the script, a banker refused a loan to an old rancher. Don't recall what he wanted the money for, but it doesn't matter. The bank man said he didn't have enough collateral. So this rancher drove a bunch of cattle into town, and intended to drive them up the front steps into the bank and offer them as collateral for the loan.

"Slim was providing stock for the picture, and he let the director know way ahead of time that getting cattle to go up and down stairs was about as easy as pulling hen's teeth. He said that they would walk up a ramp, no trouble, but stairs were another matter. It just wasn't natural for them. But, that director wanted stairs. He allowed that if Slim could get one critter trained to do it, that would still work—as long as it was a big steer with plenty of horn on him."

With a smile threatening to break into a laugh, Benson told how the movie crew's carpenters knocked together a rough set of stairs out at Slim's place, and how he tried every trick he knew—and every trick anyone else knew or could think of—to get that old steer to walk up those steps. They finally succeeded, sort of, by putting a halter on the steer and leading it. Even that wasn't easy.

"Well, the director wasn't too happy about it, as he thought a steer with a halter and a lead rope was unnatural, but Slim convinced him it was the best they could do. They set up the scene. The camera was out on the street by the bank, and it would see the old man lead his steer down the middle of Main Street, followed by a bunch of other cattle—must have been about forty head—driven by a couple of cowboys. When the old man got to the bank, he was to lead that steer up the steps and through the front door into the bank, all in one long take.

"Everything went along just fine until it came time for the steer to climb the stairs. He tried one step, then sulled up. That old steer hung back on that lead rope with the old man yanking and pulling every which way, but it didn't help. The director sent everybody back to their first position and rolled film again. Same thing. Except this time, the old man's cussing out that steer included words that you don't hear in movies.

"By now, the director decided to do what they call a 'pick-up,' where he would keep the footage of the parade up the street, then shoot the part with the stairs from a different angle." Benson laughed. "It did not help. Pretty soon, the actor got even more frustrated and his language got worse. The director took to yelling at anybody and everybody, putting the actor to shame in the bad language department. His words for Slim were particularly pointed, even though he wasn't there. The wranglers he'd sent to handle the cattle assured the director they had seen that big old steer walk up the steps out at the ranch a whole bunch of times. He told them he didn't care, the animal did not perform as ordered, and he was damned if he would pay one red cent for it—and he threatened not to pay Slim for anything else he had provided, including cattle, horses, wagons, and the whole deal.

"By then, that director was so wound up he called it a wrap for the day and stormed off. All the actors and extras and crew stood around looking at each other for a while, not quite sure what to make of it, or what they ought to do. Finally, the Production Manager told everyone to go on home—which did not make him happy, as he would have to pay them all for a day's work that didn't get done."

Latigo asked what happened after that, between the director and Slim. Benson said Slim was mad as a bag of cats when he got the report. As soon as the steer was off the truck and back home, he took ahold of the lead rope and walked that steer up the steps as pretty as you please. He sent for the director, who had cooled off enough by then to agree to a visit. He watched the steer go up the steps, and he and Slim looked things over to see if they could figure out why the usually docile animal refused to work for the camera.

"Well," Latigo said, "what was it?"

Benson stopped smiling long enough to sip some more tea. Then, "Turns out it was the stairs. They got out their measuring tapes, and the stairway they had built out at the ranch was not as steep as the one at the bank, and the rise was a bit off. When that old steer reached up to the first step at the bank, it hit him at the top of the hoof, almost on his pastern, and he didn't know what to do about it. So, the director got that carpenter crew back to work and they rebuilt the steps at the bank, with the risers and treads and angle the same as at the ranch.

"They set up the scene again later, and it went off like clockwork. The director was happy—happy as he could be with a haltered steer—and Slim got paid, and all was well in Hollywood." Benson swallowed the last of his tea and swirled the ice cubes around in the glass. "Except directors still don't like cows."

For days to come, Latigo quizzed Benson about the what and why of "Westerns."

"They say these TV and picture shows are about cowboys, but most of the people in them wouldn't know which end of a cow gets up first.

They've got more gamblers in them shows than there is cards in a deck. They've got marshals and sheriffs and deputies. They've got bounty hunters. They've got gunfighters. They've got outlaws. Mostly, they've got men that don't seem to do anything 'cept wander around lookin' for trouble they can sort out. That ain't like no cowboys I ever heard of."

John Benson could only smile.

"And when they are supposed to be cowboys, workin' on a ranch or on a cattle drive and such, they don't hardly do neither. Seems like all they do is hang around in saloons waitin' for trouble. They spend more time in fistfights or gunfights than herdin' cows. Half the time they're runnin' all over the country shootin' at Indians or rustlers or bank robbers or somebody else. Who's takin' care of the cattle while all this is goin' on?"

It was a question Benson did not attempt to answer.

"What about them outlaws and killers they make out to be heroes in some of them pictures? You look at them ol' boys like Billy the Kid or Jesse James. From what they say in the history books, the truth of it is that men like them never thought a thing about stealin' from folks that never done them no wrong, or shootin' somebody just for the hell of it. Some of them shows would have you think they was just poor unfortunate cowboys who never got an even break. It just ain't right."

Benson listened with good humor to Latigo's rants over many an evening on the front porch. He sipped his iced tea, whittled at a chunk of wood on occasion, and smiled. One evening, he set aside his pocket-knife, swallowed a long draught of iced tea, and spoke.

"You a reader, Latigo?"

The young cowboy sat up straight, squinted eyebrows furrowing his forehead. "What do you mean?"

"I mean, do you read books?"

Still wondering, Latigo said, "Not so's you'd notice. Not since school. I read what they told me to in class, but not much else. I'll read a magazine about Western history now and again."

"You remember any of it? Have any favorite books?"

Latigo did not answer. He sat for a time, brow still furrowed and pursed lips working back and forth as his eyes looked upward as if the answer was written on his brow. "Not that I can think of." He shrugged. "I don't know. I just could never sit still to read a book when there was somethin' I could be doin' outside, you know, with the horses and such."

Benson nodded. "I see." He set his glass on the side table. "All of what you say about Western movies and television shows is pretty much the truth."

Latigo opened his mouth to say something, but did not speak when Benson raised a hand to stop him.

"The thing you should know is that the same can be said of many stories—stories a hell of lot older than the Old West. You ever hear of a man called Homer?"

Latigo shook his head.

"He was a storyteller. An old Greek, lived a long time ago. Long, long time ago—maybe a thousand years before Jesus Christ came along. He wrote these stories that are still around. One is called *The Iliad*, the other *The Odyssey*. They're about a lot of people and places and things, but mostly about a couple of guys called Achilles and Odysseus. Them two get themselves involved in all manner of adventures, fighting and loving and trying to save the world—not so different from the cowboy heroes in the movies.

"You probably know some of those old stories from the Bible. Take David—a boy who killed a bad man in a fight, ran for a time with a band of outlaws, romanced the women, and went on to be king. Then there's old Moses. Murdered a fellow to protect his people. He caused all kinds of calamities for the Egyptians, and led all the Hebrews out into the desert to get away, stopping only to drown the whole Egyptian army in the Red Sea.

"If you were to read what the Romans left behind, you'd read stories about heroes and villains; gods with great powers fighting off evil. Later on, people told stories about kings and dragons and knights in armor—men like Galahad and Gawain and Lancelot who, like some of those TV cowboys, wandered around the countryside taking on evil and looking to do good, slaying dragons and rescuing princesses and such. Then there's a famous book about a fellow called Don Quixote who took it into his head to spend his life and fortune fighting for worthwhile, but mostly lost, causes wherever he would find them."

Benson stopped for a time, watching Latigo ruminate on what he had said. He sipped some tea and said, "Even what you say about making outlaws like Jesse James and Billy the Kid into heroes is nothing new. Way back in England in the Middle Ages, they told stories about Robin Hood. He came back from fighting a war to find his land had been taken by a corrupt sheriff, and to see the ruling class persecuting regular folks. So he got up a band of highwaymen and robbers. The stories say Robin Hood stole from the rich and gave to the poor." He paused for another taste of tea. "But, if he was real and not just a man in a story, I don't suppose he gave away much of what he got, any more than what other outlaws would."

Latigo sat, staring into nowhere. Benson let him sit for a stretch before asking what he thought.

"I don't know what to think. What am I supposed to think?"

Benson smiled. "That's up to you. I'm just saying that storytelling isn't new, and the shape of stories hasn't changed much since folks first started telling them. And movies are just another way to tell stories. They might not be real, and they may not always reflect the way things get done in the real world. But they are not meant to—they are meant to entertain people. If there's some truth in them that folks can take away, so much the better. People like their stories to make them laugh, or maybe cry, or to believe that the good guys will win out over the bad guys—same as stories always have done."

The two sat for a time.

"Here's the thing, son," Benson said. "When it comes to earning a living, this movie business isn't a bad way to go, if you can make a go of it. Most folks don't. But the movie we just worked on was put together by a good outfit—so you started somewhere way above the middle, if you get my drift. Not like most, who start out in low-budget horse operas where they work a whole lot harder for a whole lot less pay than what you just did.

"Howard Walsh is one of the better directors around, and you've caught the man's eye. And when that happens, word gets around. Hollywood isn't that big a town. The man told me that a good-looking kid like you, with what you can do horseback and with your rope, has got a real future. It doesn't hurt any that you've got Slim on your side, either. He can help you get work, if you want it."

After another long silence, Benson stood. He picked up his glass and tossed the dregs of tea and melted ice into the shrubbery, and did the same with Latigo's glass. He turned to look Latigo in the eye when the boy stood.

"You know, Latigo, there's a big, long line of youngsters looking to get a break in the movie business. They've got their hearts set on being the next big cowboy hero, the next big star. Sad thing is, there isn't a one of them that has much of a chance to make it. You do. But it's not going to happen unless you quit turning up your nose at the whole notion of Westerns."

Chapter Twenty

Latigo stayed on in the apartment above the garage behind the Benson's house. They were glad to have him, and offered him the accommodation for as long as he cared to stay. Elaine liked having another hungry man to cook for, and she and John enjoyed his company.

An established actor with a good reputation, Benson worked less for more money than most in Hollywood. He used his influence with friends and acquaintances to get Latigo opportunities to work, and Slim Jones sometimes recommended the young cowboy for stunt jobs. Latigo was cast in a number of television series to play a variety of small roles that lasted only an episode or two. He was hired for horseback stunts for both television programs and feature films, often unaware of the name or nature of the production. Now and then he would do some fancy roping.

John Benson took a call for Latigo one day when the youngster was away on location for a few days, acting a small role for a TV Western. Benson handed him the message when he returned.

Latigo read the name Sam Sturges, and a date and time. "What's this mean?"

"Sam Sturges is a director. He's getting ready to shoot a Western, and wants you to come in for a screen test."

Latigo's blank look alternated between the paper and Benson. "What's that mean?"

Benson smiled. "Son, the parts you've been playing don't require much in the way of casting—finding someone who can pull it off. Your work has come by word of mouth, or someone recommending you for a job. But for bigger roles, and bigger productions, there's more money at stake so the producers want to hedge their bets. One way they do that is to hire only big-name actors that they know people will pay money to see in a movie.

"But sometimes the director wants a new face, and that makes producers nervous. So they do screen tests. They'll call in actors and give them some lines to say, maybe alone or maybe with another actor, and they'll put it on film. Sometimes they want you to do something specific to the role, like see if you can ride a horse, or sing, or some such. Then they look at the film of all the actors and see who they like best—or who the producers and money men think will draw crowds at the box office."

Latigo shook his head. "I don't see as I got much of a chance. I ain't no kind of actor to speak of, and anyone else who shows up will likely have more experience or training than what I got."

"I wouldn't worry too much about it, son," Benson said with a smile. "From what I hear, Sturges wants you for the part, just from what he's heard about you. Part of the test will be done horseback, and there won't be anybody any better at that than you. But that's not all. He's also wanting to see what the actors can do with a rope—if you ask me, you're a shoo-in. Long as you don't piss your pants or fall off the horse or sull up and lose your voice, you'll be fine."

Latigo stared at the note, then looked at Benson. "I don't know. Maybe I ought to strap on a diaper 'fore I go."

Benson laughed and clapped Latigo on the shoulder. "Don't worry, son. You'll do fine. If you want, I'll go along with you—just in case you have any questions about what's going on, you understand. Oh, and one more thing. This is a pretty big part, they tell me. You'll get paid more money for this one part than what you've made all together for the work you've done so far."

Latigo blanched. "You tryin' to make this deal sound better, John? If I wasn't already ascairt enough, I sure as hell am now."

When, two days later, Benson loaded Latigo into his car to drive him to the screen test, he reassured the young cowboy that he would do fine. "I always think of it this way when I go to an audition, son—I ask myself what's the worst that can happen, which is that I don't get the part. And I tell myself that if I don't get the part life will go on, same as it did before. And that there will be another part somewhere down the road."

Latigo only nodded, fiddling with the coiled lariat on his lap.

They passed through the gates at a studio Latigo had never visited. Benson, however, was known to the guard, who waved them through. Benson drove past the complex of sound stages and offices and warehouses to the backlot. They walked past a city street that had looked bustling and busy in many a movie, but today was abandoned and eerie. Benson led them through an alley between buildings that emptied onto a residential street, likewise empty and unnatural. Just beyond that was an Old West town, different yet similar to the sets Latigo had seen on other studio backlots.

A few workers bustled about, setting up reflectors and flags, a camera, and sound recording equipment. Benson walked directly to a man sitting in a canvas chair, shaded by a flag—a big square of black fabric in a frame—held overhead by metal stands. A young woman with a clipboard stood before him, listening and writing, then hurried away. Latigo could not help thinking that whoever sold clipboards to the movie studios must make a darn good living.

"Sam, how are you?"

The man turned, saw Benson, and smiled. "Just fine, John. It's good to see you." He stood and offered his hand. "I regret to say you've wasted your trip, John. We're casting for a young man, and despite the fact that I am old enough to be your father, you are still too old for the part."

Benson laughed. "You sure, Sam? How about I wrestle you for it? We'll see who is young enough and who isn't."

"Sorry, John. My wrestling days are behind me."

"What are you doing here, Sam? This kind of thing is usually left up to people well down the pay scale from a famous film director."

Sturges waved him away. "Not this time. I know what I want for this film, but I have to convince the producers. I'm here to make certain things happen the way I want them to, so I get what I want. As you know, John, when I want something, I usually get it." A smile offset the ominous words. Sturges turned to Latigo. "And speaking of what I want, you are Latigo Brown."

Latigo nodded, but before he could speak Benson said, "He is. I just came along to see that your people treat young Latigo properly. Had I known you would be here, Sam, I would have brought Elaine along for reinforcements."

"How is Elaine, anyway?"

"Oh, she's fine. Still trying to teach me proper manners, same as always. And now she's got Latigo here to educate as well."

"Well, we'll have to have you and Elaine over for dinner one day soon—after this film is in the can. It has been too long."

The woman with the clipboard returned and told Sturges everything was ready.

"Let's start with the easy stuff, Latigo," the director said.

As if on cue, a wrangler appeared from between a saloon and a bank leading a horse. Sturges told Latigo his first scene involved riding down the street toward camera, the horse at a lively, impatient trot as Latigo studied the town. He was to imagine the street crowded with busy people going about their business. He was to look from side to side for possible signs of trouble, or to identify where trouble might come from, then rein up in front of the bank, dismount, tie his horse to the hitch rail and enter the bank.

Latigo did as instructed when Sturges hollered "Action." He felt better when the director did not call for a second take, assuming he had performed to his satisfaction. He stayed horseback for the next scene. Down the street, a worker held a mannequin. Latigo was to ride toward it and, as the worker carried it at a run, rope the dummy and drag it away down the street, all with as much haste as he could muster. Sturges ordered the camera to roll, and Latigo spurred the horse to action. He shook out a loop as he rode, spun it overhead a few times and, as he approached the running man holding up the mannequin, threw a loop and jerked his slack so the loop tightened around the dummy's shoulders without touching the man carrying it. He rode on by, taking wraps around the saddle horn, jerked the mannequin away and raced on, the dummy stirring up dust as it bounced and dragged behind.

The final horseback test involved two horses. Latigo dismounted and a stuntman Latigo knew from Slim's place took the reins of his horse. The stunt rider was to ride to Latigo, leading his horse, as Latigo ran out of the bank. Latigo was to intercept the hurried horses, run alongside, and vault into the saddle—all at the quickest pace possible, and without losing the bags of stolen money slung over his shoulder. This test required three takes, each at Latigo's request, claiming he could do it faster. Sturges voiced his satisfaction after the third performance, calling it good even though Latigo offered to do the stunt again, faster still.

Next, Latigo was handed a gun belt. He strapped it on, pulled the pistol from the holster and checked the cylinder to make sure it was empty, and replaced it. Sturges positioned Latigo in the street in front of the camera and told him that, when cued, he was to draw the gun and point it at the camera. Speed was not of the essence here, the director said. What he wanted to see was menace and determination, a look that said, *be careful, or you are dead.*

Finally, Latigo was handed a script—a single page of dialogue between his character and another man. The other actor's lines would be delivered by the young woman with the clipboard. Latigo skimmed the script, then read and reread it carefully. He thought the lines easy enough to remember, but worried that delivering them to a pretty young lady rather than the angry man on the page would be difficult.

But, again, Sturges seemed satisfied with the test. He thanked the crew and ordered them to strike the set, shook hands with Latigo, gave his goodbyes to Benson, and hurried away, the young woman with the clipboard in his wake.

Benson said nothing until they had passed through the residential neighborhood and city street sets and were in the car, outside the studio lot, and on the road home. Latigo cast repeated sidelong glances at him, wondering at his silence.

When the silence overwhelmed him, Latigo said, "Well?"

Benson looked at him. "Well, what?"

"How did I do?"

Benson laughed and clapped Latigo on the thigh. "How the hell do you think you did? Son, I do believe you are about to star in a movie."

Latigo swallowed hard.

"You won't be the lead, mind you. Top billing will go to an actor who's been around for years. An Englishman. He's a big name—won lots of awards, starred in lots of films. Does just as well Back East in Broadway stage plays."

"Who is it?"

Benson smiled. "Oh, I better not say. It will either make you nervous if you know who he is, or make you worry if you've never heard of him—either way, it won't do you any good to know his name. You'll find out soon enough, unless I miss my guess."

They rode along in silence for a time, then Latigo asked if he had learned anything more about the movie.

"Yes, some. I talked to that girl, Sam's assistant, when I could. Sturges wants you to play an outlaw threatening the old man's empire. Ranches, railroads, banks—the old man has his fingers in everything, and this young man—you—won't quit robbing and stealing from him. Makes such a nuisance of himself, the old man keeps the law on his trail, hires bounty men to hunt him down, puts railroad detectives on his trail. That's the gist of it, anyway. What do you think?"

Latigo did not answer for a time. Then, "I guess it sounds okay. I don't know that I'm all that happy about playin' a bad guy."

"Why's that?"

"Mom and Dad will be disappointed to know I've forgot everything they've taught me, and that I've lost my scruples and gone wild. And if Granny finds out, she'll think I'm goin' to hell for sure."

Benson looked at Latigo. The boy looked serious, save the twinkle in his eye. He thought the kid would make an actor yet.

Benson turned the car into the driveway, drove around back, and parked in front of the garage. Both men got out of the car, Benson opened the back door to the house, and Latigo walked to the door that led upstairs to his apartment.

"One thing I forgot to mention," Benson said from the open kitchen doorway.

Latigo stopped and turned, holding his door open. "What's that?"

"You remember that story I told you about the steer that wouldn't climb up the stairs to the bank?"

Latigo nodded.

"You remember I told you about the director getting all het up and pitching a fit over it? Cussing and cursing and carrying on?"

"Yeah. Sure."

Benson smiled. "That director—that was Sam Sturges."

Chapter Twenty-One

Latigo Brown listened to the director's instructions. In the scene, the bounty hunter—star of the television series of which this episode was a part—learned that Latigo, his quarry, was holed up in a saloon girl's room on the upper floor. As the camera watched from across the street, Latigo was to throw open the window sash and step out onto the porch roof above the saloon entrance, tugging down his hat and buckling on his gun belt as he came. He would then scurry to the edge of the roof and leap off, landing in the saddle on his horse, standing at the hitch rail on the street below.

"Yessir. I can do that easy enough," Latigo said to the director of the series. "Then what do you want me to do?"

"Ride down the street. Fast as you can."

The bewildered look on Latigo's face prompted a query from the director.

"Well, sir," Latigo said, "that horse is tied up at the rail there. How can I ride off if he's tied up?"

The director released a long breath. "Well, the horse isn't tied, I guess. Yes—that's it. You knew you might have to leave in a hurry, so you left him untied."

Latigo tipped back the brim of his hat. "Well, sir, what if he wandered off? See, a horse won't just stand there for long if he ain't tied up, or at least ground tied, if he's trained for it. He might get thirsty and mosey over to the water trough. Or go lookin' for a bite to eat. Or just get tired of standin' there and go stand somewheres else. That's why them hitch rails is there, so you can tie up your horse so he'll stay where you put him."

The director clenched his jaw as it reddened from the flush creeping up from under his shirt collar. "Who the hell cares?" he growled. "Look, kid, just do it. I've shot this same scene a thousand times."

"Yessir. I ain't seen it done that many times, but I always wondered about it every time I did see it. It just don't seem natural." Latigo shrugged and climbed the stairs inside the saloon to the platform inside the window where the room was supposed to be in the false-fronted structure.

The shot went off without a hitch, and Latigo raced down the street as it curved out of sight between the building fronts of the Western town. Once again, he had eluded the grasp of the famed bounty hunter.

The bounty hunter series was among the bit parts and stunt work that kept Latigo busy while Sturges's big film was in pre-production. Most of the jobs lasted only a few days, and few involved speaking parts. The bounty hunter series was an exception, as his role extended over two episodes, and required Latigo to act, as well as perform stunts—both his own, and some as stunt double for the bounty hunter who starred in the series.

Latigo did not care much for the part, or for the director. Always behind schedule, and hurried and tense as a result, the man belittled crew members when his chaotic instructions weren't carried out to his satisfaction. Extras and bit players likewise felt the lash of his tongue. Only the stars and series regulars were spared; that because they had let the man know, in no uncertain terms, that he had better show them the respect they deserve if he expected their best work. Otherwise, it was implied, cues might be missed, lines forgotten, or worse.

Latigo's next brush with the director's wrath came days later, when the company was on location out in the Simi Valley for chase scenes. Oddly enough, the cause was much the same as before. In the scene— leading up to the climax of the episodes and the capture of Latigo's character—he was cooking over a campfire in an out-of-the-way place, avoiding the bounty man's pursuit. But the hero ferreted out his hiding place, and, concealed in a cluster of rocks, called out to the outlaw, demanding his surrender.

"Now, as soon as you hear his voice, don't hesitate," the director told Latigo. "Leave everything behind, get on your horse, and hurry away. Now, I want you to do a crupper mount. You know that stunt, I hope—you had better know the stunt."

Latigo allowed as how he did, in fact, know what a crupper mount was. While it was not a staple of Westerns, it was not unusual. The move required the rider, after a running start toward a horse facing away from him, to place both hands on the horse's rump as he jumped, launching himself over the horse's rear to land in the saddle.

The director bristled at the look on Latigo's face. "Well, what is it cowboy? What's the problem?"

"Well, sir, I can sure do it if you're sure that's what you want."

"Why the hell would I not be sure?"

Latigo shrugged, and pointed to his mount. "A couple of things, sir. First off, the horse I'm supposed to ride is tied to a tree at yonder edge of camp there."

"So?"

"I can't see how I'm goin' to untie him."

"Dammit! We've been through this before. I don't care if the horse is *supposed* to be tied. It will be untied when you get there!"

"Yessir."

"What else?"

"It likely don't matter at all, but I been horseback all my life. Raised with horses and with cowboys. The thing is, I ain't never seen nobody get on a horse that way—'cept in movies or on TV."

His face as red as the bandana around Latigo's throat, the director told Latigo that if he wasn't so stupid, he would realize that this was television, not real life for some bunch of hick-town idiots and their flea-bitten nags. He quivered, fists clenched at his sides, and said that he, personally, had directed dozens of screen cowboys to mount just that way. And that movie cowboys had done so almost since the first frame of film was exposed on a Western. Then he turned and stomped away.

"Sir?"

The director stopped, and wheeled around to face Latigo. "What? What else could possibly be wrong?"

"Well, sir, meanin' no disrespect—"

"—Too late for that! Get on with it!"

"Seein' as how this here outlaw was camped out and cookin' a meal, most times he would unsaddle his horse."

"Dammit, kid, this ain't most times!"

"I understand, I guess. But if he didn't take the saddle off, he would for sure loosen the cinches. Nobody who knows horses would leave his horse to stand for any length of time with the cinches snugged. Easy way to gall a horse, or cause saddle sores."

The director only stood, stiff as corner post. Had the air been cooler, it is possible steam may have risen from him. All around, cast and crew stood quiet, trying to hide smiles.

"Just tryin' to help is all," Latigo said with a shrug. "Sir."

"Well, thank you, cowboy," the director growled. "Now, if you have finished educating us on the ways of the world of horses and cowboys, can we shoot this scene?"

Latigo smiled. "Of course, sir. Whatever you say."

The scene was completed in one shot, as Latigo executed a perfect crupper mount and raced away, leaving the still-seething director waving away a cloud of dust.

In Latigo's final scenes, the bounty hunter star of the show chased Latigo at high speed through the rugged terrain, blazing away at the fleeing outlaw with his six-shooter as Latigo returned fire. Latigo thought it prudent to neglect to mention that each of them had fired several cylinders' worth of cartridges, and while the prop men had been busy between takes reloading the revolvers with blank cartridges, there would be no sign of reloading on the screen.

Finally, Latigo's horse, trained to fall on cue, would stumble during the chase for no apparent reason and crash to the ground. Latigo, dazed, would be unable to regain his senses before the hero bounty hunter had him in handcuffs.

The director called for several re-takes of the horse wreck and Latigo's fall and tumble, although none of the other actors, or the crew members, had seen any fault in any of the previous takes.

*****

Over the weeks to come, Latigo, dressed as an Indian, was killed several times in horseback fights with cavalry troopers, and once while circling a circled-up wagon train. He slugged it out in a saloon brawl, crashing through the banister on a stairway to land on, and collapse, a poker table with a game in progress. He allowed a horse to buck him off. He huddled behind a small embankment as a herd of stampeding steers—numbering, perhaps, twenty head, increased in quantity on screen through different angles and repeated takes—thundered overhead.

He rode in a posse pursuing cattle rustlers; he rode in a posse chasing a bank robber; he rode in a posse after a marauding band of Indians; he rode in a posse tracking down a jailbreaker; he rode in a posse dogging a gang of train robbers; he rode in a posse hunting a notorious gunfighter; he rode in a posse shadowing the kidnapper of a fair maiden; he rode in a posse trailing the killer of a barkeeper—always at a high lope or dead run across the countryside, sometimes leaving clouds of powder smoke in his wake.

From time to time he wrote home, always inserting a note for Penny telling which famous actors he had worked with—often not knowing why they were famous. But his little sister's enthusiasm bubbled off the pages of her letters back to him, especially when he mailed home autographed eight-by-ten glossy photographs of the stars.

He encouraged his parents to make use of the money he sent home, but his mother always said the money was his, and that it was safely deposited in his account at the local bank. They never said so, but Latigo knew the money amounted to more ready cash than his family would see in return for weeks, months, years of hard work on the ranch.

For his part, Latigo spent little. Despite their objections, he insisted on paying the Bensons for bed and board. He considered trading his battered 1948-vintage pickup truck for a newer model, but in spite of the strange looks from other drivers on the streets of Los Angeles, he decided that as long as the truck got him where he was going, it was good enough for him.

If there was one thing Los Angeles had, Latigo thought, it was drivers. He grew accustomed to, but never comfortable with, the volume of traffic. He avoided the freeways whenever he could, feeling trapped in the flow and uneasy with the tons of steel racing past, or mired in the stop-and-go of traffic jams. Still, when not working, Latigo braved the traffic to see the sights.

More than once, he ventured out Sunset Boulevard to Pacific Palisades to the state park at the Will Rogers ranch. He wandered the grounds, the outbuildings, and the ranch house, walking in the footsteps of one of the few men he held up as hero. During one visit on a slow day, a cooperative caretaker in the house, who recognized him from earlier visits, allowed him to handle one of Will's lariats, and even rope the stuffed calf in the ranch house's living room, as Will himself did.

He visited the tar pits at La Brea, where scientists excavated the bones of ancient animals. He rode a streetcar. The Bensons treated him to a Mexican dinner at a famous restaurant on Olvera Street, the birthplace of the city. He and John watched a football game at the Memorial Coliseum. Latigo stood in the surf at the beach in Santa Monica, feeling the waves wash over his legs as they rolled in, and the strange sensation of the sand washing from beneath his feet as the water receded.

But Latigo, in his tours of the city, avoided one of its main attractions—Hollywood. His work provided more than enough exposure to the movie and television business to suit him. The famous stars who attracted crowds wherever they went, and whose houses were attractions themselves, did not interest him.

The only film-related place he visited when off work was Slim Jones's ranch. He never tired of lending a hand in training horses, for horseback was the place he loved more than any other. Still, the smells of horses and cattle often made him homesick, and as he worked with the horses, Latigo missed Nugget, and wished the palomino horse, put out to pasture back home, was here with him.

One day. Maybe.

Chapter Twenty-Two

It was well after dark when Latigo Brown led his horse into the livery stable. He found an empty stall and pulled the saddle from the tired animal's back. He stepped out into the stable alley. The sound of the gunshot and the force of the bullet arrived simultaneously. The lead slammed into the swells of the saddle, nearly knocking it loose from his grasp. He let the saddle fall as he dove, rolling once across the packed earth of the alleyway, into what he hoped would be a protected corner behind a storeroom wall.

He sat for a moment, back against the wall, huffing for breath. He did not bother to pull his gun, for he could see nothing to shoot at in the dark building. Nor did the sounds offer any clue—shuffling hooves, rumps slamming against partitions, snorts and neighs. The only light, and that faint, filtered in through the stable's open sliding doors, rendering the alleyway a softer shade of black.

Latigo lifted a pitchfork, knocked over in his scramble for concealment, that had been annoying his hip. He hung his hat on the end of the handle and ever so slowly reached it beyond the protection of the wall and into the alley. A shot rang out, shattering the wood, dropping his hat to ground. He reached out and snatched it back, settling it again on his head.

As he sat, Latigo's eyes adjusted somewhat to the darkness. He felt, as much as saw, the steps of a ladder nailed to the barn wall beside him, leading upward through a hatch in the planks of the ceiling, which also made the floor of the loft. The storeroom wall would protect him from the gunman, so long as the attacker remained at the front of the stable, or outside the wide doors, or wherever he was hiding.

As quickly as he could go slow, Latigo climbed the ladder, letting his weight settle easily onto each step to avoid creaks and squeaks. He emerged through the hatch and stepped away from the hole, straining to see. Pale moonlight easing through the loft doors illuminated the upper level of the stable well enough that Latigo could see the shapes of things. Hay, stacked against the rear wall, occupied most of the space. Barrels and kegs and crates and boxes and bags lined the walls; storage, he supposed, of surplus materials, or goods not needed in the everyday operation of the stable.

Edging his way along the floor toward the open doors, Latigo stepped on a board that whined at his weight. Gunfire came in answer, bullets ripping holes in the plank floor, splintering the wood as they tore through. None came near Latigo as he crouched. He waited a moment before again creeping forward toward the doors.

Reaching out from the peak of the barn above the doors was a jib with a block at the end, threaded with heavy rope, to hoist items to the loft. There was no winch or other means of providing lift; horse or manpower from below must do the work. Latigo studied the situation, then took up the rope. He estimated the length to reach the ground, and hitched one end around a 100-pound sack of feed. As he worked, he heard the horses shuffling about below, disturbed by Latigo's attacker making his way slowly into the depths of the stable, listening for Latigo as Latigo listened for him.

With the tail of the rope anchored, he tied a loop in the end. He carried the heavy gunnysack toward the stacked hay until the rope grew taut. Back at the doors, he stepped into the loop with one foot, drew his revolver with one hand, grasped the rope with the other, and stepped out into empty air.

The wooden block on the beam screeched an exasperated song as the rope turned through it. The feed sack hissed across the floor of the loft toward the doors, dragged along as Latigo's weight pulled the rope as he dropped toward the ground, faster than he had imagined. He saw the flash of fire as the assassin in the stable loosed a shot at him, and Latigo returned fire. Once alight, he kicked out of the loop that rode him down and leapt aside, both for the protection of the stable wall and to avoid the 100-pound bag of oats as it dropped, the loop on the rope whistling upward as the sack fell.

Latigo kept moving until reaching the deep shadow alongside the building next door, a general mercantile locked up and dark. He waited. After an eternity of hammering heartbeats, the gunman crept out of the stable, back pressed against the sliding door as he studied the street in both directions. He looked directly at Latigo, but saw nothing.

The gunman waited and watched. Latigo did the same. Hearing or seeing nothing, the man stepped away from the stable and took a few hesitant steps into the street, following the barrel of his gun as it probed the shadows. Latigo waited until the bushwhacker was well out in the open before stepping out of the darkness into the moonlit street.

"Right here, mister."

The gunman dropped to one knee as he spun around and fired. Latigo heard the buzz and felt the heat as the bullet passed by. Before the next shot could come, Latigo fired. His aim proved true, and the kneeling gunfighter collapsed onto the street.

"Cut!" Sam Sturges shouted from the comfort of his canvas chair positioned behind the camera in the walkway between the livery stable and the general store on the studio backlot. "Print, and wrap!"

Filming the scenes had taken most of the day, with Sturges shooting what filmmakers called "day for night" by using filters to underexpose the film and shift colors and contrast to fool audiences into believing it was night. With the sun low on the horizon, the day's work was over. The grips went about their business of collapsing stands and storing flags and reflectors. The camera crew completed their reports and stowed film magazines, the camera body, and the lenses and filters in their proper places. The property man collected the revolvers, and the lady in charge of Latigo's wardrobe collected his accessories. A wrangler led Latigo's mount out of the livery stable—his horse being the only one actually present in the stalls during the filming.

It had been an optimistic first day of shooting for Sturges's production, but the director wanted the cast and crew to start out on the right foot—working hard, moving fast, and carrying out his instructions without question. Most of the set-ups that day to capture the gunfight in the stable were completed after only one take, with the exception of those that required coverage from another angle. Sturges was particular, but he knew what he wanted and if he got it with one take, he moved on.

Unlike the ranting and raving director in John Benson's story about the steer that would not climb the stairs, Sturges seemed mild-mannered to Latigo. It would not be long before Latigo saw his other side. It happened the next day. And it involved stairs.

Well, not a stairway, exactly, but a balcony. An outdoor balcony on the second floor of a cut stone building—made of lath and plaster—serving in this production as an office block on the backlot Western town's main street.

The scene called the lead performer for his first appearance on the set. Legendary actor Ewan Broderick, a Welshman—not an Englishman, as John Benson had thought—earned his fame in the legitimate theatres of London, was lured to Broadway with money, and later to Hollywood. The trophy case in his London home overflowed with awards and honors and other recognition earned throughout a long and successful career. Although well along in years, he still worked regularly on stage and screen.

His character in Sturges's film, Paxton Harris, owned large swaths of the West, with interests in ranching, land speculation, railroads, freighting and express, and banking. Harris was known, respected, and feared, and exercised a habit of crushing opposition at his whim.

The exception, although a minor one, was the character played by Latigo Brown. The enterprising outlaw robbed and stole from Harris's empire apparently at will, and the emperor seemed unable to stop him. The law, bounty hunters, and private detectives were always one step behind the bandit, much to Harris's chagrin.

Reining up in the street in front of the office block, the town marshal, knowing Harris would most likely be found in his upstairs office behind the open doors of the balcony, called out to him. The lawman wanted to keep his distance, fearing the rich man's wrath.

Paxton Harris walked out onto the balcony and the camera, from its low angle, revealed him leaning over the balcony rail, looming above and staring down at the world from his superior position.

"I'm afraid I've got bad news, Pax."

"What is it?"

The marshal removed his hat and raked his fingers through his hair.

"Well?" the voice boomed from above.

"It's the 11:20 Express, sir. It's been robbed."

"Robbed? How the hell can you rob an Express? The train doesn't stop!"

"Cut!" Sturges stepped down from his canvas chair and spoke quietly to his assistant and to the cameraman. Cast and crew stood silent, waiting.

Ewan Broderick's patience wore thin and he asked what the matter was.

Sturges said, "Just a minor tweak, Ewan."

Broderick waited. "Well?"

"You see, Ewan, it's your expression."

"My expression?"

"Yes. Paxton Harris is a powerful man. The world is at your beck and call. You are a bull among steers. Except for this bandit. He is like a yapping little dog, nipping at your heels. He cannot do any real damage to your empire, but he is an annoyance. All your efforts have been unsuccessful in bringing him to heel. When the marshal tells you he has struck again, you are—well, frustrated. Irked. Annoyed. You feel as if you should be able to kick the little dog at will, yet it continually eludes you. You are not helpless, exactly, not yet. But you resent, again, the bandit's intrusion. You just want him to go away."

Sturges paused to allow his direction to register. "Shall we try it again, Ewan?"

"Certainly. But, please, address me as Mister Broderick, if you will."

No one could see it yet, but Sturges felt the flush under his shirt collar and hoped it would not rise. Everything and everyone was, by then, ready. He nodded to his assistant and the calls went out to roll sound, roll camera, and for the slate and clapper to mark the scene. This time, Sturges allowed the scene to play out a bit longer, the marshal offering further detail concerning the train robbery.

"CUT!"

"What is it now?"

"I'm still not seeing it, *Mister Broderick*."

Again, Sturges called for action and, again, cut the scene short. "Please, Mister Broderick—resentment—annoyance—frustration. Please, please, can we see it in your face?"

Yet again, Sturges stopped the action. "Please! Have I not made it clear, Mister Broderick? Do you not understand my direction?"

Broderick did not answer. He turned on his heel and walked back through the balcony doorway to await the call from the marshal to reappear. On cue, he walked back out onto the balcony and leaned over, looking down at the mounted lawman. But he held his peace, waiting, waiting, he believed, to build the tension he thought the director might be looking for. He waited too long.

"CUT! *Mister Broderick!* Have you forgotten your lines? 'What is it?' *That* is your first line. Three little words, each a single syllable— *what*, *is*, *it*, phrased as a question. Shall we try again? And don't forget the expression on your face!"

Broderick did not move, his hands grasping the balcony rail beneath white knuckles. He looked down at Sturges, slumped in his canvas chair. "Pardon me—Sturges, is it?"

The director looked up at the actor, his face florid.

"Sir, I have trod the boards in London's West End and on the stages of New York City's Broadway. I was acting for the cinema while your mother was still changing your nappies."

"We are well aware of you accolades, Mister Broderick. And your age. I don't see how either is getting us anywhere. Are you ready to try it again?"

"Let me say, sir, that this old face has served me well. I learned long ago, well before your time, that it can express anger. It can look happy, or sad. It can reveal fear. Communicate sadness. And it will, at will, show a blank look that says I do not understand."

This time, it was Broderick who paused to allow his statement to take root. Then, "Now, *Mister Sturges*, let us do the scene. Just tell me which of my expressions you wish to see—limited though you believe them to be—and I shall deliver!"

Without waiting for a reply, Broderick went back through the doorway to await his cue.

Sturges still sat, seething, slumped in his chair, neck craned upward toward the now-empty balcony. Lacking a target for his wrath, he turned it on the actor playing the marshal. He blamed him for not setting the mood properly for the old actor. He berated him for missing his mark on the street—a matter of the width of a horseshoe, truth be told. He chastised him for sitting his horse too casually in the presence of the powerful man. He castigated, chided, scolded, cussed, and rebuked the gaffer, the grips, the camera operator, the sound man, and the script supervisor.

Finally, frustrated, he told the assistant director to ready the next set up. This scene would be abandoned for now; rescheduled for a future date when they were all in a better frame of mind to fulfill his vision for the film.

Latigo Brown, who watched the whole thing from the shade of the saloon porch across the street, could see in the faces of the company how the steer who would not climb the stairs must have felt.

Chapter Twenty-Three

Shooting continued over days and weeks, with Sturges and Broderick maintaining a strained, if productive, relationship. Had he been given free rein, the director may well have recast the part, but the producers were banking on the star's box-office appeal and cachét. The director and actor spoke only when necessary, and Sturges allowed the actor to interpret the role according to his own vision, which, as it developed, was different from the director's original intent, but proved every bit as effective.

One day, Latigo Brown learned the purpose behind the screen test scene when he had roped the mannequin, jerking and dragging it away from the grasp of a running man. The scene in the movie had Latigo riding into town to visit the mercantile for supplies, only to be assailed by a hail of bullets. Latigo barely had time to return fire as the shooter kicked up dust, splintered woodwork, and shattered windows as his target ducked and dodged around the covered porch of the store, trying to get a shot off. But the gunman stood in the street, a revolver in each hand, throwing lead so fast and furious that Latigo, so intent on finding effective cover, could barely find time to return fire.

Then something happened that rarely, if ever, occurred in Western shoot-'em-ups; something Latigo had never seen—the gunfighter ran out of bullets.

The gunman looked askance as the hammer on the revolver in his left hand fell on a spent cartridge. He looked wide-eyed at the pistol in his right hand when it, too, responded to the trigger pull with the same sickening snap.

But it was the sound of opportunity for Latigo's character. Latigo leapt off the porch, unhitched his horse from the rail, and swung into the saddle. He smiled. Holstering his gun, he took down his rope and shook out a loop. His attacker saw it, sensed what was coming, and set out down the street at a run. Latigo rode in pursuit, loop spinning and ready to throw.

Most of the time, in most movies, such a pursuit and capture of a fleeing assailant would be accomplished by stunt men—one on the ground and one mounted, filmed at angles that captured the action but concealed their faces. Sam Sturges had something else in mind. He intended to film the climax of the scene in a different way; one that required the horseback actor himself to rope and drag the running man. The gunman was, in fact, a trained stuntman ready, willing, and able to be roped and dragged for his day's pay. Latigo, his roping ability known, and proved to the producers in the screen test, would perform his own stunt work.

Surges mounted the camera in the back of a truck. The truck would drive down the street, the gunman-turned-stuntman running along behind, head swiveling to keep an eye on the pursuing horse and rider. Latigo would come on, in full view of the camera, rope the running man, jerk him from his feet as the rope tightened, then drag his captive past the truck and out of frame.

Getting the action on film required three takes, as the truck driver got his speed worked out, the camera operator determined the limits of the frame, Sturges found the most advantageous mark for Latigo to make the catch, and Latigo adjusted his movements and timing to make it all work. Through it all, the stuntman was good-natured and cooperative, his work made easier because Latigo did not take hard dallies, allowing the wraps to run just enough to soften the jerk.

Sturges was pleased with the result, believing his vision for the scene noteworthy. He took pleasure in knowing the effect could not easily be imitated by other filmmakers, absent the talent of Latigo Brown, who was proving his ability as a featured player along with his skills as a cowboy.

Latigo, for his part, was as yet unsure of the acting business. Constantly nervous when delivering lines, he feared appearing wooden and amateurish. But Sturges assured him his work was satisfactory, if not better than that. Ewan Broderick took the youngster under his wing, never telling Latigo what he should do or how to do it, but telling him stories. The tales, often funny, and often with the star's failures the source of the humor, proved instructive in another way. Latigo came to realize that even the best, most experienced, actors made mistakes. That they were often, if not always, uncertain. And that a modicum of nervousness was necessary, even desirable, to keep an actor on his toes, to keep him aware of and paying attention to the scene he was in, and reacting to it. Acting, good acting, Broderick told Latigo on more than one occasion, was reacting.

Still, Latigo's anxiety troubled him. Then, one day, it boiled over.

Paxton Harris had a granddaughter. A refined, educated, cultured young woman played by an actress whose beauty Latigo found second only to that of Annika Eriksson, the rising star he had dropped a loop over following his trick roping display in his first movie. So, the cowboy was decidedly on edge when it came time to film a scene featuring his character and the young lady.

*****

Delilah Harris, granddaughter of magnate Paxton Harris, stands clutching her handbag. Through tear-filled eyes, she stares at the helpless carriage, standing aslant and askew in the road. The harnessed horse snorts, neck craned to look back at the stalled carriage. The left shaft hangs loose from the harness, causing that side of the conveyance to sag and twist away from the horse.

Time passes, and Delilah is seated on a rock beside the road, twisting and worrying the handbag in her lap. The tears have stopped, but their tracks are visible in the light powder of dust on her cheeks; smudges of the grime are also present on her fitted jacket and skirts. The hat pinned to her upswept dark hair has been bumped awry, and dark tendrils of her thick mane have come loose to hang free, framing her face. The downed carriage still sags in the road; the horse stands hipshot and head down, its swishing tail and twitching hide as it flicks away flies the only sign of wakefulness.

The young woman perks up, then stands, at the sound of hoofbeats. A lone rider approaches. Delilah steps out into the road to stand beside the carriage horse, now alert. She holds one of the lines in a gloved hand just below the bit chain and watches the approaching horseman.

Latigo Brown reins up beside Delilah, looks the situation over, and smiles. "Looks like you've got a speck of trouble, Miss."

Delilah nods.

"From the look of things, it ain't nothin' important. I reckon I could set it to right, if you'd care to have me do it."

Delilah lets loose a long-held breath and smiles, fear and uncertainty flushed away with a look of relief. "Oh, yes! Please! I would be most grateful for your assistance."

Latigo dismounts for a closer look, standing close to Delilah as he examines the broken harness and rubs the carriage horse's neck and shoulder. He points to the fault. "See here, Miss, right there's your problem. The shaft tug on your harness wore through and busted. That's why your shaft there is danglin' out yonder, 'stead of hooked to your horse here where it belongs." He pats the horse, clapping his hand against its shoulder. "You're lucky you got a well-trained horse here,

Miss. Otherwise, he might've spooked and tried to run off. You'd have a right mess if he did—you could've been hurt bad."

Delilah swallows hard and tries to smile. "Well. What am I to do now? Rather, what can you do, since you so kindly offered your assistance?"

"Not to worry, Miss. I'll have you back on the road in no time."

Latigo unbuckles the tug strap from the back band and lays it on the iron tire of the carriage wheel. He pries open his pocketknife and uses it to pierce holes in the broken ends of the tug strap, fetches a length of whang leather from his saddlebags, and laces it through the overlapping holes to repair the break, if only temporarily. He lifts the sagging shaft and pushes the carriage back into line, buckles the tug piece onto the back band, and around the shaft, adjusting the length of the tug until the shaft is level.

"Now, Miss, that'll get you back to town, but it ain't fixed by no means. You have a harness maker fix it proper. You might have him look over the rest of harness, too. Could be it needs fixin' in other places."

"I don't know how to thank you. If you will accept payment, my grandfather will compensate you, I am sure."

"Oh, no, Miss. I couldn't take no money just for helpin' out a damsel in distress. It ain't no more than what a man ought to do, and what any man would. Not worth botherin' old Paxton Harris over."

Delilah perks up and her eyes widen. "You know my grandfather?"

"Oh, no, Miss. Can't say as I do. But ever'body knows *of* him." Latigo smiled and thumbed back the brim of his hat. "I have done business with the old man, in a manner of speakin'. I've been seen on his trains and express coaches, and in his banks, and on some of his ranches. But, no, I don't know Mister Harris."

Latigo helps Delilah into the carriage and hands her the lines. "If you don't mind, Miss, I'll ride along with you on into town, just in case my repair don't hold up."

Delilah smiles, her expression countering her words. "Oh, I'm sure that will not be necessary. Your work strikes me as being of the highest order."

"Just the same, Miss, I'll ride along. I'm goin' that way anyhow, and I'd be happy for your company."

Delilah responds with another smile, fluffs the lines and makes a kissing sound to put the carriage horse into motion.

The carriage arrives in town, and Delilah stops at the livery stable. Latigo dismounts, and offers his hand to help her step down. They stand close, and she lays a hand on his forearm.

"Thank you again, sir. Your assistance is appreciated. And your company has been most enjoyable." Face turned upward, she leans close. "Are you certain there is nothing I can do to thank you...personally?"

Delilah's lips part and her eyes close. Latigo leans in and touches his lips to her forehead, quickly retreats, and steps back.

"CUT!"

Latigo took another step back, turned, and found the director.

"Latigo! What are you doing?"

The cowboy shuffles a bit. "Did I do somethin' wrong, Mister Sturges? On the script, it says to kiss her."

"You call that a kiss, Latigo? She is not your grandmother! Kiss her, for heaven's sake!"

Latigo flushed. He looked at the smiling actress, then back at the director. He shuffled some more. "Can I have a word, Mister Sturges?"

"What is it?"

Latigo walked to Sturges, sitting in his canvas chair in its usual place behind the camera. The crew members watched Latigo as he walked.

The smiles on their faces deepened as did the blush on his. He stopped in front of Sturges and took off his hat, holding it against his chest with both hands grasping the brim.

"Well, Latigo? Spit it out. What is it?"

"I—I—I'm a not sure I can do it."

"Do what? Kiss her? Good hell, Latigo!" Sturges waved his arm, taking in the cast and crew and the world beyond. "I could pick out any man here, and he would *pay* me for the opportunity to kiss that girl. And we're *paying you* to do it! What's the problem?"

"I don't know, sir. I'm just nervous."

"Surely you've kissed a girl before!"

"Yessir." Latigo looked around, taking in all the grinning faces watching him. "But I ain't never kissed no one in front of a bunch of people like this."

Sturges sat, smiling and shaking his head.

"Fact is, Mister Sturges," Latigo looked up at and nodded toward the hotel building across the street. "I'd a lot rather you asked me to get shot and fall out of a third-story window in that hotel yonder, than make me kiss her in front of all these people."

Sturges, more amused than angry, said, "I am sorry, Latigo, but you've got to do it." He stood. "Okay, everybody, back to one! Let's get this scene shot and call it a day!"

Latigo, head down, scuffed slowly back to the carriage in front of the livery stable and the smiling actress. She reached out and held his forearm and leaned close, craning her neck to whisper in his ear. "Don't you worry, Mister Latigo Brown. I will make it as painless as possible. You just take a deep breath, put your lips on mine, and I will take it from there." She leaned back and pinched his cheek. "As a matter of fact, I'll bet that once I get started on you, cowboy, you'll forget there is anyone else around."

A wrangler drove the carriage back to the starting point. Latigo walked beside the actress, she clutching his arm, he leading his horse. They played out the scene, Latigo anxious all the while he would forget his lines. Then he remembered he had no lines in the scene—his only job was to help the young woman step out of the carriage, then give her a kiss when she appeared to ask for it. He hoped the makeup he wore concealed the flush he felt rising as she stopped the carriage and he stepped out of the saddle.

On cue, he kissed her. Or, rather, she kissed him. Long and deep. And, as she predicted, he forgot where he was in the world, and became an active and appreciative participant in the scene.

"Cut!" Sturges said. "That's a wrap!"

Latigo heard the director as if from a great distance. The woman broke the seal, leaned back, and asked if it was as bad as he expected.

"Oh, no, Miss. That was right fine."

He came to his senses and looked around, wondering why the assembled members of the company were all looking at him. Smiling. And applauding.

Chapter Twenty-Four

Having an actor able to convincingly perform his own stunts freed Sam Sturges to attempt camera angles and setups seldom, if ever, seen on film.

A rider racing to, and running parallel with, a moving train, then reaching out to take hold of a train car and slide out of the saddle and onto the train was a staple in Westerns. The risky scene was accomplished with the actor's stunt double boarding the train, while the actor relaxed somewhere in relative comfort and safety. But Sturges mounted a rear-facing camera on the side of the train and photographed the action with the actor—Latigo Brown—head on as he approached and reached the train on a running horse, and slid out of the saddle to swing onto the platform on the tail end of a rail car.

Latigo's intention in boarding the train—one of many in Paxton Harris's railroad empire—was to stop the train, locate the mail car, and free it of the riches it carried. Latigo wondered how he would make his getaway, and how he would carry away the bounty—he had, after all, abandoned his horse miles back in boarding the train, left to run loose and wander to who-knows-where. Sturges assured him no one would care.

Another action scene seen in many Westerns featured a man or men—usually bandits, sometimes with one of the good guys in pursuit—running along the tops of the cars on a moving train, jumping from car to car as they went. This, too, was accomplished by stunt doubles, to avoid the risk of injuring—or killing—actors.

But, again, Sturges took a fresh approach. He parked the camera in the gap between cars, looking back along the top of the train. Latigo Brown would run along the tops of the cars, leaping the gaps as usual.

But, as he approached the camera, it would become obvious to viewers that it was the actor himself atop the rushing train, with no way to fake it. In his final leap in the scene, Latigo had to leap over the camera with its protruding film magazine as well as across the gap to the next car. The camera operator assured Sturges the sequence had looked great through the viewfinder, and would bring theater goers to the edges of their seats. Seeing it happen for himself when viewing the "dailies" inspired in the director the belief that he may well reach the pinnacle of creativity and artistry in Westerns with this film.

As for Latigo Brown, who was making it all possible, he continued to question the reality of many of the things he was asked to do. And, always, Sturges assured him that no one else would care, and that it would look great on the screen.

Still, Latigo questioned why he would be able to rustle unbranded steers from Harris's ranches, when the branding crew, or even a cowboy hunting strays on the range, would brand a bull calf at the same time it was roped and thrown and tied to be turned into a steer. An unbranded steer, he said, defied logic.

He wondered why he was so often asked to rear his horse; to cue it to stand on its hind legs and paw the air with its forelegs, while he doffed his hat and used it to wave goodbye, or hello, to whoever else was in the scene. Such behavior was not natural for a horse—or a cowboy, for that matter.

He asked about the believability of shooting the pistol from an attacker's hand—not only because such accuracy was all but impossible with a revolver, but also because killing, or at least wounding his assailant to put him out of action, would be his intention in a gunfight.

He challenged the notion that the gunmen sent to bring him to heel would trail him through miles of open country, and only attack when a cluster of boulders, a copse of trees, an arroyo, a building, or some other place of concealment was at hand where he could find shelter.

And he expressed doubt about his relationship with Delilah Harris. Given that her grandfather, Paxton Harris, devoted considerable time and much money and an endless string of hirelings to bring him to bay, yet seemed oblivious of the fact of their budding, even flowering, romance, defied belief.

The response to his concerns and objections amounted to nothing more than a pat on the back and a reminder that it was only a movie. So, like a good boy, Latigo Brown performed as directed, and always gave it his best effort.

One day, as filming was winding down, the arrival of a publicist from the studio caused a stir and enlivened the weary company. Latigo, a neophyte concerning the production process, had no idea that while the actors and crew were at their work, others were at work on the movie behind the scenes.

Technicians in the lab were developing film from the cameras, with spools and rollers unwinding the reels and feeding seemingly endless lengths of film through tanks filled with chemical baths, developers, fixers, bleaches, washes, and rinses. And they were creating work prints, experimenting with printer lights and timings to create the levels of color, tint, contrast, and brightness the director of photography and director desired.

Film editors used those work prints to sort out the scenes and takes and assemble them in sequences that would be strung together in a "rough cut" of the film when complete.

A composer developed musical themes and melodies for the movie's score; ideas that would be developed and arranged and recorded to enhance the action on the screen.

And the publicity department studied the script, viewed segments of film, looked through stacks of still photographs taken on the set, or posed with actors for promotional purposes, as they devised a plan to capture the essence of the movie and create excitement and anticipation among prospective viewers with film trailers for theaters, posters, magazine and newspaper advertisements, and other publicity materials.

The visitor to the set on the studio backlot that day carried with him a rolled tube of paper. With a good deal of theatrics, he removed and pocketed his sunglasses, tacked the end of the rolled paper to the big sliding door of the livery stable, stepped aside, and let the roll unwind. With a flourish and a toothy grin worthy of a medicine show salesman, he extended his arm and hand to direct attention to his revelation. Latigo learned it was a "one sheet," a poster advertising the movie, that would hang in theaters and elsewhere, and would serve as the source from which other printed publicity materials would derive.

The cast and crew gathered round, allowing Sam Sturges space front and center. The director was one of the few members of the company not surprised by what he saw, as he had worked closely with the artists and designers in the publicity department in the creation of the poster.

Across the top in blazing red letters was the film's title. An illustration of Ewan Broderick dominated the space, as in the character of Paxton Harris he stared down at the world from his perch on the balcony outside his office. Second only in size to the film's title was his name, under the word "Starring."

When Latigo was able to get a closer look, he was surprised to see beneath Broderick's name, in somewhat smaller letters, the words, "Also starring Latigo Brown," followed by the name of the woman playing Delilah Harris. Smaller illustrations created a border along each side of the poster, and Latigo was further surprised to see himself depicted waving his hat while atop a rearing horse, and in another illustration pointing a drawn pistol at the viewer.

As the crowd dispersed, Latigo asked the studio man if it would be possible for him to get a copy of the poster.

"Certainly, Mister Brown. Anything you please. What you see here is a press proof. The one sheets have not been printed in quantity yet, as we await final approval. If you like, you may keep this copy, as we have others back at the office."

"Thank you kindly, Mister. See, this is the first time my name's ever been on anything like that. I'd like to send it back home—my little sister Penny will get a big kick out of it."

The publicity man rolled the poster from bottom up, pulled the tacks affixing it to the stable door, and, with a bow, handed it to Latigo.

"Thanks again, sir. Like I said, I ain't never had nothin' like this happen before. It all seems kind of strange."

The publicity man again flashed his toothy grin. "If I were you, Latigo Brown, I would get used to it. Unless I miss my guess, you are well on your way on the road to stardom. Why, I wouldn't be surprised to see you become the most famous cowboy star of the big screen."

With that, the publicity man put on his sunglasses, showed off his smile, and walked away. Latigo watched him go, thinking the man was either off his rocker or full of bullshit—deciding the latter to be the case, most likely a requirement in his line of work.

That evening in the Benson's kitchen, Latigo spread the poster across the table, which it covered nearly as well as a tablecloth.

"My, my, Latigo," Elaine said. "That certainly is impressive."

"Son," John said, wrapping an arm around Latigo and clapping him on the shoulder, "it looks to me like you're on your way. It took a good many years before I ever saw my name on a one sheet."

Latigo did not know what to say, but the flush on his face betrayed him.

John clapped his shoulder again, and squeezed tight. "Not bad for a ranch kid from west of nowhere who hasn't got any better sense than to climb aboard bucking horses for fun, wouldn't you say?"

Latigo shook his head. "I don't know what to say, sir. It don't none of it seem real. All I do is just show up where they tell me to, say what they want me to, and do whatever else they say, no matter how silly it is. It don't seem like real work, even."

Benson laughed. "Maybe not. But you've got to admit it pays a whole lot better."

*****

Even with filming completed, Latigo was called on by the production company from time to time over the coming weeks. A few times he was back in costume to re-shoot a scene flawed for some reason the first time, or to bridge a gap or fill a hole in continuity revealed as the film was edited.

But, most of the time, he was called in to work in a stuffy little room with a big glass window by himself. There, he would stand at a microphone and watch his filmed self on a screen. "Looping," it was called, and Latigo could see why. The segment of film he watched was spliced end to end to form an actual loop, so what he watched repeated itself over and over and over. His job was to speak the lines he was speaking on the film, again and again until the synchronization of his voice and the moving lips on the screen was perfect, or as near to it as possible.

Sometimes the sound recorded on location during filming lacked the fidelity required; other times extraneous sound was recorded, and sometimes the director wanted the line spoken with different emphasis or feeling. It was all part of the complexity of creating the soundtrack for the movie, and part of the larger post-production process. As Sturges and the editors refined the assembly of the scenes and takes into a visual story, others worked to support and enhance with sound what was seen on the screen.

Latigo nosed around the studio sometimes after completing his work, watching the activity and, more often than not, wondering what was going on. He saw people called foley artists and editors create and record footsteps, hoofbeats, door slams, gunshots, wheel squeaks, window breaks, splintering wood, crackling fire, slaps and smacks for fistfights, and all manner of other sounds. Their ingenuity fascinated him, as the sounds were made with little boxes filled with sand and gravel and dirt or floorboards, in which people walked in place, timing their steps to film of a walking actor. The sound of running horses came from coconut shells pounded by hand into a box of sand. Kneading a box of discarded film for crackling fire, clapping boards together for gunshots, opening and closing tiny doors, and other inventive effects, although wholly false, added realism to the movie.

He watched a small orchestra in a big room play music while watching a film sequence on a large screen, with the composer-turned-conductor beating time with his baton. The songwriter's themes and melodies were timed to the action on the screen, arranged and orchestrated to heighten suspense, intensify violence, embellish a touching or romantic scene, amplify sadness, or elevate whatever emotion the scene called for.

One day, after finishing a looping session and hanging around watching editors feeding rolls of film with pictures and others with sound through their Moviola machines, scrolling back and forth over and over again to find the exact frame for a transition to another angle, shot, or scene. A studio assistant opened the door and motioned him out of the cutting room and led him to the building foyer. There, a messenger awaited him, and, after getting Latigo's signature on one of the film business's ever-present clipboards, handed him a plain envelope with only his name on it. How the messenger had tracked him down, he could not imagine.

Latigo slid a thumb under the flap and tore the envelope open. Inside was an engraved letterhead from another studio. The typewritten letter requested his attendance at a meeting to discuss Latigo Brown's participation in a major motion picture project now under development. After spelling out the time and place for the meeting, the letter closed with a scrawled signature Latigo could not decipher.

Typed beneath the scribble was the name: T.C. McGill.

Chapter Twenty-Five

John Benson sat in his favored chair on the front porch holding the letter, reading and rereading it. He set the letter on the side table, took off his reading glasses and laid them atop it.

"Son, do you know who T.C. McGill is?"

Latigo shifted in his chair. "Not sure that I do, sir. Name rings a bell, so I guess I've heard it somewhere. Don't know where or why. He must be somebody in the movie business, from what it says."

Benson smiled, sat upright in his chair and looked at the cowboy. "He surely is in the movie business. He's a director." He took a sip of his iced tea and set the sweating glass back on the table. "You know, the directors you've worked with on these movies—Howard Walsh and Sam Sturges—they're good at their jobs. Respected. They're kind of at the top of the game when it comes to making Westerns. Higher in the pecking order than the directors of those TV shows you've worked on. You see what I'm saying?"

"Yeah. I guess so," Latigo said with a shrug.

"T.C. McGill, now, he's something different. I suppose he's the most successful filmmaker in Hollywood these days. Has been for years. The man's a bigger star in the business than the people who show up on the screen. He'll make a Western from time to time, but Westerns are kind of a sideline with him, if that. The man has so much power and influence he can make any movie he wants. Mostly, he makes these big epic pictures; stories from the Bible or ancient history or big battles. You've heard that phrase they hype some pictures with—'a cast of thousands'—well, that was probably invented to describe T.C. McGill's productions. He can raise all the money he needs to make a movie with a couple of telephone calls, then has to make more calls to turn down people who want to give him more money."

Benson relaxed in his chair to let Latigo think about what he had said. He sipped his tea while he watched the cowboy, imagining he could see the wheels and gears and sprockets inside his head whirring and turning.

"You getting the idea of what this letter means?"

Latigo stared off into the distance somewhere, but his eyes did not appear to see anything. He blinked, and looked at Benson. He shook his head, a motion so slight as to be barely noticeable. "I guess so. Maybe." He sighed and sagged. "No."

Benson sat upright again, then leaned toward Latigo. "What it means, son, is that you've made it. You're about to become a star. If McGill casts you in this film, whatever it is, you'll become a big star."

As Latigo looked at Benson, his eyes glazed over and again saw nothing. The brain behind them also went blank.

*****

"Mister McGill will see you now," the woman at the desk said. Latigo stood up from his chair and gave the room another look. The production offices he had visited in the past tended to be cramped and cluttered, bustling with activity as people came and went. This one was quiet, reverential. It was spacious, and furnished with fine overstuffed chairs to accommodate those waiting to conduct business.

The receptionist stood and walked to a set of double doors of heavy, dark wood, opened one, and waited for Latigo to pass through then closed it, the latch whisper quiet. The room before him was likewise large; large enough to dwarf an oversized desk near the far wall. Its expanse gleamed with light from a chandelier, the surface bereft of anything save an old-fashioned blotter and a fancy pen set at the front edge that looked to be out of reach for anyone seated in the tall, wide, upholstered chair behind the desk. The chair sat empty. Latigo stood, hat in hand, and wondering if he was to continue waiting here, or if he should take a seat in one of the twin upholstered chairs facing the desk.

Before he could make up his mind, someone spoke from another part of the room he had not noticed.

"Latigo Brown, I presume?"

The cowboy turned toward the voice, and saw that it came from an alcove branching off the main part of the room. The spacious nook featured a u-shaped assemblage of plush sofas, opening onto a fireplace of stacked stone slabs. A fire flickered on the grate, but it was not fueled by logs, or even coal. Rather, it was one of the newfangled gas fires.

Flanking one side of the fireplace was a young, bespectacled man in a business suit, hair slicked back, face shaved so smooth the skin glowed. Cradled against his chest was a clipboard, but rather than the standard-issue variety, it appeared to be made of varnished and polished inlaid wood and gold-plated hardware.

The young man, unsmiling and sober, shifted his gaze from the cowboy to the man standing at the other side of the fireplace, and the source of the voice. This, Latigo thought, must be T.C. McGill. His dress was less formal. He wore a necktie, but his shirt was khaki-colored with flapped pockets and shoulder straps. High-topped polished boots of black leather reached nearly to his knees. Tucked-in pants bloused over the boot tops, then spread wide at the thighs. Latigo did not know what they were called, but the pants looked like those he had seen in magazine pictures of fox hunts in England. Latigo judged the man to be somewhere beyond middle age.

Latigo nodded to the men and stepped forward, offering his hand to the man he assumed to be the director.

"That's me, sir. Latigo Brown." He grasped the man's hand and shook it firmly. "I guess you wanted to see me."

"It is a pleasure to meet you, laddie." He did not bother to introduce himself. "Please, do take a seat."

Latigo sat in the center of the sofa facing the fire, sinking into its depths. The other men sat, each on one of the sofas at right angles to the one Latigo sat on.

"Now, Mister Latigo Brown, I am a busy man, so let us get down to business. What do you say?"

"Sounds good to me, sir. But I ain't at all sure what business it is we've got to get down to." Latigo looked from McGill to the young man, who looked up from his note taking, his eyes gone wide and face pale. He looked back at the director.

"Well. Yes," McGill said. "I have heard about you, Latigo Brown. I understand you are an authentic cowboy of the American West."

"I guess you could say so. I was raised that way. Growed up on a ranch. Worked horses and cattle all my life. Rodeoed some."

McGill nodded. "I see. And how did you come to take up the acting trade?"

Latigo collected his thoughts. "Well, it all just kind of happened. Met this stunt man up in Las Vegas, fellow by the name of Clete Holman—"

"—Ah, yes! I know Clete Holman! He has performed for me in many productions. First rate, Mister Holman! First rate!"

"Well, anyway, he was tellin' us stories about bein' in the movies. Then I met John Benson, and he told us more stories." Latigo shrugged. "It all sounded kind of interesting, so I thought I'd come on down here to Hollywood and give it a try. Mister Benson, he said he could maybe get me some jobs as a stunt rider. Which he did. That's about it."

"Ah, laddie, you have done that and more. I have heard tell of your finesse with a rope—what is the word, lasso?—and that the lines you speak are well delivered."

Latigo shrugged. "So what is it I can do for you, Mister McGill?"

"I am, as you may have surmised, making a movie. A Western. Aye, but it is not the kind of Western you can find playing at any cinema, nor is it related to the serials on the telly. No, laddie, this production will be larger in scope, much larger; a saga to chronicle for all time the romance and heroism prevalent in the mythos of the Old West. The Western, if I may say, to end all Westerns. Speaking figuratively, to some degree, of course—but I intend to make a film against which all others on the subject shall be measured and found wanting."

"That's a pretty tall order, ain't it?"

"Perhaps. Some back home in Scotland—God bless the Dear Green Place—would say I am all bum and parsley for saying it."

Latigo's forehead looked like a plowed field; his eyes like dry wells.

McGill smiled. "I have heard the same sentiment expressed in a manner you will find familiar. All hat and no cattle. But, truth be told, neither adage applies to me. I say what I'll do, and I'll do what I say."

Latigo nodded his understanding. Then his brow wrinkled again. "But I still wonder what all this has got to do with me."

The man in the suit stopped scribbling on his clipboard and stared at Latigo. The cowboy looked at him, and saw a face displaying something between shock and disbelief and surprise looking back at him.

"Aye, laddie!"

Latigo's gaze snapped back to the director.

"Have you not ferreted it out already? You are to be my star, Latigo Brown."

Latigo swallowed hard. "Sounds like a tall order for a guy like me. I'm new to this movie business, as I'm sure you know."

"Aye. I know it well."

"Then why would you want me for the job?"

McGill smiled. "I am in need of a fresh face. I want an actor not already tainted by fame, whose very presence on the screen will not distract from the story. And that fresh face, without question, is yours, Latigo Brown."

"Still, why me? I mean, there's all kinds of folks out there who ain't famous. Lots more than there are famous ones. What makes you so sure I can pull it off?"

"As you may have surmised in your time here, brief though it may be, Hollywood is a small town. Word gets around. To answer your question, I am acquainted with the man who was director of photography on the Sam Sturges film now in post-production. That cameraman has worked for me on occasion—"B" camera, of course, or second unit. But I trust his judgment. I have spoken with him, and he assures me of your competence, and your ability to take direction."

Latigo said nothing.

The director cleared his throat. "And, I must say, there is one other thing."

"What's that?"

"I believe you know Miss Annika Eriksson."

Latigo nodded.

"A bonny wee lass, she. Destined, I believe, to become a major star. Which she shall be, incidentally, before the curtain falls on this film. Annika has been cast as the female lead in the picture. And it is her request that you play opposite her. The decision is not hers, you understand—but it is her wish."

Wide-eyed, Latigo said, "Why, I can't hardly believe that. I don't hardly know her. I roped her once in a movie, but that's all. We ain't spoke but ten words to each other."

McGill shrugged. "That is at it may be. I can only say the young lass was—is—quite taken with you. She is of the firm opinion that you, laddie, you, and you alone, are the best man to take on the role of her romantic interest."

Latigo blushed, and McGill said, "On screen, of course."

For what seemed an eternity, Latigo sat without speaking, head bowed and eyes riveted on the carpet. The director and the office assistant who had yet to speak a word also remained silent. Latigo, holding the brim of his hat in both hands, rotated it around and around. Then, he wagged his head and looked up at McGill.

"I'm mighty flattered, sir. But I don't know."

"Don't know what?"

"I guess there's a whole lot of money ridin' on this here movie of yours. I'm afraid I might mess it up for you."

McGill did not speak for a time. The only sound was the scratching of the pen as the man in the suit wrote something—Latigo had no idea what it might be—on the pad on his clipboard.

McGill cleared his throat. "I'll only ask that you leave that worry to me, laddie. There is a saying back home. 'Failing means you're playing.'"

"I ain't sure what that means."

"Let me explain. It means that it is better to play the game and do poorly than to sit on the sidelines and not play at all. Assuming, of course, one gives it his best effort."

"I see. I guess." Latigo stood. "I'll sure think it over. I guess I can find you here if I need to?"

McGill stood, his jaw clenched so tight that Latigo feared the man would soon be spitting out pieces of broken teeth. He spoke but one word, and it snapped like the lash of a bullwhip. "Robert?"

The man with the clipboard scrambled to his feet. He extracted a sheaf of papers from underneath his notepad on the clipboard and held them out to Latigo, then spoke his first words during the entire course of the meeting. The words came out with the staccato rhythm of a typewriter fingered by a capable typist. "Here. Take this. It is a contract. Look it over to see if it is to your satisfaction. Which I am sure it will be. The telephone number for our legal representative is on the forms. Contact him if you have any questions. Return the signed contract to this office at your first opportunity. Good day."

Latigo did not look at the papers. He settled his hat on his head and, with both hands, rolled the papers into a tube and carried them out the door. He nodded at the lady at the desk in the reception area as he passed through. He dropped the contract on the seat of his old truck, turned the key, stepped on the starter, and drove home.

"Whoooeee!" John Benson said with a whistle as he examined the contract. "You've really hit the big time, son. This is more money than most actors will ever see in their whole lives."

"What should I do?"

"Do? Sign the damn thing!"

"You think so?"

"Of course I think so. This is the opportunity of a lifetime!"

"I guess so. But there's a lot riding on it if I do sign it. I'm afraid I could screw the whole thing up."

Benson took in and let out a long breath. "Latigo, it isn't all up to you. You've seen how many people it takes to make a movie. And there will be a whole lot more than you've ever seen before working on this one. T.C. McGill is no fool. If he thinks you can do the job, then you ought to take his word for it."

Latigo shrugged, and made a half nod. He reached out for the contract, but Benson drew it back.

"Son, as you know, we're talking a whole lot of money here. A man in your position needs legal help. Pretty soon, you'll be hearing from lawyers and agents and managers wanting to handle your career. Some of them are shysters and will rob you blind. But a good one will take good care of you. Take care of your money and deal with all the legal mumbo-jumbo and see to your best interests. What I'm saying is, you ought to have someone look at this contract. Just to make sure."

"Heck, John, I don't know no lawyers."

"I'll tell you what. I'll have my manager look at this. He's an attorney, and he won't steer you wrong."

"You think he'll take me on?"

Benson shook his head. "No, I'm afraid not. He's up there in years and wanting to retire. Fact is, I'm going to have to start looking for someone myself. But he'll look this over as a favor to me. We'll go see him tomorrow."

Latigo thanked Benson and stood up from the kitchen table and walked out the back door. He climbed the stairs to his apartment over the garage, hung his hat on the peg, and collapsed on the bed.

Chapter Twenty-Six

Latigo Brown sat in T.C. McGill's office. This time, he sat in an overstuffed chair across the desk from the director. The expanse of the desktop spread before him, holding only the blotter and pen set, and a stack of papers Latigo assumed was the contract just delivered. Latigo also took note of a detail he had not noticed on his first visit. McGill and his desk sat on a higher plane; perched atop a dais elevated six or so inches above the rest of the room. From his seat, McGill always looked down on his visitors, who were forced to look up at him.

Latigo had handed the signed contract to the woman at the front desk, who asked him to wait, then carried the sheaf of papers through the big doorway into the boss's office. She soon returned, waited at the door, invited the cowboy to enter, then closed the door behind him. Latigo sensed a change in McGill's attitude from their first meeting. His effusive manner had turned abrupt, almost cold.

The bespectacled assistant, again dressed in a sharply tailored business suit, sat at small writing desk butted against the wall beside, but somewhat behind, McGill's. His desktop was as empty as his boss's, holding only his clipboard with its writing pad affixed, and a pen lying beside it.

"Latigo Brown," McGill said. "I am pleased to see you have come to your senses and signed the contract. Frankly, laddie, I was surprised you did not sign it on the spot."

Latigo swallowed hard. "I didn't mean no disrespect, sir. As you know, I'm new at this acting business. And, to tell you the truth, you liked to've scared the daylights out of me. I never expected no such thing as to be asked to be the main actor in your movie. I thought maybe you wanted me to do some stunt ridin' or somethin'; maybe a little speakin' part, if I was lucky."

The chill in McGill's demeanor melted away with a smile. "No harm done, laddie." Still, the director stayed on his perch, maintaining his distance from the actor. "Now, to business."

McGill outlined the story of the film. He offered no script, as it was undergoing yet another of many rewrites ordered by the director. Latigo was surprised at what he heard. The story was built on the same foundation as every short, every "B" Western, every horse opera, every oater, every shoot 'em up, and every dime novel celebrating an overblown, heroic version of western expansion.

There were ranches and railroads, road agents and rustlers, battles with Indians and gun battles in the streets, saloon brawls and bank robberies, horseback pursuits and hangings. And the usual rivers of blood offset, to some degree, by a touch of romance. Annika Andersson's character, much like the one in the Sturges film, was a relative—daughter, in this case—of a powerful man. The story had everything, it appeared to Latigo, that moviemakers thought the Old West was made of. Except, of course, cattle. And truth.

"Sounds like quite the story, Mister McGill."

The director smiled. "Aye, that it is, laddie. But it is the making of it that matters, and I will make a movie of the West unlike any heretofore projected on the silver screen. And it will make you, Latigo Brown, a star."

The cowboy swallowed hard.

"Now, we shall need a horse for you. Not an ordinary nag, but a noble, picturesque beast—striking and photogenic, handsome in the extreme." McGill steepled his forefingers and tapped them against his lower lip. The scratching of his assistant's pen resounded in the silence. Then, "Tell me, laddie, do you know of such a horse? Perhaps among the mounts in the stables you are familiar with—but a horse held back for a special time?"

Latigo did not have to think. "I believe I've got just the thing, sir." He told McGill about his horse back home, Nugget. Told him it was a stallion, well-muscled and powerful, even though not yet fully grown. Said it was a rich, golden palomino, the gold enhanced with the silver of its mane and tail. Boasted of its ability under the rein, its catlike quickness, its speed and surefootedness, its endurance and even temper.

"Please have the horse shipped here," McGill said. "I sense definite possibilities if what you say is so."

"You can bet on it, sir. I ain't one to brag most times, but with this horse it's different."

"I assume the horse is trained—or can be—for film work. Not just the usual things, you understand, but actions in keeping with his partnership with the hero. You know the thing—nicker or neigh on demand, snort and blow as needed, come when called, allow the crupper mount, flying mounts, vaults, that sort of thing."

Latigo allowed that Nugget had not been taught those things, but was surely intelligent enough to pick them up quickly with training.

"And, of course, he must be able to stand on his hind legs for a considerable period, rearing up with you in the saddle."

"I reckon he could learn to do that. But I got to say, Mister McGill, that that ain't a thing a horse would normally do on his own. Ain't natural."

McGill shook his head "No matter. It is a beautiful thing to see, and we shall see it." He paused, steepled index fingers again tapping at his lip. "Now, one more thing concerning the horse. This mount of yours is destined to become a star, right along with you, Latigo Brown. This name, 'Nugget,' you say?" He shook his head. "That will never do. He will need a moniker more majestic, more deserving of the magnificent beast that carries it. What do you think?"

Latigo thought. "Well, sir, I don't reckon there's any harm in givin' him a different name for the movies, like some of them actors do. Heck, 'Latigo' ain't my given name, come to that. Still, that horse'll always be Nugget to me."

McGill nodded. "Fine. I will put the writers to work coming up with something suitable. Robert," he said to his assistant, "make a note," as if the young man was not already writing down what Latigo assumed was every word they spoke, the way he furiously worked the pen.

The director's eyes locked on Latigo's face, his gaze so intense the cowboy squirmed. He squirmed more as the scrutiny persisted. He looked at the floor. He studied the walls. He looked out the window. He looked at McGill, and saw the director's eyes still boring holes in his face.

"Smile."

"What's that, sir?"

"Smile."

Latigo managed a lopsided grin, his face in no mood to show amusement at the ongoing inspection.

"Oh, come on, laddie! Smile!"

Latigo tried harder. He forced a smile that soon turned to laughter as the absurdity of the situation overcame the discomfort.

McGill held up both hands, palms outward. "Enough. You have a fine face, laddie. I believe the camera will like it."

Latigo blushed.

"One thing. That smile. Some of your teeth appear to be a wee bit crooked. And one of them, one of the front teeth, is chipped, I see."

Latigo's flush continued. "Yessir. Got that rodeoin'. Bareback horse tried to tip over in the chute with me, and we kind of bumped heads. His poll turned out to be harder than my face—broke that tooth, and give me a fat lip and bloody nose besides. Then the next mornin' I had two black eyes—looked like a racoon."

McGill smiled. "All good and well." He turned to Robert. "Arrange an appointment with the dentist." He turned back to Latigo. "We'll get that smile put in proper order for you."

"Oh, I don't know, sir, I...."

"You'll thank me for it later, laddie. Where you're going, a bonny braw smile is money in the bank."

McGill pontificated a while longer concerning this and that. He told Robert to make an appointment with the wardrobe department to take Latigo's measurements so they could get started on his wardrobe. He ordered Robert to contact the publicity department and have them set up a photo session with Latigo as soon as wardrobe had a suitable costume. He instructed him to have them start planting stories in the trade papers about Latigo Brown, the rising cowboy star. Better still, he said, include Annika Eriksson in the photo shoot, and tell publicity to hint to the gossip columnists that there might be romance in the offing for the co-stars of the forthcoming T.C. McGill epic of the Old West.

Latigo sat through this and more, overwhelmed and embarrassed and insecure with it all. Finally, McGill reminded the cowboy to have his horse brought to Hollywood post haste, and to commence with the required schooling. "If funds are required for the transport or training, see Robert here. He will see you get whatever you need. And don't be shy in the asking, laddie."

As soon as Latigo made it back to his apartment, he placed a long-distance call home. After being cast in the Sturges film, he had had a phone installed in the apartment, saving him the trouble of calling from a pay phone, tying up Benson's line, calling collect on their telephone, or using their line to call long distance then haggling with John or Elaine to convince them to accept payment for the privilege.

Penny answered. Hearing from her TV-and-movie-star brother never failed to animate her already bubbly personality. She asked if he had seen any of her favorite actors of late, and if he had collected autographs or glossy photos or both from them. He finally convinced her, after she made him swear up and down on his oath to provide more scrapbook fodder, to hand the phone off to their father.

After the usual niceties, Latigo asked his father if he would bring Nugget in from the pasture.

"Sure, son. What you got on your mind?"

"Well, I believe I'm goin' to use him in a movie they want me to be in." His father laughed. Latigo explained that the man in charge of the movie wanted him mounted on a flashy kind of horse, and that Nugget filled the bill as well as any of the horses in Hollywood.

"So is Nugget goin' to be famous, like Trigger and Champion and Silver and Topper and them?"

"Oh, I don't know. Could be, I guess. Not sure it's a good thing, though. Come to that, I still ain't sure about this movie stuff at all." He could hear his father chuckle on the other end of the line.

"It ain't for me to say, son, but the size of them checks your mother is puttin' in the bank for you make it look like a pretty good deal. Pays a hell of a lot better than puttin' grass in one end of a cow and gettin' a calf out the other." There was a pause, and Latigo could hear talking in the background. "Here, son. Your mother wants to talk to you."

"Orval, how are you doing? Are you getting enough to eat? Are you getting enough sleep? They're not working you too hard down there, are they?"

Latigo assured his mother all was well, and that John and Elaine Benson were taking good care of him, and that he was more concerned about all the sitting around he was doing, both between jobs and waiting around on the set, than he was about working too hard. His mother spurred him to plan a visit home soon, and assured him that Raymond and his father were staying on top of the ranch work, and not to worry. "This call must be costing you a fortune," she said, then passed a kiss down the line and hung up the phone.

The next call he placed was to his rodeo buddy and best friend, Harley Warren.

"You busy, Harley?"

"Oh, y'know—not much."

"How's the rodeoin'? Winnin' anything?"

Harley laughed. "You might not know it, livin' down there in the tropics like you are, but it's still wintertime up here. Ain't no rodeos goin' on in these parts these days."

Now, Latigo laughed. "You're right, Harley. Weather here don't change much from one day to the next. Sun's up most ever' day. Come to think of it, I don't know as I could find my coat if I was to have need of it."

He explained his need to have Nugget trailered to Los Angeles, and wondered if Harley was up for the job.

"Oh, hell yes! I been wantin' to see that country down there since you went. And Lord knows I could do with a little sunshine. It's so cold up here I have to keep bustin' the dog loose from the truck tires."

They discussed details, and Harley allowed that if Latigo could find his way around the big city, he could do it with his eyes closed. Latigo said he would send a check to cover expenses. He reminded Harley he was not on the way to a rodeo and running late, so he should take it easy, lay over along the way, see that Nugget got plenty of rest, and to feed him up on oats, as he was likely to be ganted up some from a diet of hay and whatever pasture grass he could paw out from under the snow.

"Oh, and Harley—bring your war bag. I hear tell there's some rodeos around here—leastways up in them towns in the hills. Maybe we could get entered up in one or two of 'em. It's been too long since I saw you get piled by a bull."

Chapter Twenty-Seven

Latigo Brown walked into the dentist's office and checked in with the receptionist. By now, his face was a familiar one in the office. He took a seat in the waiting area, doffed his hat, and laid it crown down on a table next to his chair. The only other patient was a girl who looked to be about ten years old, sitting across the room with her mother. The girl looked away when Latigo smiled at her. He pawed through the outdated magazines on the table, then picked one up at random and riffled through the pages. From time to time, he would sneak a peek at the girl, and, like the first time, she would look away. Then, she held his gaze. He smiled. He winked.

She swallowed hard and said, "Are you a cowboy?"

"Why would you think that?"

The girl pointed at the hat on the table and the boots on his feet.

"Well, young lady, I guess you've got me. I reckon I am a cowboy, for a fact."

She waited, then said, "Where's your horse?"

Latigo smiled. "Y'know, people ask me that all the time. What I wonder is, why don't anybody ever ask me, 'Where's your cow?' "

The girl giggled.

Later, Latigo drove home, his face tingling in places and numb in others from the anesthetic. He checked in with Elaine, alone in the house as John was working away on location. Finding everything as expected, he changed into work clothes—older versions of what he was wearing—and left for Slim Jones's place. Harley's trailer stood in the line of other towed outfits along the lane, parked there since his arrival with Nugget. He had been working for Slim around the place, handling chores and working with the horses. Harley bunked with Latigo, and the Bensons insisted he occupy a chair at their table for meals. He seemed content, for the time being, to enjoy Southern California's fine weather. Compared to home, he said, you could hardly believe it was winter.

Not long after his arrival, they all sat together at supper. As Elaine kept the boys' plates full, John asked them about their plans for the weekend.

"Well, there's a little rodeo up north of here in some town called Springville," Harley said. "We was figurin' on enterin' up and maybe win us some money off these California cowboys."

John's brow furrowed and he looked at Latigo. "You too, Latigo?"

Latigo nodded. "Yeah. Thought I might as well. Ain't nothin' I got on that won't wait."

John shook his head. "Son, you better read that contract you got with T.C. McGill."

Latigo sat upright. "What do you mean?"

"Well, there's a clause in there—standard in most contracts for big productions—forbidding you to participate in any activity unrelated to the production that could conceivably involve danger, hazard, menace, peril, threat, or risk, where injury, trauma, impairment, misery, mutilation, disfigurement, or death may result. Those may not be the exact words the lawyers put in those contracts, but close enough."

"You mean all that fancy talk means I can't rodeo?"

Benson shook his head. "Not until the movie is in the can."

Latigo looked at Harley and shrugged. Harley looked at Benson, who shrugged. Harley shrugged. "Well, so much for rodeoin'." He smiled. "I reckon Latigo would've got bucked off on his head anyway—he's gone soft in all this good weather, and all that idlin' around at them movie studios."

Latigo picked up a dinner roll and made as if to throw it at Harley. Harley held up both hands in defense. "Now, Orval, you put down that bread roll. What would your momma say to see you misbehavin' so? Mind your manners, or I'll tell her how you repaid Missus Benson's hospitality with rude behavior. Show a little couth!"

And so the rodeo weekend was spent, as was most every other day since, at Slim Jones's ranch, with Latigo working with Nugget—or, as the horse was to be known thanks to McGill's screenwriters, *El Fuego*, which Latigo was told was Spanish for flame, or fire. He had to admit the name had a certain ring to it, and suited the stallion.

The horse was coming along well in the training. He learned to shake his head and snort, raise his head and nicker, and stand and bugle on cue, and to come running at Latigo's beck and call. Latigo worked him on the long track, vaulting in and out of the saddle at a run, hanging from the sides of the saddle in concealment, and, just for the fun of it, standing in the saddle as Nugget walked, loped, and galloped. For good measure, he accustomed the horse to his repertoire of rope tricks, and even ran a few calves and steers through the chute in Slim's arena to school Nugget in the fine arts of handling stock at the end of the rope.

And Latigo trained the mighty El Fuego to stand for the crupper mount, which the cowboy considered absurd, and was sure the horse found demeaning. Rearing up and pawing the air, likewise ridiculous, was also now in the horse's bag of tricks. One thing McGill instructed Latigo not to teach the horse to do was fall—too dangerous, he said. They could not risk injury to a horse destined for stardom.

El Fuego also looked more and more like the fire whose name he carried. His shaggy winter coat fell to repeated sessions with currycomb and brush, and his hide grew lustrous and shiny on a diet of sweet hay of a good grass and alfalfa mix, supplemented with a regular ration of rolled oats. His deep, golden color fairly glowed, and the flaxen hair in his mane and tail grew long and silky, rippling and shimmering in the slightest breeze.

Slim Jones, whose experience with horseflesh was both long and wide, admired the stallion. "Say, Latigo, what would it take to take that sorry excuse for a horse off your hands?"

"Oh, I don't know, Slim. He might be too much horse for the likes of you."

"I wouldn't get on him, myself. A man's got his pride, you know. But I believe I could shift him to some hobby rancher who don't know no better. They like horses like this one—they think they look good standin' in the pasture. And I'll admit, he is a purty horse. Thing is, looks ain't everything. That horse might as well be hollow, for all the smarts and sand he's got in him."

Latigo laughed. "Well, if you want to buy him, Slim, you're goin' to have to name a price."

"Now, c'mon, Latigo—what'll it take? I can't buy him and sell him both, you know."

Latigo shook his head. "I don't know, Slim. How much you got in your pocket right now?"

Slim smiled. "I ain't fallin' for that, boy. You got to remember, I been doin' this a long time. You can't get me to tip my hand with a tired old trick like that."

"I don't know what to tell you. I ain't got the experience tradin' horses that you do, for sure. So I got to be extra careful you don't take advantage of me."

"Oh, son! Ol' Slim wouldn't never do that!"

"You're probably right. But if you don't mind, I think I'll call home first and see what Momma says. I ain't sure, but I think she warned me about men like you."

Slim laughed and clapped Latigo on the back. They had had essentially the same conversation before, and they both expected they would have similar ones in the days to come. But Latigo was convinced of one thing—Nugget, El Fuego, was not for sale.

Evenings at home often found the cowboys sitting in the shade of the Benson's front porch. They sat for long periods without speaking, sipping the iced tea Elaine kept in their glasses, comfortable in one another's company. Or, when the mood struck, they told what rodeo cowboys called "re-ride stories," remembrances and reminders of their— and others'—exploits in in the arena. Sometimes it was boasting about a particularly successful rough-stock ride or timed-event run. But, more often than not, the stories involved wrecks and crashes and other misfortunes that did not seem funny at the time, but now made fodder for laughs.

"Speakin' of wrecks, whatever become of Danny Wickham?" Latigo wondered one evening.

"Oh, he healed up all right—he can't ride broncs no more, and he creaks and rattles like an empty hay wagon, but he gets around without too much trouble. He's been up there in Jackson Hole workin' for ol' Junior Blevins and his tourist rodeo."

Latigo mused for a time. "Junior Blevins, huh? I think about him now and then. Sounds like he got that rodeo goin' then. You ever go up there?"

"Yeah. Once. It's quite the deal. Blevins, he rides around town in that big convertible car of his all day. He's got it hung with banners and wired for sound, and he drives around and around the town square and up and down the streets playin' music and talkin' on his microphone all about the rodeo, invitin' folks to come out and see real cowboys."

Latigo laughed. "So what's Danny doin' for him?"

"He mostly sees to things out to the arena. Puts boys on horses that people bring in to see if they'll buck enough to put in the string. Sees to the feedin' of the animals, and pennin' before the rodeo. Then he acts as arena director and chute boss and what-all durin' the show, while Blevins sits up in the crow's nest and announces the rodeo. I swear, I don't know how the man can talk as much as he does. He uses up more words in a minute than what regular folks use all day."

"You win any money up there?"

"Not to speak of. I only hung around about a week or so. Won a little in the bareback and bull ridin' and some in the bulldoggin', but there wasn't enough in entry fees to amount to much of a purse. It was mostly just local boys wantin' to be rodeo cowboys, and a few real hands who'd pass through once in a while on their way to a rodeo somewhere else. But, like I said, most of 'em was just local boys startin' out. They'd be lookin' for a place to land soon as the chute gate opened, or tryin' to rope off horses that wasn't no better trained than they was. I couldn't find no heeler good enough to do any good in the team ropin'."

Latigo smiled. "Missed me, then, did you?"

"Oh, hell no! Bad as them heelers was, they were a damn sight better'n you!"

"Why'd you leave? As I recall, Junior Blevins offered to keep us on full time."

"He'd make good on his claim, all right. He paid me for the days I was there. I helped Danny out around the place. Got on a few range bulls ranchers would haul in to see if they'd buck enough that Blevins would buy them. Ran fresh calves and steers through the chute like you do to get 'em used to it. That kind of thing. But, a man would have to be able to survive on cold-water sandwiches if he was to live on the wages ol' Junior paid."

"Cold-water sandwiches?"

"You know—two slices of bread and a glass of water. Not enough nourishment in it for a hungry boy like me. So, I moved along. Besides, it was comin' on fall and they'd be shuttin' down the place for winter pretty quick, anyhow."

One morning Latigo got a call to come to the studio for a wardrobe fitting. His previous experience with the wardrobe department on other productions amounted to some assistant handing him a hat, shirt, and bandana, and making sure the colors were the same as he had worn in related scenes filmed earlier. Even on the Sturges film, the clothing was typical run-of-the-mill cowboy clothes. So, he did not know what to expect at the fitting—but it was not what he found.

The costume designer and seamstresses rolled out a whole rack of shirts. Latigo swallowed hard when he saw the yokes and shoulders and cuffs in contrasting colors, brightly colored piping on the seams, arrow-pointed slash pockets, even fringe on the front and back yokes of some shirts, and the sleeves of others.

"Holy cow! This is what I'm supposed to wear? I ain't never seen or heard of no cowboys wearin' anything like this. Why, I'll look like one of them Nashville opry singers! Has Mister McGill seen this stuff?"

The costume designer sniffed and said that he had, and, in fact, had approved every design and requested further embellishment to some.

The neck scarves were fairly ordinary, but of a higher quality fabric than Latigo was accustomed to. The pants were mostly light in color—unlike the usual shades that tended to conceal dirt and grime rather than accent it, as these would.

The wardrobe people sent him behind a screen to try on a shirt and a pair of trousers to check them for fit, telling him to leave his boots behind. He came out glad to be in sock feet, as he would have been unable to stretch the tight legs of the pants over the tops of his boots. It turned out that would not be a problem.

Feeling uncomfortable and embarrassed in the gaudy outfit when he came out from behind the screen, he found a pair of boots standing on the floor. Almost reaching his knees, the shafts of the boots were inlaid with multiple colors of brightly dyed leather, in floral designs featuring winding stems and leaves and big blossoms. Even the toes were adorned with contrasting caps inlaid with even more contrasting colors. When he sat down to put them on, pulling up his pants legs, the wardrobe designer waved him off, saying the pants were to be worn tucked into the boots.

Latigo looked at the man, wide-eyed. "Mister, I been wearin' boots my whole life, and I ain't never stuffed the cuffs of my britches into 'em. Can't say I know many that do, and there ain't none of them real cowboys."

With his head on a tilt and his eyes aimed down the bridge of his nose, the designer informed Latigo that none of that mattered. He was no longer a real cowboy, but a movie star, and this was how movie stars of the cowboy kind dressed.

He was also handed a pair of gloves, the high leather cuffs of which were stitched with floral designs similar to those on the boots. He was shown several pair, with various colors of stitching to coordinate with the variety of shirts.

Then came the hat. White. The edge of the wide, wide, brim was whip-stitched with leather cord, with a wide ribbon around the crown in the same color. He was informed there would be several identical hats, save the color of trim, again to coordinate with the colors of his shirts. Beyond that—or above that—the crown of the hat was taller than normal, almost as high as a sombrero, with a Montana crease.

Latigo could hardly wait to get out of there. But leaving did not provide the relief he hoped for. For, as he left, he was handed a package containing a shirt and trousers, the hat, and the boots, and told by Robert—who had been hanging about on the fringes of the activity—to show up at a photographer's studio two days hence for publicity photos.

Chapter Twenty-Eight

The photo shoot occupied the better part of a day. The photographer—a fussy little man in a berét—sat in a canvas chair fluttering his fingers and waving his hands as his assistants bustled around the studio shifting lights, hanging backdrops, moving props, and shuffling film holders. From time to time, the photographer would rise from his perch to duck under the black hood on the camera and stare at the image on the ground glass as he fiddled with the bellows and fidgeted with the focus.

He instructed Latigo, his face caked with makeup, to pose with a foot propped on a fake boulder. To sit on a plaster log. To stand, arms akimbo, and show his remodeled smile. To look menacing. To draw his twin silver six-shooters and threaten the camera. To gaze into the distance. To stand with lariat in hand, both coiled and with a loop. And, as if such a thing were possible, to look "normal" for a series of what the photographer called "head shots," with both serious and smiling expressions.

Latigo left the studio and thought nothing more about it until a week or so later when Benson, back at home after the film he had worked on wrapped, tossed a copy of one of the trade papers from the film industry on the kitchen table. He had folded it open to a particular page, and when it landed in front of Latigo, he looked down to see his own face staring back at him. He did not move.

Harley reached over and slid the newspaper away and picked it up. He smiled, then laughed, as his face caught up with what he was seeing. "Well, would you look at that! Sorry rodeo hand Orval 'Latigo' Brown has got famous on us!"

Latigo snatched the paper back, and read the brief text accompanying the photo. He dropped the paper, his face turning from wan to flushed.

Harley took the paper back, cleared his throat ceremoniously, and read. "Word on the street has it that T.C. McGill has crowned the next king of the cowboys. According to sources, budding actor Latigo Brown has been cast to star in McGill's forthcoming Western extravaganza, opposite Scandinavian enchantress Annika Eriksson. Studio officials refused to confirm the rumors." Harley laughed again. Latigo's blush deepened.

"What do you think, Latigo?"

"I don't know what to think, Mister Benson. It's kind of embarrassing. And to be seen in them clothes...."

Benson smiled. "I wouldn't worry, son. I've had my picture taken in a lot worse outfits. Hell, one time I had to wear a powdered wig and knee britches for a Revolutionary War picture. Then there was the time I wore nothing but a loincloth when I was stunt double for a jungle savage. I even appeared wrapped in a sheet one time, wearing a little crown of olive branches, to play a Roman politician." He shrugged. "It's all just play-acting."

Latigo thought on that for a time. Then, "I see what you're sayin'. Thing is, you was just playin' a part. That there's supposed to be *me*— Latigo Brown—not some character in a movie."

"I suppose you've got a point. Still, there are worse things than being a famous cowboy star. I know most all of them, and they don't seem to mind it much. Oh, they might have been a bit bothered by it all at first, but they got used to it. Some of them even like it. And I don't suppose any of them object to the money."

Harley retrieved the newspaper. "If you don't mind, Mister Benson, I'll keep this here newspaper. Ol' Latigo might not think much of it, but I know his little sister Penny'll be tickled pink to see it. I can't wait to send it to her."

The weeks ahead brought more notice in the trade papers of McGill's forthcoming epic, with many of the articles featuring Latigo and Annika Eriksson. McGill's words spoken in the office—which had not meant much at the time—echoed in Latigo's mind. He had instructed his man Robert to have the publicity department start planting stories like these. Then, another of McGill's brainstorms started appearing in the gossip columns, not only in the trade papers, but in the daily newspapers as well—tidbits that hinted, intimated, implied a romantic relationship between Annika and Latigo. This, despite the fact that the pair had not laid eyes on one another since their appearance together in the barn dance scene all those months ago.

One day a package arrived for Latigo. Enclosed was a fancy tuxedo with a Western cut. The attached message informed him of the pending arrival of a car early the next evening. Dressed in the formal attire, he was to accompany the car and driver to the residence of Annika Eriksson. He was to call for her at the door and escort her to the car, which would deliver the couple to a banquet at a hotel ballroom in Beverly Hills.

The car arrived as scheduled. However, it was not what Latigo expected. The stretch limousine was of a dimension to put Junior Blevins's oversized car to shame. Its polished black surface mirrored its surroundings, and the chrome adornments sparkled bright enough to cause him to squint. The driver, dressed in an odd uniform and cap, stood beside the open back door of the car, several steps to the rear of the front door. Latigo and the driver nodded greetings to one another, then the cowboy stepped through the open door into the passenger compartment.

Stretched across the full width of the compartment was a bench seat, padded and plush. Latigo sat in the center and extended his legs, the soles of his boots falling far, far short of the seatback ahead. He imagined he could sleep comfortably stretched across the seat, or even on the soft carpeted floor. He laid his hat crown down on the seat beside him. Reaching out in both directions, he propped his hands atop the seatback and pillowed his head against it. Not hearing, and barely feeling the hum of the engine or surface of the road, Latigo dozed off during the journey to Anna Eriksson's home. The driver braked the car to an imperceptible stop. Latigo started when the driver opened the door.

He stepped out of the limousine, positioned his hat, then tugged at the hem of his jacket and smoothed the lapels. Only then did he look around. The car was parked on the curve of a horseshoe-shaped driveway, its interior arc bordered by flower gardens, manicured lawns stretching away from its outer edge. The top of the drive abutted a staircase with the same curve, the steps low and wide, leading to a broad, deep porch. A row of fluted columns defined the perimeter of the porch, a wider gap in the row and a carpet runner marked the walkway to the front doors.

Latigo had to crane his neck to see the tops of the twin doors, and their width would not be out of place in a hay barn. A velvet rope hung at the seam between the doors. He touched it, drew back, then grasped it and gave a gentle pull. From inside, he heard the faint sound of a gong. Within seconds, one of the doors swept open without a sound, revealing a man attired formally, wearing a dark suit, white shirt, and bow tie.

The man bowed slightly. "May I help you, sir?"

"Yessir. I'm here to call for Miss Eriksson, if you please."

With a half bow, he swept the door open farther. There, a few paces back into the room, stood Annika Eriksson. Her feet were not visible beneath the long hem of her black dress, which swept upward to her waist. From there, it flared out again to hug her torso, but ended there, her shoulders and back bare. Had Latigo not been able to see most of what kept the dress from sliding down, it would have been a mystery.

Latigo took off his hat and swallowed hard. "Miss Eriksson. I—I'm—it's good to see you again."

She smiled, and the cowboy's knees felt it. "I could say the same, Latigo Brown." She let the words sink in, admiring the flush on the handsome cowboy's face. "I see you did not bring your—what do you say? Lasso rope?"

Latigo shuffled his feet, but had no response.

Annika's smile somehow became more brilliant. "It is okay. I will come willingly. There is no need to capture me."

Latigo somehow mustered the presence of mind to crook his elbow. Annika placed a gloved hand onto his forearm and he led her toward the limousine, where the driver stood at attention beside the open back door. Latigo wondered where the photographers with their flashing bulbs and the reporters with their shouted questions had come from, having noticed no evidence of them when he arrived. The couple did their best to ignore them.

At the car, Annika released her hold on his arm, he embraced her elbow and guided her into the limousine, then followed her through the door. She slid across the seat, but stopped short of the center. Latigo sat beside her, gripping the armrest on the door when it closed.

He did not sleep on the trip to the banquet. Neither did he offer much in the way of conversation, his mind muddled and voice strangled. Only his eyes functioned properly, riveted to Annika's face, watching her lips as she attempted to draw him out, noting the lustrous locks of honey-colored hair arranged so perfectly on her head, then gazing into the sky-blue depths of her eyes. He looked away only when he feared his look too penetrating. But, unable to look elsewhere for any length of time, his gaze soon returned to the beauty beside him. They arrived at the hotel, and ran a gantlet of photographers and reporters to reach the entrance.

They were halfway through the meal before Latigo regained enough composure to speak coherently to Annika. "What do you think of this movie Mister McGill is making?"

Annika shrugged her bare shoulders. "I do not know. I am told that for much of it, we shall be on location in the desert. I do not like to be away from home. 'Roughing it,' as you call it here in America, is not in my nature. Sunshine is not kind to my skin. I detest the buzzing around and biting of insects. And there will be horses, which I fear."

Latigo smiled. "Oh, there ain't nothin' to fear from a horse. If you mind yourself, naturally. Heck, I been horseback since I was a baby— my dad would take me ridin' long before I could walk. First, I rode in front of him in the saddle, but it wasn't long 'fore he put me on the back of a gentle ol' horse by myself. I been ridin' 'em ever since."

Annika smiled, but Latigo saw little sincerity in it. Still, she forged ahead.

"I am told you ride the rodeo?" She pronounced it *ro-day-o*. "Bucking broncos? I am afraid I know nothing of the rodeo. In Sweden, there is no rodeo."

"Oh, it's just a way for cowboys to get together for braggin' rights on who's the best riders and ropers and such. It's all kinds of fun. I should take to see one some time."

"But is it not dangerous?"

"A feller can get hurt all right. But it ain't no more dangerous than drivin' around in Los Angeles. Drivers here is a whole crazier than any bronc or bull I ever seen."

Annika shivered. "Still, horses are so…so…big!"

Latigo smiled and went on with his meal. After a few bites he asked Annika what she thought of what the newspapers were saying about them.

She waved the notion away with a fork on which three long, skinny, string beans were impaled. "It is nothing. I have been romantically linked in the gossip columns with every actor I have appeared with, and half the other men in Hollywood besides. It is all publicity. I pay it no mind." She nibbled at the green beans with a teasing smile. "Still, one never knows."

Latigo blushed. Annika laid her fork on her plate, folded her gloved hands in her lap, bowed her head slightly and looked at Latigo through the veil of her eyelashes. "You are, after all, a handsome man, Latigo Brown."

His blush reddened, and he inserted an index finger into his shirt collar and tugged.

She looked directly at him and smiled. "You have a lovely smile."

The cowboy squirmed. "Ah, that ain't nothin'. Mister McGill, he had that done. I got enough porcelain in my mouth to line a bathtub."

Annika clapped her hands together and giggled, drawing notice from diners at other tables.

They left the banquet early, neither of them interested in the ceremonial portion of the event, or even knowing its purpose. The ride back to Annika's mansion differed from the drive to the banquet. On the return trip, Latigo was able to hold up his end of the conversation. But his eyes were drawn to his companion as much as ever, and he made no attempt to avert his gaze.

He held her hand as he escorted her to her door. She turned toward him and grasped his other hand. His eyes widened when she leaned in and kissed him lightly on the cheek. She had no sooner drawn back than the big door swished at the hand of the butler.

Annika smiled, squeezed his hands, then walked through the doorway.

On the way back to Benson's house, Latigo tried to talk himself out of his attraction to the young woman. He realized he was hopelessly smitten. But he also knew that Annika Eriksson was way out of his league. No one in his right mind would even consider pairing up a thoroughbred filly with a scruffy, half wild mustang fresh-caught off the range.

Chapter Twenty-Nine

Latigo Brown sat horseback in the center of a dirt street in an Old West town. He looked around at the buildings, lined with wooden sidewalks, hitchrails, and the occasional watering trough. None were what they seemed. Some of the structures were built from wood, others looked to be brick or cut stone, but were, in fact, lath and plaster. Some were facades fronting emptiness, others hollow shells. The saloon was finished inside, as was the hotel lobby, the main floor of the bank, the front part of a general store, and the livery stable. While he had never worked on the backlot of this particular studio before, it all seemed strangely familiar.

Shooting was to commence today—finally—on T.C. McGill's movie. Latigo had yet to see a script. Apparently, it was still being rewritten under McGill's direction. Only he had a vision of the full story. The actors would, for the time being, see pages only for scenes they would play that day or the next. So, for reasons he did not know much about, Latigo was mounted on Nugget—El Fuego—in the middle of the street, lariat in hand, waiting to perform some rope tricks.

The scene would be much like the barn dance scene from his first encounter with Annika Eriksson, except outdoors, horseback, and without musical accompaniment. From what McGill told him, his character—Latigo Brown—was smitten with Miss Elizabeth— "Libby"—Wainwright, daughter of the powerful judge, Montgomery Wainwright. Libby was shopping in the mercantile, and would step out carrying a few packages wrapped in brown paper and tied with string. When she emerged, Latigo was to commence his fancy roping display to impress the young lady, the scene ending with Libby wrapped in a loop, and his inviting her to go riding with him that evening.

McGill gave Latigo no other direction, trusting him to devise his own sequence of rope tricks and to remember his few lines. The cowboy saw nothing untoward; the only possible complication being that Libby would be standing on the board sidewalk under a porch roof. But he saw no reason he could not thread his catch loop into the space under the roof and between the porch posts.

Latigo waited while the crew fiddled with the arrangement of lighting fixtures, the set dressers added their finishing touches to the store windows and the porch, the assistant director saw to the placement and performances of the extras acting as bystanders going about their business in the town until becoming spectators, and the camera crews tinkered with lenses and magazines and mounts. Latigo had already learned that McGill captured most every scene with two cameras, each focused on the action from a different angle.

Through it all, Nugget stood quiet beneath Latigo, alert and curious as to what went on around him, but displaying no nerves or anxiety in the strange environment. The saddle he carried was considerably heavier than what he was used to. Provided by the prop department, it was mounted with polished silver adornments on every possible surface, from the top of the horn to the roll of the cantle, on the corners and borders of the skirts and jockeys, and with saddle strings emerging from glittering conchos, all contrasting brightly with the gleaming black leather. The breast collar and bridle likewise carried their share of silver ornaments.

"Are you ready, Latigo?"

"Yes, sir, Mister McGill." Robert had informed Latigo to *always* address the director as *Mister*. There was to be no familiarity on the set, and there would be no speaking to McGill unless spoken to. If there were questions, he was to direct them to the assistant director, to Robert, or, as a last resort, to McGill's production assistant. McGill's authority was absolute, and his directions were never to be questioned. The same held true, Latigo was assured, for the entire cast and crew. The cowboy wondered how long he would be able to hold his tongue, should there arise a situation he did not agree with.

"Do you wish a rehearsal?"

"No, Mister McGill. I believe I can pull it off."

After the usual preliminaries to get the sound equipment and cameras rolling, the scene marked, and the background players in motion, McGill called "action" through his megaphone.

Latigo watched the door of the general store through hopeful eyes, and when it opened and Annika—Libby—walked through, he urged Nugget—El Fuego—forward a few steps, then turned him broadside to the door.

As he turned, Latigo kicked free of the stirrups, pulled up a knee, propped it on the seat of the saddle, and lifted himself to stand on the seat. The instant he stood upright, he flipped out a butterfly loop and started working it back and forth, feeding more of the length of the rope into it. As it grew, he stood up a vertical loop that almost touched the ground, then lifted it overhead and stood it up to spin on the opposite side.

While his attention was fixed on the whirling rope, from the corner of his eye, Latigo caught a glimpse of Libby standing at the edge of the porch, packages cradled at her breast, watching the display through wide eyes, lips open to match, framing a faint smile.

Latigo again hoisted the wide loop, raised it overhead, and lowered it to spin around himself and Nugget in a trick called a "wedding ring." He spread his feet and dropped into the saddle, all the while keeping the loop on the go. Once settled, he signaled Nugget to move, and the horse, as if his tail were nailed to ground, spun in a tight circle. Latigo signaled him to slow and stop, facing Libby.

Hoisting the loop overhead, Latigo spun it vertically alongside as he drew it into a tighter, smaller loop, then again started the figure-eight-style spin of the butterfly loop. Once established, he let the twirling rope spin away to sneak under the porch roof and drop over Libby's head and shoulders. He pulled in the slack in time for the loop to snug up around Libby's waist. Latigo urged Nugget forward, coiling the rope as they went, and stopped with the horse's head inches from Libby's face. She drew back, but only a bit, as Annika tried to control her fear of horses in order for the scene to work.

"Afternoon, Miss," Latigo said with a tip of his hat and a grin that showed off his smile. "I wonder if you would care to go ridin' with me this evenin'?"

"Why, Mister Brown! It appears you have me in your clutches already. You do not give a girl much opportunity to refuse."

Latigo smiled at her for a long moment. "It's up to you, Miss. I wouldn't want to pressure you none."

Libby cast off her feigned annoyance and smiled. "I should be delighted to accompany you." The smile disappeared. "I shall have to ask permission from the judge, of course."

Latigo smiled again. "Oh, there's no need to worry yourself over that. I stopped by the courthouse already. Judge Wainwright, he says it's fine with him, so long as I have you back home 'fore dark."

"Why, Mister Brown! I do declare—you are such a gentleman! My father is not so forthcoming with all my callers."

After another long moment of locked eyes and lingering looks, Latigo informed Libby he would be by after supper, with a gentle horse for her to ride.

"Cut!" came McGill's voice through the megaphone.

He said nothing to the actors, instead huddling with the director of photography and camera operators about repositioning the cameras for

232

closeups and cutaways of the conversation between the principal actors. Latigo sat horseback, waiting. Annika signaled one of the grips, who hustled onto the porch carrying a chair. She sat, and like Latigo, waited. She fanned herself with a folding fan kept concealed somewhere on her person or among her packages.

With the trick roping part of the scene declared good, the actors played out their lines twice more for the cameras. McGill called the scene a wrap, and the crew went about moving gear and equipment for the next scene, which did not involve Latigo. He led Nugget off the street and through an alley between buildings to the staging area behind. Harley walked with him. He had come along this morning to get a first-hand look at the movie business, and to see his friend in action.

"Is it always thataway," Harley said, "waitin' around and waitin' around, then doin' somethin' for a minute, then waitin' around some more?"

"Pretty much. Kind of like waitin' around till the bull ridin' for a re-ride for a saddle bronc that run off. The hard part is stayin' ready, and not fallin' asleep."

Harley chuckled. "Well, I guess it all pays the same—waitin' around, or doin' what passes for work."

Latigo led Nugget to a pen set up for the horse, shaded by a canvas fly, and with a water trough fashioned from a cut-down oil drum, the other half of which served as a hay manger. After pulling the saddle, Latigo took a currycomb and brush to the sweaty patch where the saddle had ridden on the stallion's back, replaced the bridle with a halter, and shut the horse inside the pen. He fetched two bottles of soda pop from a tub of ice and handed one to Harley and they sat down on chairs under a shade next to a long trailer divided into dressing rooms for the actors.

Harley took a long sip from his drink, then waved the bottle in the direction of the tub it came from, which sat next to a long table covered with fruit, sweet rolls, doughnuts, wrapped candy bars, and all manner of snack food. "What is all that?"

"Oh, that's for the crew—for anybody on the set, really. They call it 'craft service' for some reason. Don't know why. Whenever they ain't workin', the crew guys come around and stuff a bunch of groceries down their throats." He grinned. "If ever you're around when them grips come, you best take cover. They'll swarm that table like a horde of locusts. Them big ol' boys work pretty hard when they're workin', and they eat pretty hard when they're eatin'."

The cowboys sat without talking, sipping their drinks and enjoying the shade. After a while, Harley swallowed off the last of his bottle and set it on the ground beside his chair.

"Y'know, Latigo, I'm thinkin' of headin' on back home."

Latigo did not answer.

"Spring's comin' on up there, and it won't be long till they start puttin' on some rodeos. I ain't been on a bull for so long I fear my butt's gone soft. Besides, there's a girl I been wantin' to see."

Latigo turned and looked at Harley and smiled. "You think she'd want to see you?"

"She might. I been gettin' a letter from her now and then."

Sitting upright, Latigo leaned forward in his chair to get a better look at his friend's face. "No shit? A girl, writin' to you? What's she say in those letters?"

"Oh, I don't know. Mostly just wonderin' why I don't write her back more often."

"Who is this girl? Do I know her?"

"Nah. I never met her till you'd already run off to come down here to Hollywood."

Latigo sat back in his chair and shook his head. "Poor kid. She likely don't know what she's gettin' into. She must be pretty hard-lookin', this girl."

Harley walked over to the craft services table and came back with a doughnut and another bottle of soda pop. He sat down, took a third of the doughnut in one bite, then washed it down with a long draught from the soft drink. He shook his head. "Nope. She's a right pretty girl, if you must know. Oh, she ain't no Annika Eriksson, but she's awful easy on the eyes."

After a long moment of thought, Latigo said, "You want to be careful, Harley. There's many a good hand bit the dust on account of a woman. You'll end up sellin' your saddle and takin' a town job."

"Nah. Her daddy's got big ranch. Kind of a haywire outfit, but with a little work, a fella could make it a right nice spread." Harley did away with another chunk of the doughnut and lowered the level in the pop bottle. "Best of all, she ain't got no brothers or sisters—only child."

They sat in silence for a time, Latigo sipping at his drink and Harley finishing off his food and drink.

"You thinkin' of gettin' hitched, Harley?"

He shrugged.

"Would you be marryin' this girl, or marryin' the ranch?"

"Don't know. Most likely both, I guess."

"Well, son, you had best be sure about her. You know as well as I do that keepin' a ranch goin' is a hell of a lot of work. If the two of you don't get along, you'll be pilin' a heap of misery on top of all that work."

Again, the silence stretched.

"How come you ain't never said anything to me about this?"

Harley shrugged. "I don't know. Guess I was just tryin' to figure it out for my ownself. Besides, you ask too many damn questions." Harley reached out and landed a light punch on Latigo's shoulder.

Latigo took off his movie hat and swatted Harley. He cussed himself and drew it back, holding it out front with both hands, studying the crown and brim for dents.

*****

Over the next few weeks, Latigo showed up at the Old West town on the studio backlot, or on a sound stage for scenes on interior sets. Unlike the Sturges film, where his character spent his time breaking the law then avoiding law officers and bounty hunters, "Latigo Brown" was the epitome of the "good guys," typified by his big white hat and its colored stitching and crown ribbon. He stopped in to see the judge from time to time, as well as the local marshal and county sheriff, to learn what scofflaws needed dealing with. As far as Latigo knew, he dealt with the lawbreakers absent any office or official capacity. He was just a good guy doing good.

McGill watched carefully as Latigo continued to perform his own stunts, fearing his leading man might get hurt. But no misadventure occurred, and McGill, like Sturges, enjoyed the freedom of shooting the scenes with the actor, rather than having to shoot around a stunt double. Still, when it came to stunts, McGill proved more demanding than any other director in Latigo's experience. He expected the stunt performers to throw harder punches in fistfights, fall farther from windows, balconies, and rooftops, bear the brunt of more blows from chairs, clubs, and bottles, fall harder from bucking horses, drag farther from stirrups, and roll longer when tossed off a racing wagon.

Latigo went about his business as expected, often wondering why he was doing what he was doing, never seeing the big picture, but never questioning McGill. The man was a perfectionist, and did not mind wasting what seemed like miles of film with retake after retake after retake, searching for some subtle difference in a performance, with the actors seldom understanding what was wanted of them. He paced around in his high boots and jodhpurs, his neckties or cravats, his dark glasses and safari helmet, carrying his megaphone. The cast and crew knew the man was near to boiling over when he stopped talking.

Then, after long, uncomfortable minutes when cast and crew stood by wondering when the storm would hit, he would take up the megaphone, aim its bell at the offending party, and, in a loud and often profane tirade, berate their lack of skill, their dearth of talent, even the circumstances of their birth, and tell them to get out of his sight. The result was a mad scramble to rearrange the rest of the day's schedule to shoot around the absence of the offender.

The next day, it was as if nothing untoward had happened, except that McGill refused to speak to the object of his ire. Instructions were conveyed through the assistant director, and McGill never commented on the offender's performance. Latigo somehow escaped the director's wrath, following instructions as best he could, and never questioning the great man. For, as much as McGill ignored or abused those he did not approve of for whatever reason, he pampered those he liked, extending latitude and privileges unavailable to others.

Latigo got along well with everyone, for that matter. He respected the work of the lowliest members of the crew, accepted advice from stuntmen in choreographing stunts, and showed nothing but kindness to his fellow performers. His only failure was in overcoming Annika's dislike and fear of horses. She avoided going near them except as required in a scene, and even then she stayed as far away as possible and hurried away before the director's call of "cut" reached "t." But, like a good trouper, she donned her split skirts, put on a brave face, and mounted up whenever the scene called for it.

Latigo wondered how the delicate girl would deal with the weeks ahead, when the company would pack up and move to the desert, where the bulk of the movie would be shot on location.

Chapter Thirty

Latigo woke up and looked around the dim room, waiting for his mind to realize where he was. A motel in someplace called Moab. In Utah. They had arrived in the night, when he was already asleep in the car, as were the other actors who shared the vehicle.

He sat up in bed and used the palms of his hands to scrub away the sleep that smeared his face. After lifting his hat from the bedpost and putting it on, he found his jeans and pulled them on, then slipped into his shirt, but did not bother with the buttons. Socks and boots went on next. The door stuck to the frame a bit when he turned the knob and pulled, requiring a jerk to pull it free. He checked his pants pocket to make sure the key was there, and stepped outside.

Latigo stopped before taking another step. Spread before him and looming high above was a cliff wall a thousand feet high, the sandstone glowing orange and red in the light of the sun still rising somewhere behind him. "Holy cow!" he said in a voice he thought only he would hear. He flinched at the sound of nearby voice.

"It is something to see, is it not?"

He turned to see Annika Eriksson, sitting in a metal chair beside an open door two doors down from Latigo's room. Wrapped in a robe of shiny fabric with a feathery collar, she cradled a paper cup in her hands, filled, Latigo assumed from the steam rising from it, with coffee.

"It sure is. I never saw none of it when we got in. Too dark."

"The night does get very dark here."

"You been here before?"

Annika shook her head. "Oh, no. But I was unable to sleep well. I walked about. I believe I was the only one stirring in the town. So many stars."

Latigo stepped off the walkway onto the gravel parking area that fronted the row of rooms. He looked one way then the other, then turned in a slow circle, taking in the cliff wall, which seemed to intersect another in one direction, boxing in the valley. In the other direction, the sheer wall led away into the distance. The other side of the narrow valley was skirted by a steep mountain ridge. The abrupt ridge was more broken than the opposing cliffs, and brush clung to footholds here and there among house-size sandstone boulders. Lining the street in both directions were small commercial buildings—two cafés, another motel, a bank, and an assortment of stores, all dark and awaiting the day.

"Where did that coffee come from?"

Annika nodded toward the motel office at the end of the row, with its "No Vacancy" sign glowing in red neon through the window. "The night manager—who I also believe is the day manager—has a hotplate with a percolator. I am afraid the coffee is bitter, and spent a wakeful night as I did."

Latigo smiled. "Well, long as it's hot and wet, I reckon it'll do." He opened the office door to the ringing of harness bells hanging from it on a leather strap. The jingle startled the manager out of a nap—or what passed for a night's sleep. He stood up and placed both hands on the high counter to steady himself. He cleared his throat. "Good morning. What can I do for you?"

Latigo nodded toward the coffeepot sitting on its hotplate on a low cabinet against the wall that looked to serve as a desk as well, cluttered with a stack of ledgers, a file box, loose papers, a pile of towels, an old typewriter, and a telephone. "Could I trouble you for a cup of that coffee there?"

"Sure thing." The motel man poured a stream of the thick, dark liquid into a paper cup with foldout handles on the side and passed it across to the cowboy. "No charge. Courtesy of the establishment for our guests."

Latigo left the office sipping the bitter brew, thinking it not quite worth the price. Annika no longer sat in the chair in front of her room, so he passed it by and took a seat in the matching chair by his own room. He sipped the coffee and watched the shifting light and shadow on the cliffs as the sun rose. Halfway down the cup, he decided he had had enough, and tossed the rest onto the gravel of the parking lot.

Forcing the door past its sticking point, he closed it behind him, reversed the process of getting dressed, and stepped into the bathtub under a showerhead that sprayed water in random directions, and let the water flow off his head and down his body. He tried to remember if he had ever before spent a night alone in a motel room.

On the rodeo circuit Latigo followed, where most of the cowboys led a hand-to-mouth existence, bunking together was the norm. In fact, it was not unusual to stack four or more cowboys in a room, sleeping crosswise on the bed to allow more bodies. If the room was big enough—an eventuality that seldom occurred—they might even shift the mattress to the floor, and fill the box springs with another row of snoring cowboys. All, of course, outside the knowledge of motel management. Standing under the hot stream, Latigo remembered the many mornings he had endured a cold shower and attempted to dry off with a wet towel—the early risers in the room having depleted the supply of hot water and fresh towels.

Dressed again and outside, Latigo milled around with the cast members now waiting in the parking lot, along with a few of the crew members, most of whom were at other lodgings. Some sipped coffee from the paper cups from the office. Given the lack of complaints, Latigo assumed the manager had percolated a fresh pot. The Assistant Director and Robert, each with clipboard in hand, huddled together comparing notes. The "A.D." as he was called, got the attention of the small crowd, informing them that cars and drivers were on the way, and to be ready to leave for the location in five minutes.

"What about breakfast?" came a voice from the crowd.

"At the location," the A.D. said. "Caterers are set up out there, and there'll be a hot breakfast for everyone who wants one. And I'll guarantee the coffee will be a hell of a lot better than this sludge," he said, raising his paper cup high. The announcement was met with cheers from the group.

The loaded cars turned onto the street of the town and headed toward what looked like the dead end Latigo had seen earlier, where cliff walls met just outside the town. But such was not the case—a wide river—the Colorado, Latigo was to learn—flowed out of a narrow gap in the cliffs. The highway crossed the river and turned into a narrow canyon beyond the loop of the river which then disappeared downstream into another defile. But, just before reaching the bridge, the cars turned off onto a smaller road into the river gorge from which the river came. For several upstream miles they hugged the river, hemmed in by thousand-foot-high sheer cliffs that left no room to spare.

After a dozen miles or so, the gorge opened out into a valley, carpeted with green fields and pastures, sagebrush and sandy ridges. The cliffs broke into canyons and gorges, with a pale blue backdrop of mountains with snow-covered peaks in the middle distance.

They arrived at an orderly camp, with tents of various sizes arranged in neat rows. Trucks carrying equipment, and trailers containing dressing rooms and the production offices lined up along a stream bank. A large temporary corral held some two dozen head of horses. A few smaller pens held the mounts ridden by the principal actors, with Nugget enjoying a private enclosure with a canvas fly for shade.

Latigo wondered about the horse herd, a question answered as he sat at breakfast. The A.D. came by with that day's script pages. He told Latigo not to bother reading them, as there were no lines for him in the first setup. The bulk of the day's shooting consisted of a chase, in which cowboy hero Latigo Brown, accompanied by a small posse, pursued a band of horse thieves and their plunder.

Before Latigo finished his breakfast, the horse wranglers on the crew, with help from the stunt riders who were playing horse thieves, turned the horse herd out of the corral and pushed the bunch into and across the river. The move was not without danger, as the current in the river, while not swift, looked to be steady and carry some force. The horses kept their footing on the riverbed for more than two-thirds of the distance across, then were forced to swim. The opposite bank was steep, and required scrambling, clawing hooves to clear the water. Latigo watched the whole thing from his seat at the breakfast tables.

"What do you think, Latigo?"

Latigo turned to see the crew's stunt coordinator standing behind him. "Looks like I'm goin' to get wet." He knew the man, having worked with him at Slim Jones's place. The man was a good hand, with years of experience working with horses and film crews.

The man smiled. " 'Fraid so. Water's a bit higher than what it was when we worked this out last week. Still, it ought not be any trouble unless somethin' goes wrong."

"Ain't that always the way it is?" Latigo said with a smile. Then, with a more serious expression, "Other than havin' his nose in a water trough, Nugget ain't never been in the water."

"Well, I guess we'll find out what kind of a horse he is. I wouldn't worry none if was you—from what I've seen, he's the right kind."

Latigo said he did not doubt the horse would be fine, but expressed concern about the heavy, silver-mounted saddle the prop department had fashioned.

"No need to worry 'bout that. Those boys have painted up a lighter rig for the swim. You'll be all right. McGill's got three cameras set up to shoot this, so we ought to get it in one take—if, like I said, there ain't some kind of wreck."

Latigo made his way to his dressing room in the trailer and put on the fancy cowboy outfit left hanging there by the wardrobe people. He thought it absurd to go chasing around the country after outlaws in such garb. But, as he had been told a thousand times by now, this was the movies.

As he stepped out the door, he watched a motorboat ease up to the riverbank. An odd-looking affair, twin rows of metal oil drums kept it afloat. The deck was flat, enclosed by a waist-high rail. As workers secured the boat with lines tied to stakes driven into the bank, the front of the rail opened like a gate and one of the grips laid down boards topped with sheets of plywood to form a gangplank.

At the corrals, a wrangler curried and brushed Nugget and, when Latigo arrived, was just snugging up the cinches on the painted saddle. Latigo admired the handiwork of the prop people, thinking their work more than enough to fool the cameras, and grateful his horse would not have to ferry the heavy silver saddle across the Colorado River. He led Nugget down to the riverbank, where the stunt coordinator and A.D. waited. A saddle lay at the stunt man's feet. The A.D. studied his clipboard.

"Would you look at this damn boat, Latigo?" the stunt man said. "It's a newfangled outfit they call a pontoon boat. It's usually got rows of seats on it—they use it to give tourists rides on the river."

"What're we goin' to do with it?"

The stunt man smiled. "We're goin' to give you and El Fuego there a ride across the river. Don't want you nor that horse to get your fancy outfits wet 'fore you have to." He picked up his saddle. "If you don't mind, I'll ride along. My horse went over with the herd. Now, let's see if that critter of yours has got sea legs."

Latigo handed the reins to the stunt man. "Hold him for a minute." He walked onto the gang plank and bounced up and down to test its stability, then stepped onto the boat. It was unsteady, and rocked back and forth some, but the deck seemed solid enough. He left the boat and took Nugget's reins, scratched the horse's muzzle then patted his neck, whispering something to him. Then he turned and walked onto the boat, the horse following without complaint. The stunt man and his saddle followed along, the A.D. behind him.

The grip disassembled his gang plank, stowed it on the deck, and jumped aboard—the movement rocking the boat, causing Nugget to arch his neck and perk up his ears, but he calmed at Latigo's word and touch—and closed the gate. The noise of the motor pitched up and the boat reversed slowly into the stream, then turned about and accelerated across the channel. The operator butted the front end against the bank on the far shore, and the grip jumped onto the bank, which was about a foot higher than the deck, with another shallow rise above that. He hitched the lines around the stakes already driven there, and rebuilt his gang-plank.

It took some coaxing from Latigo and a swat on the rump from the stunt man to convince Nugget to make the jump onto the shore, but he lunged forward and cleared the edge. The A.D. came ashore with them.

"Gentlemen," he said to the two cowboys. "Here's how this will work. This boat will anchor a little offshore from where the horses jump into the water. The camera on board will be over-cranked to get the shot in slow motion."

"Hold on a minute!" the stunt man said. "That ain't how we set this up! When them horses come off that jump, they won't be lookin' to dodge no damn boat!"

The A.D. shrugged, and said McGill had decided to change things up. He thought the shot would be more dramatic this way.

"Well, I'll have to shift the jumpin' off place, then."

"No. You won't. Mister McGill wants it this way. Just do it like you set it up."

"That old man don't give a damn who the hell gets hurt or killed, just so he gets his shot!"

Latigo stood back, watching the back and forth.

The stunt man said, "Is he goin' to be on that boat?"

"No, but I will."

"Well, I hope to hell one of them horses lands in your lap." The stunt man turned away, hefted his saddle, and stomped off in the direction of the horse herd, held in a loose bunch by the other stunt riders.

The A.D. watched him walk away. "What do you think, Latigo?"

"Beats me. The man knows what he's doin'. Could be you're invitin' trouble."

After a long moment of looking from the horses to the boat and to the far shore, tapping his pencil against the clipboard as he thought, the A.D. said, "I guess we'll see what happens. But we'll shoot it the way the boss says. It will take a few minutes to get back over and rig the camera. I'll be talking to Mister McGill on the walkie-talkie." He pulled a pistol from the pocket of his jacket. "The stunt men already know this, but this is loaded with blanks. First shot means be ready. Second shot means action. Let's make this work. I don't want to take any more chances than we have to."

When the boat pulled away, Latigo tightened the cinch and swung aboard Nugget. The stunt coordinator had his horse saddled when Latigo reined up El Fuego at the group of stunt riders, all dismounted and standing in a circle. Latigo soon learned from their mumbling that they were not pleased with McGill's change. But they all agreed the added danger was not enough to refuse to do the scene. They mounted up and pushed the horses over the low ridge, atop the crest of which the running horses would first be seen by the cameras, with the horse thieves in front of, among, and behind them, pursued at a short distance by Latigo Brown and his posse of two. Latigo and the stunt coordinator stopped at the top of the rise, from where they could watch the activity below and see when their time drew near.

Chapter Thirty-One

Latigo Brown and the lead stunt man heard the first shot, and turned their horses off the rise and rode toward the horse herd. The stunt man shouted final instructions to the other stunt riders, and they dismounted to tighten their cinches—but not enough to hinder the horses' swimming—and check their rigging, then remounted. Latigo did the same. The cowboys stirred the loose horses, herding them into a tight bunch. After a few nervous minutes, the second shot sounded.

With whoops and hollers, waving arms, and the slap of coiled lariats against chaps, the bandits hazed the horse herd up the hill and pushed them into a run, stirring up a cloud of dust. Latigo gave them a short head start, then told his posse of two to "Come a-ridin'." Nugget reached the top of the low ridge in a hurry, and Latigo had to slow the stallion to avoid overtaking the herd. He gave Nugget his head, and the horse dodged brush and boulders as he made his way down the slope.

Latigo watched the first of the riders and loose horses leap off the bank, sending sheets of water skyward. Some horses balked, but were forced off the edge by the animals behind. One or two swimming animals nudged the anchored pontoon boat as they surged past it on either side. Checking his position, Latigo adjusted his course so that Nugget would reach the riverbank directly in front of, and at a slight angle to, the pontoon boat. He touched the horse's belly with his spurs just as they reached the edge, encouraging Nugget to make a long, airborne leap before hitting water.

When they landed, Latigo slid out of the saddle, grasping the horn and letting Nugget tow him through the stream. They passed within inches of the boat. When he felt the horse's hooves strike the riverbed, Latigo swung his leg over Nugget's back and found his seat and the stirrups as the horse stopped swimming and started running. He set a course directly at a camera on a scaffold on the shore, Nugget's hooves sending up a sparkling spray of water droplets as they churned through the shallower water near the shore. After passing the camera, Latigo glanced back to see his posse, just then reaching the shallow water. He had gained ground on the stolen horses, tasting the dust cloud they raised.

After running a half mile or so across the valley, the lead stunt man signaled a stop, and the other riders turned the herd, slowing it and, finally, tightening the bunch and herding it back at a trot to the temporary pasture and through the gate.

Latigo rode Nugget on a long circle to cool him down. He was surprised to find the horse calm after all the activity. Back at camp, he tied him to a fence rail at his private pen, and pulled off the wet saddle. Other than the sweat stain on his back where the saddle had ridden, Nugget was already dry in the spring heat. The wrangler assigned to his care came with brush and currycomb, but Latigo took the grooming tools and told the young cowboy to go to lunch, as he would see to the horse.

The mess tent was close to empty when Latigo got there. He took a tray and the caterers filled it with food. T.C. McGill, the A.D., Annika Eriksson, and the actor playing her father the judge, sat a table in the far corner of the tent. McGill waved Latigo over.

"I believe we captured some beautiful film this morning," the director said.

Latigo only looked at the director, his mouth busy chewing.

"What did you think?"

Latigo swallowed, and shrugged. "I only saw it from horseback, and that mostly through dust and splashing water."

"Yes, yes. It was glorious."

"Kind of dangerous, don't you think, parkin' that boat right in the middle of it?"

McGill's eyes narrowed. "We got the shot."

"Someone could've got hurt—one of the men. Or a horse."

"Laddie, all that matters is that we got the shot. You will appreciate it when you see it on the screen. A marvelous piece of film." McGill left the table. The A.D. glared at Latigo, then followed his boss out of the tent.

Latigo kept at his lunch in the silence. Then the old actor spoke.

"Young man, you will do well not to question Mister McGill like that. It is not a wise career move."

Latigo shrugged, but did not stop chewing.

"I have worked on many of the man's films. You might say I am a regular. Long ago I learned to do as he says. He does not take kindly to criticism, or even questioning. If you stay on his good side, he will ask you to appear in other films in the future. Otherwise...." The man cocked his head and arched his eyebrows.

"Well, I guess you could say I was lookin' for a job when I got this one," Latigo said. "Only thing is, I wasn't. This movie stuff just kind of came along. If I go back to chasin' cows and ridin' buckin' horses for a livin' I won't feel much loss."

The old actor sniffed and, like the others had done, left the table.

Annika smiled. "You are unlike anyone I have yet encountered in the business."

Latigo smiled back. "I guess that's 'cause I ain't really in the business."

"You do not care to be famous? To be a star?"

"Can't say I see much to recommend it."

"Not even the money?"

The cowboy smiled again. "Well, I can't complain about that. I ain't never been paid so much to do so little in all my life."

Annika stood, and smoothed her dress over her lap. "Well. I must dress for work. We have a scene to shoot later, you and I."

Latigo looked at her with furrowed brow. "Oh? What's that?"

"The scene with the carriage—your conversation with the judge and myself."

"Darn. I guess I better go learn my lines."

He wolfed down the rest of his meal and hurried off to find the lady who kept track of all the scripts. He got the appropriate pages and sat on the step leading into his dressing room in the trailer and pored over the lines. He breathed a big sigh of relief to learn his words were few—most of the talking would be up to the judge. Latigo would ride alongside the judge's carriage as he drove along with Annika, pontificating on the law and justice and truth and right. He decided he could remember his occasional response to the judge's oration, even given the unsettling proximity of Annika Eriksson.

They shot the scene during what the movie people called "golden hour" and "magic hour," just before and after sunset. The light then is soft and warm, and shadows fade and disappear, lending an atmosphere to the scene not available at any other time. In truth, they had about half an hour to capture the scene. But the old actor playing the judge was an experienced professional, and he spoke his lines with perfection, and Annika's and Latigo's brief contributions to the conversation came off without a hitch.

McGill, riding along in the back of the camera truck driving beside the carriage, declared the first take good, then repeated the scene once more to add closeups of the characters.

The next morning, the cars again delivered the actors to the base camp. The day consisted of several setups in various locations to com-

Rod Miller

plete the capture of the horse thieves and recovery of the stolen horses. There were panoramic shots of the chase across the valley, with the spectacular cliffs and spires and rock formations as a backdrop; close-up shots of pounding, churning hooves; flowing manes and tails and flaring nostrils; bandits firing at the pursuers from the backs of running horses, and Latigo and his posse returning fire. The scene culminated with El Fuego surging past the herd and turning the leaders, and Latigo roping the outlaw leading the chase out of the saddle in the process.

Other aspects of the story were recorded in the days to come. Then the company called it a wrap for that location, and moved on to an even more isolated, iconic location for Westerns—Monument Valley.

Interrupting the open expanse of the broad valley were tall buttes, their flat tops and vertical walls skirted by scree shed by the sandstone over centuries. Some buttes stood thin and delicate, others broad and strong, and some formed walls and fences over wide stretches of the sandy desert and its scant vegetation.

Headquartered at a rustic trading post, the company moved from location to location led by Navajo guides—whose reservation encompassed the valley. They shot scene after scene among the towering spires and buttes, never knowing whether they were shooting in Utah or Arizona, the border between the states transecting the desert basin.

The schedule one day called for filming what McGill called his "money shot." The scene would close out the movie, drawing the curtain on the story and providing a splendid backdrop for the chiseled words "THE END" on the screen.

The director spent all day setting up the shot. The camera, positioned on a low, sandy ridge, looked out on a wide expanse of the valley, creating a path through the sandstone spires pointing directly at the sun setting out of an even broader expanse of the sky. The action in the scene was simple—Latigo Brown and Libby Wainwright riding off into the sunset, their figures becoming silhouettes against the flaming orange disc as it dropped out of a salmon-colored sky to disappear beneath the desert horizon.

McGill positioned and repositioned the single camera he would use for the shot, shifting to the right, then the left, moving up the ridge then down, and peering through the viewfinder to evaluate lenses and filters and exposure settings. He pointed out, repeatedly, Latigo's and Annika's path, identifying landmarks to keep them on course. He demanded a costume change for Annika, even though her clothing would not be identifiable in the distance of the shot. He harangued the wrangler to be sure the horse Annika would ride would be lively, yet easily controlled. He asked Latigo's assurance that El Fuego would prance properly, looking and acting as a wonder horse should in his shining moment. Latigo allowed that the horse would be fine, unaccustomed though he was to traveling at anything less than a dead run when cameras were rolling.

When the sun reached the proper point in the sky, McGill declared the preparations finished, and let everyone on the crew know that heads would roll if everything did not go as planned.

The wardrobe people made final adjustments to Annika's clothing, pinning her hat securely atop her well-coiffed hair, causing Latigo to muse about how a woman could be so clean and well-groomed at the time and place the movie was set, particularly given what the girl had gone through, and would yet go through, in reaching the end of the story.

Latigo tightened the tuck on his shirttails, fluffed the bandana around his throat, and cocked his broad-brimmed, high-crowned hat at the proper angle. He selected a pair of gauntleted gloves from the prop table, along with one of the identical gun belts, each with double holsters in which nestled silvered revolvers. He strapped on the pistols, tightened the cinch on his saddle and mounted. A wrangler helped Annika aboard her horse, then led the animal to stand beside Latigo and El Fuego.

McGill rushed over with a last-minute change, asking Annika to ride to the right of Latigo, rather than the left. He once again pointed out the path they were to follow, warning them to stay on course, and sent them on their way.

No one on the crew spoke as McGill watched his stars ride away. When he judged their position suitable, he ordered the camera operator to roll. He watched with a slight smile as the heat waves shimmered, the sky flamed, and the desert glowed in the perfect picture of his creation.

One of the grips heard it first. A faint hum, barely discernable. Others perked up as the sound increased to a growl. Someone pointed. McGill blanched. There in the perfect sky, coming from slightly south of west, flying to somewhere a bit north of east, was an airplane. A passenger airliner, lights on its wingtips and elsewhere blinking and glowing against the darkening sky.

The airplane came on. No one spoke.

McGill stood out of his canvas chair, his face no longer wan, turning a shade that would not be out of place in the sky surrounding the sun. Without a word, he strode to the prop table where lay Latigo's second gun belt, with its twin holstered pistols. He pulled both revolvers from their sheaths. He pulled back the hammers. Taking careful aim, he fired one, then the other, in turn at the airliner until the hammers fell on spent cartridges.

Still, no one spoke. Someone snickered. Jaws clenched, McGill spun around, searching faces to find the offender. The snicker became a chuckle, then a laugh.

"You!" McGill shouted at the stunt coordinator. "Come here!"

The cowboy tried, without much success, to suppress his smile as he approached the director. McGill yelled, long and loud, about the ruined shot, all his careful planning gone for naught, the time and film wasted. He even reverted to the language of his homeland, telling the stuntman to be quiet, to "Haud yer wheesht!" He exclaimed the day was "Tatties o'wer the side," a complete and total disaster. He huffed. He puffed. He steamed and smoked. Then, after his ire ran down, "What, you daft fool, is so funny?"

The stunt coordinator ducked his head, hiding his face behind his hat brim, scratching at the sand with the toe of his boot. He cleared his throat and looked at the director. "Sorry, Mister McGill. It just struck me as funny, is all."

"What, dammit? What is funny?"

The cowboy swallowed hard. "It's you, sir—what you're doin' there—I mean, what you done."

McGill only stared, his eyes aflame.

After a long moment, the stunt man spoke. "Well, you see, sir, it's like this—that there airplane is maybe ten thousand feet up in the sky. You couldn't possibly hit it with them pistols. Besides, them guns is shootin' blanks."

Off in the desert, Latigo and Annika rode on. They wondered about the airplane. They wondered at the sound of gunfire. Then, having lost all concern for what McGill might say or do, Latigo reined up Nugget. With a hand on the cantle, he turned in the saddle to look back at the crew on the ridge, barely visible in the deepening dusk. Annika stopped also. Latigo looked at her and shrugged.

"I reckon we might just as well head on back."

They turned the horses around and rode, no longer into the sunset, but away from it.

Chapter Thirty-Two

It took days for T.C. McGill to recover from the spoiled shot. He cussed the airlines, he cussed airplanes, he cussed manned flight all the way back to and including the Wright brothers. He did not speak to the stunt coordinator for the remainder of the shoot, relaying instructions through the A.D. Even Latigo and Annika got the cold shoulder, never mind the fact that their participation in the scene had nothing to do with its ruin—they were guilty by association in the director's eyes.

Still, shooting continued. McGill cooked up another scene with the judge and Libby conversing in a moving shot. He framed them seated on a buckboard, from behind, to capture their faces in profile as they drove, with the majesty of Monument Valley as the backdrop. Crowded into the back of the small wagon rode the camera, with its operator and his assistant, the soundman with his recorder and microphone boom, and McGill in his canvas chair.

The team pulled the buckboard along a desert two-track road. As always, the sandstone buttes and spires in the background dominated the scene as the actors conversed. McGill was almost smiling at the beauty of it all when a jackrabbit barreled out from under a sagebrush beside the road, darted under the hooves of the team pulling the wagon, then burst out in front of the frightened horses. The horses bolted, nearly spilling everyone in the back of the wagon over the end gate.

The judge, unaccustomed to handling a team at anything beyond a trot, sawed at the lines without effect. Annika, one hand grasping the seat and the other holding her hat down, held her breath to avoid screaming. The crew members scrambled to secure the camera and recording equipment even as they bounced and jolted along with the careening buckboard. McGill, hands grasping the arms of his chair, shouted at the actor to control the horses and stop "this damn wagon."

The desert hare had no sooner erupted from the brush than Latigo ran to where Nugget was tied, awaiting the next scene. The cowboy took an instant to tighten the cinch as he turned the horse away from the fence and urged him into motion with his voice. He stepped along as the horse gathered speed, straightening the now-snug latigo strap as the length of his strides reached their limit. He grabbed the saddle horn and vaulted into the seat.

As if reading his rider's mind, or forming his own opinion of the danger below, Nugget ran down the hillside, kicking up sand and tearing through brush. Sensing the angle between his approach and the course of the runaway buckboard on the two-track road, Latigo adjusted his direction, Nugget responding to the touch and increasing his speed as the ridge met the valley floor and leveled out.

Nugget's breathing was becoming labored when they reached the wagon, but he put forth a burst of speed to overtake the panicked team. As he ran beside and slowly moved past the near horse in the team, Latigo leapt out of the saddle onto the horse's back. He grabbed the cross-check lines where they passed through the ring, as well as the line on the horse he now rode and pulled with steady pressure and the occasional jerk. The horses soon responded, and as they slowed, Latigo steered them off the road into the deeper sand and into a circle. Hauling the team to a stop, he spoke to the quivering, sweating, blowing horses as they tossed their heads, sidestepped, and pawed at the ground until they quieted.

He turned to look at the occupants of the wagon. "Ever'one all right?"

The judge eased himself off the wagon, staggering a step when he lit, grabbing the wheel to steady himself. Latigo swung his leg across the lathered horse's neck and slid to the ground, keeping a hand on the line. He gestured to the judge to step up and take hold of the horses' lines next to the bit chains. "I don't think they'll give you any trouble," he told the trembling actor. "These horses is all run out." Latigo crossed in front of the team, speaking to the horses in a soft voice and rubbing their faces and necks as he passed.

He went to Annika and offered a hand. She took it, and fell off the buckboard seat into his arms. Her breathing was ragged, almost coming in sobs. "Horses. I hate horses," she gasped.

"You're all right now, Miss."

Two of the company's trucks rolled up, and the men that came with them helped unload the camera and sound gear. It would have to be taken apart and tested for damage from all the jolting and jostling. A wrangler who came along checked the team for injury and gave the wagon a once-over, looking for breakage.

"These horses seem all right to you, Latigo?"

"I believe so. Give 'em a rest and they'll be fine."

"That's how it looks to me. I'll see to gettin' 'em back to the barn. You want I should take El Fuego along?" He nodded toward Latigo's horse, standing a few yards away, cropping at the bunch grass that sprouted out of the sand among the scattered brush.

"Nah. I'll ride him on back." He again assured Annika all was well, and walked her to one of the trucks and helped her into the cab. "Don't you worry none, Miss Eriksson. You're all right."

"Damn horses!"

"Now, Annika, don't you be cussin' them horses. They only did what horses do. If anything, you ought to be cussin' that jackrabbit—he's what caused it all."

She reached out and laid a hand on his shoulder. He grasped it with his hand and gave it a gentle squeeze, then stepped back and closed the door. He turned to find T.C. McGill standing a few feet away, waiting.

The director stepped forward. "You saved our lives, laddie."

"Oh, I don't know. I reckon the judge would've got them horses sorted out 'fore too much longer."

"Aye, laddie. Yer bum's oot the windae when you say that. I know what you've done. And I shan't forget it."

Latigo went to Nugget, and felt up and down the horse's legs. He lifted each hoof to check the sole for lodged stones or injury or loose shoes. Satisfied the horse was well, he climbed aboard and started for base camp, deciding to take a long, easy ride back rather than return to the location and the trucks and trailers that would transport the crew and equipment.

Annika Eriksson watched him ride away, man and mount growing small in the distance of the vast desert and its towering buttes.

*****

The next day, McGill ordered the company to prepare for another try at his "money shot." Since the actors' presence would not be required at the location until late afternoon, they lazed around base camp at the trading post. Latigo thumbed through Los Angeles newspapers and Hollywood trade papers brought in by the pilots who flew exposed film back to the city for processing.

"These here newspapers is still talkin' about us—you and me," he said to Annika, who sat fanning herself in a chair fashioned from pine logs and covered with a woolen Navajo blanket.

She flipped her fingers as if shooing away a fly. "It is nothing."

"I don't see how those folks could think a pretty lady like you would have any truck with a no-account saddle bum like me."

Annika smiled the smile Latigo had seen a hundred times, every one of which caused a flutter somewhere deep inside. "Think nothing of it. They have linked me romantically with every actor I have appeared with. Such rumors and gossip are their stock in trade. Do not pay it any mind. Already, they are hinting at my involvement with the man cast to play opposite me in my next film—and I have yet to meet him. In reality, I have no intention of entering into any relationship with a man. I cannot afford to let such foolishness distract me from my career."

Latigo nodded, and turned back to his newspaper.

"I am reading that the film you acted in for Samuel Sturges has been released to rave reviews," Annika said. "Soon, every ingenue in Hollywood will be begging to appear in your films. Directors will be knocking at your door. You are a big star, Latigo Brown, in spite of your reluctance."

Latigo tipped the newspaper enough to see Annika's teasing smile, then raised it again to conceal the flush he felt rising from under his shirt collar.

The sunset scene that evening worked to perfection—superior, in fact, to the spoiled effort, as layered clouds hanging above the western horizon filled the sky with flame and color even more impressive than before. All that remained on the schedule was the film's climactic scene; an ambitious undertaking involving a hijacked stagecoach, an Indian attack, and a courageous rescue by cowboy hero and star of the show, Latigo Brown.

Several previous scenes in the script, all shot on the studio backlot and sound stages, led to the story's climax: the leader of an outlaw band, found guilty at trial of stealing horses, languished in jail awaiting sentencing by the judge. His gang of desperados, in an attempt to free him, snatch Libby off the street, stuff her into a stolen stagecoach, and light out for parts unknown, leaving the judge a ransom note—the demand being the release of their leader. The judge summons Latigo Brown and informs him of his plight—and the peril facing Libby. During the kidnapper's flight, the stagecoach is set upon by marauding Indians, who fire the coach with flaming arrows and kill the bandits—leaving Libby on her own to face the ferocious warriors.

Latigo watched the filming leading up to his appearance. The Indians poured out of the desert, outrunning, cutting off, and stopping the stolen stagecoach. As the bandits fell to rifle fire and arrows shot by the circling Indians—played by stunt men and Navajo extras dressed, for reasons Latigo could not fathom, like Sioux or Arikara or Blackfeet of the Great Plains—the coach caught fire, kindled by flaming arrows.

Latigo took note of the fact that McGill's demand for realism result-ed in injury to some stunt riders, run over by other horses after executing a fall with their own mounts. An arrow, though blunt, hit one of the bandits with sufficient force to penetrate his skin. The stunt double dressed as Libby was burned by the flaming coach seriously enough to require medical attention, as McGill, with his megaphone, urged delay in crawling out of the inferno, seeking maximum dramatic effect.

And then, it was time for Latigo Brown, cowboy hero, to save the day—or, at least, the fair maiden, the damsel in distress. The absence of threat from the now-dead outlaws held no comfort for the captured Libby, now facing an even more imminent and dangerous fate from the attacking Indians.

Latigo topped a low ridge above the wagon road, reined up El Fuego, and eyed the chaotic scene below. The howling Indians continued circling, the ring drawing ever tighter around Libby, standing in the dust and smoke, her white skirts and bodice glowing in the sun's penetrating rays, as did her lustrous golden locks. The bodies of her captors lay round about her, dead from arrow wounds, or with flesh and organs obliterated by bullets.

The cowboy on the ridge touched his spurs to his mount, and the magnificent palomino stallion rose on its hind legs, its front hooves scratching at the sky as it bugled a warning to the marauders. Down the hillside, horse and rider flew, passing through the racing Indians as if invisible. Latigo rode to the imperiled maiden.

"Don't worry, Miss, we'll make it through!" He swept her off the ground to a seat on the horse's back, crosswise across the animal's rump, her arms entwined around him. "Grab aholt, Miss, and don't let go," Latigo said, but Libby already clung to her only hope with a vice-like grip.

Again, El Fuego reared, threatening the Indians with flailing hooves. Latigo let loose of the reins, drew his twin pistols, and sent shot after shot at the circling attackers, every bullet finding a mark, horses falling, unhorsed riders tumbling, wounded Indians spilling from their horses' backs. El Fuego whirled and danced beneath Latigo, offering a new target with every turn. The prop people reloaded the pistols with blank cartridges at every scene break, and the revolvers fired round after round, Latigo realizing as he pulled the triggers that on the screen, the guns would shoot more bullets than earthly possible, all without his reloading a single chamber. But, he reminded himself, it's only a movie.

In the final scene of the sequence, the overmatched Indians realize the futility of taking on the fearless cowboy, and retreat into the desert. Latigo raises each pistol barrel to his mouth, blows away the feathery smoke, spins the revolvers around his trigger fingers, and slides them into their twin holsters. He says nothing to the rescued woman clinging to him, face nestled into the muscles of his back.

At his rider's silent signal, the resplendent El Fuego turns away from the flaming stagecoach and the killing field surrounding it and prances away, following an unseen trail leading toward the setting sun as it sets fire to the sky.

McGill cut the scene. Annika demanded that Latigo let her off the "damn horse." He smiled and tipped his hat, telling the star she would hurt Nugget's feelings. She huffed off toward the tent that served as her temporary dressing room in this wild and distant location. Latigo rode over to McGill to verify the scene was good, offering another take if necessary. Upon assurance all was well, he rode to the makeshift corrals where Nugget could relax in the shade of a canvas fly until time to be trailered back to base camp.

He had yet to reach the place when a scream ripped the desert air. Without a thought, he reined Nugget around and spurred the horse into a mad dash toward Annika's tent. Stepping down even as Nugget slid to a stop in the desert sand, Latigo flung open the tent flap and stepped inside.

Annika cowered in the corner, fists clenched, arms pressed to her sides, hands at her mouth. Latigo surveyed the tent in a trice, but saw nothing threatening among the hanging clothes, the vanity table and mirror, the wooden chair with the padded seat, the woven rug on the tent floor, or the trunks shoved against the canvas walls.

The wide-eyed woman gathered her wits well enough to unclench a fist, and, with a quivering finger, point toward the floor in the far corner. Latigo saw nothing in the dimness, and stepped across the floor in two strides. There, backed into the angle, jointed tail arched over its back and waving the stinger at its tip, pincers on front legs raised and working, was a three-inch-long scorpion.

Latigo lifted a foot, stretched his leg into the corner, and with the pointed toe of his boot, stepped on the nasty arachnid. At the decisive crunch, Annika inhaled sharply. She stepped to Latigo as he turned and threw her arms around his neck, sobbing and drawing him into a tight embrace. After a moment, he clutched her shoulders and held her as he stepped away.

"It's all right, Miss Eriksson."

She nodded, and dabbed at her eyes and nose with a lacy hanky that appeared as if from nowhere. She managed a weak smile. "Thank you. Oh, thank you, Latigo Brown."

"Oh, it weren't nothin'. No big deal."

She laid a hand on his cheek and drew a deep breath. "I am sorry that earlier I spoke disrespectfully of your horse."

With a laugh, he turned away. He pushed aside the door flap to reveal a good share of the company, including T.C. McGill, standing in a semicircle around the front of the tent. He stepped out, looking from questioning faces to inquiring eyes to wondering expressions.

Latigo Brown shrugged. "It weren't nothin'," he said, hoisting his foot and pointing at the sole, stained near the toe. "Just one of them curly tailed bugs."

Chapter Thirty-Three

Latigo Brown sat in the spacious, plush reception area studying the framed photographs that covered the walls like wallpaper. There were actors, singers, musicians, magicians, comedians, and entertainers of every sort, from years gone by to the present. He recognized some, but most were not familiar.

The office belonged to the man said to be the most powerful and influential agent and manager in the entertainment business, with offices in Hollywood and New York bustling with busy functionaries arranging deals, negotiating contracts, making demands, reaching compromises, and promoting the professional and financial interests of their many clients, among them some of the most popular and in-demand entertainers of the day.

Latigo had an appointment with the man himself. The request for the meeting had come by letter during post-production of T.C. McGill's movie. Latigo handed the letter to John Benson, who read its two lines, then smiled and handed it back to his young cowboy friend.

"Looks like you've really hit the big time now, son."

"Think I ought to go see this man?"

Benson shrugged. "Couldn't hurt. At least hear what he has to say."

"Would you hook up with him?"

Benson thought for a long moment. "Can't say. He's good at his job, there's no doubt about that. The people he represents tend to get the best of everything—best parts, best pay, best deals on the back end, best endorsements, you name it. Still, I have heard more than once that he can be ruthless, and that sometimes he pushes people into deals they don't want. And that he's not above taking unfair advantage when he can get away with it." He sighed. "But, that's the business he's in, I guess.

Listen to what he has to say, but don't let him talk you into anything right off. They say he can talk the eggs out from under a broody hen, so be careful."

When an office worker ushered Latigo into the big man's presence, he noted the office was even larger and more richly appointed than T.C. McGill's. But, as with the director's quarters, the room could not quite swallow up the expansive—and expensive—desk that was its focus. The occupant sat behind it, cradled in the largest chair Latigo had ever seen. He could barely see the man in the chair, let alone make out his features, as the bright light streaming through the window glass that covered the entire wall behind him almost rendered the man and chair in silhouette, and caused Latigo to squint.

An orange glow brightened in the chair, then faded, and Latigo realized the man was smoking a cigar. The cowboy stood before the desk without speaking, hat in hand, assuming he was being scrutinized. He heard the man expel a cloud of smoke, which flowered above him and dissipated.

"I'm sorry," said a voice from the chair. "The sun is in your eyes. I forget."

Latigo saw a finger reach out and touch one of a row of buttons on a panel on the desktop. With a hum, translucent window shades lowered over the glass wall.

"Sit down," the voice said, the hand with the cigar waving at the chair beside Latigo and in front of the desk.

As the blinds lowered and Latigo's eyes adjusted, he took note of the man in the chair. He could not say what he had expected, but whatever picture appeared in the back of his mind, it did not match the man sitting before him. He was short—enough so that it was obvious, even as he sat—and rotund. The bald top of his head was framed by a fringe of gray hair, wild and in need of a trim. The fat cigar had dribbled ashes down the lapels of his rumpled suit coat, the tie was loosened and pulled off center, the collar button of the shirt undone.

"Look kid," the man said. "You know who I am, and I know who you are, so let's don't waste time with small talk." He flicked ashes from the cigar into a cut crystal ashtray that bristled with the stubs and butts of prior smokes. "I know all about your stunt work, and I don't care about that—stunt men are a dime a dozen. That film you made with Sam Sturges is pullin' in pretty good box office. Word on the street is that the work you did on McGill's film is first rate." He flicked nonexistent ashes from his cigar. "You see, kid, nothing goes on in this town that I don't know about. So I know all about your fancy work with a lasso." He shrugged. "That could come in handy. Set you apart, if you know what I mean."

He paused to suck on the cigar, then blew the smoke upward and watched it swirl. "Say, kid, I don't suppose you can sing and play the guitar?"

Latigo chuckled. "No, sir. Fact is, I couldn't carry a tune with a packsaddle."

Another flick of the ashes. "Too bad. Singing cowboys are a hot commodity these days. Maybe we could get you lessons."

"Well, I...I don't know about that."

The man waved the cigar. "Don't worry about it. We'll see what happens." Another puff. "Here's the thing, kid. Movies are nothing. Well, not nothing, exactly, but they're not the point."

The silence stretched as the man stared at Latigo. The cowboy told him he did not know what he meant.

He waved the cigar. "You've got to be on the big screen, sure. But that ain't where the money is. Between pictures, see, we'll get you on television. You've done television. We'll get you your own series.

You'll be on every week, building your audience. But that ain't it either. The real money's in spinoffs, and endorsements."

The man crushed the end of the cigar in the ashtray and leaned forward, propping his elbows on the desktop. "Think of it—lunchboxes, air rifles, cap guns, lasso ropes, cowboy outfits, trading cards, comic books, storybooks, watches, clocks, you name it—all with your name and picture on them. That horse of yours—what is it, El Fuego? We'll do the same thing with him. That nag will be as famous as you are before I'm done with him. We'll make a killing."

"I ain't so sure about all tha—"

"—Don't worry about it, kid" the man said, waving his hand to brush the words away. "We can talk about it later. For the time being we'll work on making you more famous—get your name out there. Everywhere. Sharpen your image. Another movie, maybe two—no, I think one will do it. Then we'll get into this other stuff. But it's there, you know. All you got to do is grab it. You'd be a fool not to, kid. And I'm the man who can do it for you. Without me, you're just another shit kicker who was in a movie."

Latigo sat. Keeping up with the man's chatter left no time to think, let alone formulate a reply.

"Now, about your next film. I've got just the thing. I'm shopping a script right now—all the big directors want it—T.C. McGill being one interested party—and it'll be next year's big deal. Actors will be coming out of the woodwork to be in it. But I could make your playing the lead part of the deal. It might take some rewriting on the script, but that's no problem."

The man stopped talking. He opened a fancy humidor and pulled out another fat cigar. He rolled it around in his fingers, admiring it, then ran it under his nose with a loud sniff. "Want one?" he said, tilting it toward Latigo. The cowboy shook his head. The man clipped off the end of the cigar with a little gadget he then put back on the desk next to the humidor. He stuck the cigar in his mouth and torched the end with a robust lighter, sucking and puffing and spitting out smoke until the tobacco was well kindled.

"Well, whaddya think, kid?"

"About what?"

"The film. The movie. The script I told you about."

Latigo's brow furrowed. "What's it about?"

The man shrugged, blew out a cloud of smoke. "Who cares? It don't matter—it's a Western. It's got horses."

Latigo thought about it as the man worked over the cigar, attempting, he supposed, to get it smoldering to his satisfaction.

"So?"

"So?"

"So what about it, kid?"

"Well, sir, I don't rightly know."

The man smiled around the cigar and said through the mouthful, "It'll pay you a million dollars."

"A million dollars?"

"A million dollars."

The shock dissipated slowly, like cigar smoke, before Latigo regained his voice. "Is it any good?"

"Any good? Who cares?"

"I do. Is it any good?"

The man shrugged. "It pays a million dollars."

Chapter Thirty-Four

The arena lay in a puddle of light in the deepening dusk. The air had a bite to it—still gentle, but enough of a nip to warn that autumn had arrived in the high country and that winter was buttoning its coat. The number of tourists visiting Jackson Hole was on the wane, and the end of the nightly tourist rodeo for the season wasn't far off.

Junior Blevins stood in the crow's nest atop the bucking chutes, microphone in hand. The grand entry—the parade of flags and banners, cowboys and cowgirls, and horses, horses, horses—trailed out of the arena. He picked up his banter where he had left off seconds before. "Ladies and gentlemen, boys and girls, it's rodeo time at the Grand Teton Stampede!"

Down in the arena, Danny Wickham, clipboard in hand, hobbled back and forth in front of the chutes. Bareback riders straddled the chutes, standing over or sitting on the backs of skittish horses, adjusting riggings, testing handholds, pulling another inch of slack out of latigo straps and cinches. "Get 'er pulled down," Wickham told a nervous young cowboy. "You're third out." He moved down the line. "You'll be second. Be ready," he told the rider tussling with a jittery horse that kicked the slide gate, reared up, then came down and stomped and pawed, snorting and blowing.

"You're up," he told the rider in the next chute.

The cowboy, seated on and leaned over the horse, lifting on the handhold of his rigging, turned and looked at Wickham. "Sure, Danny. Almost there."

He looked up at the man standing on the gate, the toes of his boots tucked into the gaps between boards, holding the latigo. "Pull 'er a little more, Harley." The man stretched the leather strap. The rider lifted on the handhold again, and, finding the rigging's give against the horse's withers satisfactory, said, "That's good. Tie it off."

The man he called Harley threaded the tail end of the strap back through its top loop through the D-ring, pulled it snug, and laid it over the horse's neck in front of the rigging. The rider tucked it into the opposite D-ring to keep it secure and out of the way.

"Rodeo fans, it's time for our first event at the Grand Teton Stampede—the bareback bronc riding! Cowboys come to Jackson Hole from all over our fair land to test their skill against our bucking stock. In the bareback riding, the cowboy's only hold on the pitching horse is one hand in the rigging, holding on for dear life to a handle much like the one on your suitcase! His spurs must be over the point of the horse's shoulders as it leaves the chute, and he must stay aboard for eight seconds. If he makes the whistle—and that's a big if—the cowboy will get a score from our two judges—half for his effort, and half for how hard the horse bucks."

Junior Blevins paused in his patter and leaned over to look down into the bucking chutes. He saw the cowboy sliding forward on the horse's back, scooting under the arm and hand in the rigging. "It looks like our rider is just about ready, folks! This is the first time we've seen this cowboy at the Grand Teton Stampede, and we hope it won't be the last. Ladies and gentlemen, give a warm welcome to our first rodeo contestant tonight—Orval Brown!"

THE END

"I think you're going to find out that westerns will be coming back.
It's Americana, it's part of our history, the cowboy,
the cattle drive, the sheriff, the fight for law, order and justice.
Justice will always prevail as far as I'm concerned."
—Clayton Moore

About the Author

Winner of four Western Writers of America Spur Awards and a Spur Award finalist on six other occasions, and recipient of two Western Fictioneers Peacemaker Awards and a four-time finalist, Rod Miller writes fiction, poetry, and history about the American West. A lifelong Westerner raised in a cowboy family, Miller is a former rodeo contestant, worked in radio and television production, and is a retired advertising agency copywriter and creative director. Miller's award-winning poetry and short stories have appeared in numerous anthologies, and several magazines have carried his byline.

Find the author online at:
writerRodMiller.com
writerRodMiller.blogspot.com, and
RawhideRobinson.com

Coming Soon!

ROD MILLER'S
A THOUSAND DEAD HORSES

Based on a historic horse-stealing adventure…
A Thousand Dead Horses **dramatizes the**
violence and perils of the Old West.

Young Daniel Boone Trewick, caught in a compromising position with a young woman, flees Missouri believing he has killed the girl's father in a fight. He joins a freighting outfit heading out on the Santa Fe Trail, intending to join a mountain man-enclave in Taos. There, he meets mountain man Thomas L. "Pegleg" Smith, and is invited to join him, "Old Bill Williams," Ute leader Wakara, and others on an expedition to California to steal horses and mules. Along the Old Spanish Trail, the party faces dangerous river crossings, a flash flood, Indian raids, and other dangers...

For more information
visit: www.SpeakingVolumes.us

Now Available!

MORE ACTION/ADVENTURE WESTERNS BY SPUR AWARD-WINNING AUTHOR
ROD MILLER

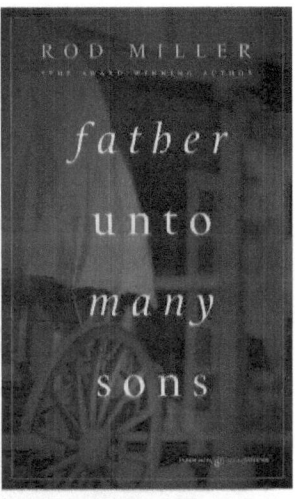

**For more information
visit: www.SpeakingVolumes.us**

Now Available!

J.L CRAFTS
ACTION/ADVENTURE WESTERN

**For more information
visit:** www.SpeakingVolumes.us

Now Available!

ACTION/ADVENTURE WESTERNS BY AWARD-WINNING AUTHOR ROY V. GASTON

Now Available!

R. G. YOHO'S
ACTION/ADVENTURE WESTERNS

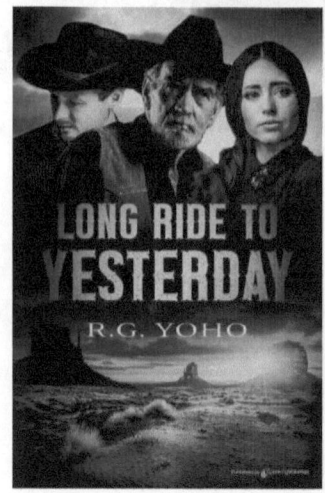

For more information
visit: www.SpeakingVolumes.us